A
Cellist Soldier

Robert J Fanshawe

Clink
Street

London | New York

Published by Clink Street Publishing 2020

Copyright © 2020

First edition.

ISBN:
978-1-913340-41-4 paperback
978-1-913340-42-1 ebook

*To my family, all those I love and to all
who suffer injustice in war.*

Prequel to *The Cellist's Friend*

"Author Robert J Fanshawe has a way with words
that will draw you in from the first paragraph –
from the very first sentence actually." Hollywood
Book Reviews, *The Cellist's Friend.*

" A perfect story written with optimism and originality."
Amazon customer review, *The Cellist's Friend.*

"For me the mark of a good read is that I would be happy
to read it again in case I missed something. This is one of
those books. Definitely one of the best books I've read in a
long time." Amazon customer review, *The Cellist's Friend.*

"The horrors of World War 1 are vividly depicted in
this searing novel of self-examination….Fanshawe
proves himself as accomplished a storyteller as he is a
writer. " The US review of books, *The Cellist's Friend.*

"Although The Cellist's Friend is set in WW1
its stories and themes are timeless." Pacific
Review of Books, *The Cellist's Friend.*

"The Cellist's Friend is raw and thought – provoking,
from the cruel opening of the music played before a firing
squad to the hopeless brutality at the front, to the hospital
wards and beyond….a sad story but one that is told with
compassion and honesty." Emily-Jane Hills Orford,
review of *The Cellist's Friend* for Readers' Favourite.

Glossary of terms

Army Units

Artillery – Main support for infantry, grouped into Regiments and Batteries.

Battalion – Smallest Infantry unit with its own logistic and headquarters elements (500 – 700 men).

Brigade – Higher formation from Battalion with usually 4 battalions and support elements.

Company – Sub-units of the Battalion, usually 3 rifle and 1 headquarters company (150 – 200 men).

Platoon – Sub-unit of the Company, usually 3 to each Company (30 men)

Regiment – Battalions formed from Counties, cities and other groups from Britain. Each Regiment has its own badges.

Sappers/Engineers and other elements – Civil engineers for building and major explosive tasks.

Section – Sub-unit of the platoon 3 to each (8/9 men).

Ranks and Appointments

Brigadier – Commander of a Brigade.

CAG – Corps Adjutant General, a senior staff officer (Colonel) who dealt with Courts Martial.

Captain – Company Commander or Adjutant.

CinC – Commander in Chief.

Colour Sergeant – Rank up from Sergeant, usually appointed as Company Quartermaster Sergeant.

Company Sergeant Major (Warrant officer 2) the Senior Non-Commissioned Officer in a Company.

Corporal – Junior Non-Commissioned Officer (JNCO) commands a section.

Lieutenant Colonel/Colonel – Battalion Commander/senior staff officer.

2nd Lieutenant/Lieutenant – Platoon Commander.

Regimental Sergeant Major (RSM) (Warrant Officer 1). The Senior Non – Commissioned Officer in a Battalion. Holds a special and powerful place in the Battalion.

Sergeant – Senior Non-Commissioned Officer (SNCO). Every Platoon has a Platoon Sergeant.

Expressions

Blighty – Britain.

Blighty One – A wound that gets you back to Britain.

No Man's Land – The space between the front lines of armies facing each other.

Stand Too – Around dawn when all soldiers man the trench, often used for inspection.

CHAPTER ONE

The photograph

A cancer of bitterness spread through the Battalion on realising that it was a photograph that caused the death of the Old Man. Those who had waved their helmets and laughed along felt it the most as they saw the falsehood in it. Soldiers will always see through something like that.

The Old Man might not have seen it at the time.

The turning point came before they heard that the photograph had been published in a newspaper under some headline about how good the morale of the troops was, and then made into a postcard. That sealed it. But the bitterness started when the new RSM arrived.

The Battalion had been on its way to the front, redeploying after a night's rest. There was some joking amongst them, as they had heard that a push was coming. The photographer noticed this. "I want to capture the smiles and the humour of these men. They look happy, RSM."

"They have a good morale about them, I'll give you that." The 'Old Man,' the Regimental Sergeant Major, the Battalion's most Senior Non-Commissioned Officer, stood fully six inches over the photographer. His words were strained out through a vast moustache which twitched with pride. He was proud of the morale. It was his battalion. He owned the men and their morale.

He loved and was loved by almost every one of them, from the oldest hardest Senior Non-Commissioned Officer to the newest, palest, shaking recruit, to whom any harsh words were tempered with a whispered encouragement such as; 'don't worry son, you'll soon get the hang of things. Remember the parade ground. React to sounds as you would to my voice. Look after yourself always and those around you.' Sometimes he even put his arm around their shoulders.

He had gathered the men in a wide, dry crater which was strangely clear of war rubbish, and big enough to accommodate the whole Battalion. They shouldn't have been there, all grouped together. But the RSM took the risk in order to have a private word with the men and get the best setting for the photograph.

"I trust you all had a good sleep last night," he said in his deep resonating voice which he hardly had to raise to address all five hundred men. "You will separate into your companies over the edge of the crater and move into your own areas. We move up after last light to relieve the; ahh humm." He never disparaged another battalion by name in public. "They are a tired and dispirited lot. You will want to be like that many times in the future, as you have in the past…Try to resist those feelings. Try to maintain your self-respect and your spirit. Believe in yourselves… and look after each other." He paused and searched the faces of the men, his men.

"Now we have an unusual event, a photograph, for posterity. I want you to make the best of this, to show the people back home that we are up for this fight, any fight. Some of you have been here before. Some of you are first timers. Good luck to all of you."

He walked back to where the photographer had set up his stand, with the black box on top. "Now are we all set, sir?"

"Yes, could they just move forward as groups from the other side over there and perhaps they could demonstrate their morale?" The photographer smiled at the energy in their movement and anticipation. He knew he could make a good picture.

The RSM returned to the men. "Right as company groups; not a parade ground is it, just move forward across in front of the camera and show off a bit. Let's have some helmets in the air and a laugh and a cheer perhaps."

Bayonets were not fixed. Rifles were slung over one shoulder. The older soldiers strode forward unworried by holes in the knees of their trousers, or mud caked puttees. They had had no resupply during the evening before, no chance to change clothes. The new reinforcements, of which there were a lot, had joined them, with their new uniforms. Then a hearty meal had come up with an extra ration of rum, followed by a long sleep, out of range of trench weapons.

Bravo Company went first but they did not show quite enough enthusiasm and the photographer pursed his lips as if he was watching a football match where no effort was being displayed. He had a word with the RSM, who twirled his arms, pumping up support. He shouted to Alpha Company. They got the hang of it. "Come on Alpha, the number one and only," shouted Ben in one of the sections. With that sort of encouragement they made a better effort. The photographer waved. He was happy.

"Relax where you are," called the RSM. Men found the nearest piece of raised ground at the side to sit on and pull out woodbines and pipes, creating a kind of gap in the middle which only the RSM and the photographer inhabited.

A noise came as though the gods had screeched a sudden warning; alas too late. A thump followed, and dry mud started flying in the flash and smoke. They still had about six kilometres to go to the front but a stray Five-Nine shell had found the space. *"Fuck this!"* Men screamed fumbling for gas masks. No yellow gas emerged, but as the smoke cleared no sign could be seen of the RSM. The shell had made a direct hit on him, standing a little distance from the photographer savouring a quiet moment.

Men searched around in vain. Word went round the Battalion that the only recognisable things they found of the RSM were his boots with the feet still in them. Of him there were only bloody bits and pieces of body and uniform. How could such a big heart and soul be brought down to a few pieces of flesh and bone and cloth and webbing? That cut men to their own bones. A body is a body, you can pay respects to it. But when the bits of it can hardly fill a few undignified sand-bags, men would find it more difficult to believe that the character and what was in the heart, had ever existed.

The camera and the cameraman were still intact, battered, and in the case of the photographer concussed and with a piece of shrapnel embedded in his hand, but most photographic plates were intact, and they would be reproduced. "Won't have the Old Man's face in it though will it," commented one of the SNCOs. They referred to the RSM as the Old Man in view of the service he had seen; from Omdurman and the Boer War. They would search for a picture that did show him, but none could be found, even though he had arranged for the photograph to be taken. "He was like a father to us, that Old Man," added the newly promoted Sergeant from A Company, smoking in some rare evening sunshine outside the HQ dugout waiting to move up the same evening.

"Better than a father. I hate my dad. He knows nothing about what we doing here. The Old Man knew everything," replied the Company Sergeant-Major looking down at his neatly tied puttees, from ankle to just below the knee, covered in dry mud, the colour of the wood revetting they were sitting on. His helmet was off, leaving dark hair plastered with sweat to his forehead. He took a deep breath and shook his head momentarily, his eyes not seeing anything.

"Maybe, they'll make you RSM, Sar-Major," said the Sergeant. He was aware that the Sergeant-Major's influence on his own life would then increase.

"Not me boy, they'll send someone else in, mark my words." He picked up his helmet, just as sounds emerged of shovels on soil, which the Sergeant knew to be a sign that it was time to get back to work. He was a bit peeved by the handle 'boy', which being newly promoted he had to accept, probably down to his small stature and inability to grow a decent moustache because of his blond hair.

He stumbled over the lip of a shell hole to where his platoon was gathered. "Well don't just sit there gawping at me, get yourselves spread out into section positions, get out of this crater, don't want us caught napping as well." Newly promoted or not he was determined to show his leadership. He scrambled each section corporal up to the lip of the crater to show their arcs of observation and fire, linking up to the other platoons whose positions had been indicated to him by the Sergeant-Major.

"What's occurring then Sarge?" asked one section corporal.

"Don't know yet, officers at their final briefing ain't they. Once it's dark we'll move into our final position."

"But we thought it wasn't final, just a holding position before the push forward."

"Like I said, don't know yet. Wait till the officer returns."

They smoked and waited, looking moodily out over No Man's Land, whatever they could see of it with darkness rapidly approaching.

The Platoon Commanders returned, carefully boundering

the craters, and gave their orders from folded canvas map cases, which hung around necks along with binoculars and gas respirator haversacks and pistol lanyards. Straps and slings and web belts and canvas pouches, some with ammo clips; uniforms creased with wear and rain and sleep and some bulging pockets hanging the uniform out of shape; weighed down every soldier. The officers incongruously also wore ties with a pin holding the collar tightly around the knot.

The Battalion conducted the late evening relief in line impeccably, following tape that had been laid down by reconnaissance parties. But when the Old Man's Battalion moved up into position there was much evidence that the morale of those relieved had been as he had predicted. Proper latrines had not been dug so there was the smell of fresh faeces everywhere. They did leave a sizeable stash of unused ammunition and enough shovels and tools to repair the trenches that they seemingly had not bothered to do.

"Why didn't they wait till they got back to their rest area, Corp?" asked Ben referring to the smell.

"What does a dirty dog do in his territory as he leaves it," commented Jack, Ben's friend and rum partner, who was not new to the Section, or the Company.

Such was the respect between units and the views of certain 'old sweats' who had been through much and become cynical.

The trenches were in a very bad state. They had been blasted apart. There were not many deep shell holes. It was just a pockmarked patchwork. So men were lying almost in the open where previous shallow trench walls had been broken down.

But the night was strangely quiet which encouraged the speculation that the Germans opposite supposedly at about four hundred yards, had moved out as well and not been relieved.

In the morning they saw how bad the trenches were. The thought that maybe they would not be here long, encouraged a reluctance to start work on repairing them. A soldier sees no point in unnecessary work. His heart will never be in it. Winning the hearts of soldiers was something the Old Man did without effort. It came naturally to him. Some officers and Non-Commissioned Officers were natural leaders. It might have been their intelligence, humility, hard work or honesty that made them so. Bravery didn't come into it. A man could be brave but regarded as incredibly foolish by his fellows and not therefore followed. Fear was the air they breathed. Courage was a moment, a reaching out beyond, or ignoring, the everyday calculation of an activity, whether something had to be done or not and the risk involved.

Risk was also a commodity, to be traded. A leader had to take risks otherwise how could he ask his men to take them. Thus platoon commanders had to lead patrols out into No Man's Land. They had to go on wiring parties. When an officer or NCO sat in his bunker, shaking and giving orders for this and that, without doing anything himself, he very soon lost his men.

Knowing this unspoken contract, some officers chose not to give orders for anything, except when something was passed down. Orders from above were not part of the risk contract. They were simply being passed on.

Had the Old Man been alive he would have toured the front line in the morning, immediately after Stand Too, quietly advising platoon commanders who seemed reluctant to do anything, of their housekeeping duties. 'Need some protection down there, sir. Don't leave those men in the open,' he might have said. His priority was always to look after the men, which made every loss of life a tragedy rather than a normality.

He didn't deliberately give instructions for immediate work that would lead to men being at risk. When there was nothing to do, he favoured sleep under as much cover as possible. The men loved being chided for not being asleep. 'Get under cover lad, get some sleep.'

'Yes *sir*,' would have been the enthusiastic response. Sometimes men just laid a cape over themselves and scraped any loose earth over it and fell asleep. Earth was the best friend and shield.

Shell holes gave some deeper protection and a crawl trench could be quite quickly dug to enable communication and some safe passage between sections occupying them. 'Straighten the line here sir, you'll need to dig that Lewis in as well and dig a comms trench to it otherwise the Lewis team will be isolated.' The Old Man instinctively knew how to use his machineguns even though he had begun his service before their full introduction. 'Get them dug in to waist depth at least, with some sand-bags above.'

He was conscious of everybody.

A Lewis gun planted on top of a mound of earth was certain to attract attention before long, even being seen from a spotter aircraft. But if they weren't sited somewhere that would give good observation, they could not do their job.

Jack and Ben sat in a shell scrape as they called it. They had hollowed out more of the original hole. "We must be the point section here," said Jack, screwing up his already tight face more.

"But it's so quiet," responded Ben.

"Yes, but we don't know anything do we. It's quiet now but it might not be in five minutes."

Ben nodded, looking down at his rifle. He pulled the small lever in front of the trigger to release the magazine, checked the four rounds inside, then eased the heavy bolt up and back to extract the round from the chamber. There was always a round in the chamber ready to fire. A minor skirmish could happen at any time. He replaced it in the magazine.

The chamber was a well-oiled metal void with no hint of mud or rust. Some men, when cleaning their rifles, were content to put a film of oil on the woodwork and metal on the outside, hardly daring to remove the bolt or pull the barrel through.

Some even released a round accidentally with trembling fingers which were meaning to release the magazine catch. It was a chargeable offence, an accidental discharge and if someone was killed or badly injured, the culprit would get a good beating as well from his comrades. Of course some would be happy to be injured with a 'Blighty one' that was not self-inflicted. The opposite happened as well with some men releasing the magazine when they meant to pull the trigger, rendering the rifle useless after firing only one round at the point it was probably most needed.

It was an instrument of some beauty, the .303 Lee–Enfield rifle, the smooth grained woodwork, the stock and butt which felt so good, the little compartment for the cleaning materials conveniently cut into the end of the butt, the black metal parts, heavy bolt and chamber; the sound it made when the bolt was lifted and ratchetted back then forward to pick up a round from the magazine and feed it snugly into the chamber, ready to fire.

Ben hefted the rifle, almost lovingly. The weight and solidity of the weapon spoke of quality and a reliable mechanism which didn't jam too much as long as it was kept free of mud and ice. The expert marksmen could work, fire and change the magazine when its five rounds were emptied and fire again, up to sixty rounds a minute. Ben looked up at the clouds scudding with a sort of spring gaiety around the sky. Rain would change everything about this balmy late March morning. Enemy action would turn it into hell. But now all that was needed was to enjoy the moments of calm.

Other weapons were being cleaned, but only half of the total number at any one time. The Lewis was on top of their crater on lookout. They took it in turns on sentry duty with the machine gun, though some were more able to fire it than others. The dedicated team of which two had their Lewis gun badges had to clean it, at night when it was not needed for look-out duties.

Drum magazines contained forty-seven rounds and the bigger ones ninety-seven. Loading the magazines, storing them, keeping them mud free and carrying them into battle was every soldier's job. At least it was now that every section had a Lewis gun. Before the team had been five strong. But they created a target all huddled together so now it was more a section weapon and the team was cut to three.

Men lounged around. They dozed and cooked a little bully on their individual soldier's stoves. There was nothing like the luxury of dry mud, sun and nothing flying through the air that would kill them.

"So what about this big push then, Corp?" asked Ben, calling across the crater.

The Corporal was sitting on his own, on a rock, of which there were not many amongst this excoriated earth. Smoke curled upwards from his pipe which he was obsessed with. He spent hours playing with it and thinking with it. As if it was doing the thinking for him.

He dragged on it now and a furnace erupted inside its great bowl. Where he got the tobacco was a mystery, but everyone had a way of getting stuff. Those that could work the system or knew the right NCOs did.

"You communicating with the Hun again, aren't you?" observed Jack. "No one's gonna miss your smoke signals. How we gonna conceal ourselves when you stoking that thing up. I'm sure they know about the 'big push'."

The corporal, Fred, thought some more and looked into

the bowl, as if it was a witches cauldron. "Sure they do. That's why we gonna keep 'em guessing."

Other men paid scant attention, though their ears were tuned in. The Lewis team were half-eyed on the opposite bank of the shell-hole. Alfred and John, a pair of friends, who did everything together. They looked like farm hands and sat cooking in the middle a few feet from the Corporal. A frightened new recruit lay doggedly behind the Lewis.

"Yea, they keeping us guessing an all," said Ben, jerking his head back towards his own side.

"Who's that 'they', you talking about Ben?" asked another, something of a loner, whose name was Ernest. He called himself that as well and invited mockery for it, seeming unwilling to go for the shorter more familiar Ernie. "My mumma called me that so I ain't gonna change it now," someone had heard him say in the bunker when he thought he was only speaking to the young Lewis gunner. Despite his sometimes naïve attitude he was a married man with children who had been called up from the reserve list and seemed to feel hard done by for being in France having left his family at home. Unlike the last of the section, Bert, a regular who had been involved since 1914 and seemed to take everything for granted. He was like an anchor to the section.

"'They', my good old Ernest, is them generals," said Bert.

"Oh, well we could be here for a long time then."

That sank the section into silence and the Corporal looked into his pipe, unable to counter the comment.

Times like this were when men sorted some things out between them, verifying rumours or amplifying them; then setting things in stone in their memories, whether they were true or not. But they didn't talk about the bad things. Hence they didn't talk about the Old Man's death. They didn't share feelings about it. That was not the soldier's way.

"Generals are all bastards," said Ernest. "Never see any of them blowed up right in front of your eyes."

"Some have been blowed up," commented the Corporal.

"How do you know?" asked Jack.

The Corporal shrugged. "I suppose they would have been," he said defensively, but he had only been out in France for a week, so everything he said was taken with narrowed eyes.

"But you never seen them here, in the front line have you?" demanded Ernest.

"They have been here, well in the front line," said Ben, with certainty in his voice.

Few had evidence of it, but somehow there was a knowledge that generals were soldiers too, though very distant ones. Senior NCOs were closer. The Old Man was the closest. He was always wandering through the trenches. Everyone talked of him when they had seen him and hoped they might do so again.

CHAPTER TWO
The new man arrives

All was confusion. The big push was off or delayed and the battalion went back into reserve. They went back without joy in their hearts to a billet that was also joyless.

"The Old Man would never have stood for a place like this," commented Jack as they surveyed the broken, almost roofless small barn, that was allocated to the section. Underfoot many years of cow dung, had been trodden, dried, then mixed with rain, mud from other boots, then dried again.

But now it had started raining afresh.

"Maybe we could get a fire going in the middle, a real fire," said Ernest.

"Yes, you can't do a real fire in a building that's got a roof but I bet Sarge would allow it here," Ben agreed with an edge of excitement in his voice

"Yea and we could catch a chicken and have us a real meal," said Ernest hopefully. There were some very skinny looking hens pecking about in the debris of the abandoned farm buildings.

The Corporal sucked on his pipe which for once was black and empty. "Can't see Sarge agreeing it," he said dismally. "I'll ask him though."

The uncertainty in his voice made the section doubt that

the asking would take place. They settled as best they could, looking for the driest piece of floor, easing kit off wet shoulders, but laying their capes down on the dung pack first.

"Go on then, go and ask him," challenged Jack.

"Let's get ourselves settled first," the Corporal replied.

Everybody wanted something to give comfort. "Where's the fucking straw?" complained the Lewis gunner, Alfred. He was moody and taciturn but that went unchallenged because of the expertise on his gun. Then they all suddenly fixated on the comfort of straw.

"He would never agree a fire if we had straw in here," challenged the Corporal.

"They got straw next door," complained Ernest, a man destined never to be happy in life.

"So what do you want, fire or straw?

"Corp, right now we want food!" injected Ben.

This put an end to the bickering. The Company was billeted in buildings grouped around a small village square. The whole Battalion was there. Each company had its cookhouse, from which smells wafted outwards, drawing men in, impatiently. But they had to wait until the cook sergeant made a signal, usually banging mess tins together.

They had heard the signal. The stew was ready. There might be fresh bread also for dipping in the stew. There would be rum issue afterwards. Joy, hardly dimmed by the drizzling rain, abounded. Mess tins were yanked out of dirty webbing. A quick inspection deemed them satisfactory for use even if they had mud and stains from food created in the trenches still in them. Those who wished could rinse them from a jerrycan of water before presenting them to be filled, hopefully to the brim. Most ignored the water.

Slinging their weapons, including the Lewis; they ran. "First in the queue, Corp," shouted Jack.

The Corporal just sucked on his pipe, worrying at its lack

of fire. He was last up, sitting in the departing dust stirred from against the walls where the soldiers had started to establish a home to return to.

They brought the smell of hot food back with them to help make it home.

"There's a parade tomorrow," the Corporal commented between mouthfuls. He had seen the Platoon Sergeant and the intelligence had been passed on.

None of the section responded. The importance of this did not surpass the meal. Time out of the trenches was a time for training, eating and sleeping. A parade was not normally part of it.

Food, a haze of smoke and the satisfaction of rum, over-came the smell and clamminess of wet clothing and brought sleep. They didn't need sentries.

Deep sleepers awake with sluggishness. Bodies unfold unwillingly in the morning, clothing creased by sleep sticking to them. No uniforms were removed for sleep, exhaustion usually robbed them of any willingness to do anything except lay down and surrender. That morning it was the Platoon Sergeant who woke everybody, marching up and down the mud street between the barns where the sections were billeted. "Let's be 'avin' you; parade at zero eight hundred, rifles cleaned, shaved and breakfasted before then."

He looked into the cowdung barn with a mouth turned down in disdain. The section coming out would hardly be clean and tidy. They had not received any new uniform or personal equipment resupply yet.

Men murmured themselves into wakefulness and scrambled things together.

"C'mon, corporal get your men moving, new RSM joining today." The Sergeant grinned. He knew this news would get everybody out. It made his job a whole lot easier.

But it created confusion. Ernest sat straight upright,

which was not easy for such a lanky thin man who never seemed to eat enough to keep his body upright and always moved about the trenches hunched, to avoid having his head taken off. "Not this quick, surely Sarge, Old Man hasn't been gone more'n a couple of days."

"Do you know how important an RSM is to a battalion, you silly carrot headed buffoon?" shouted the Sergeant. It was an unnecessary jibe, which took Ernest by surprise and made him jump up without another word, though all the others knew he would complain bitterly for days afterwards. Small things seemed to get under his skin while the others merely laughed them off. He was conscious of his 'carrot' coloured hair but men generally didn't rib him about it.

Men, still befuddled by sleep, drifted towards the village square, some dragged their rifles behind them. It was a very different Battalion to the one on display in the photograph taken only three days before.

On arrival, a strange sight greeted them. A figure was standing in front of a small monument that adorned the centre of the village. He was diminutive. He carried under his left arm a pace-stick, of the kind only used on the parade grounds of military depots and barracks. The only use of these pace-sticks was to measure the length of a soldier's marching stride. The official length was twenty-eight inches. The pace-stick was in fact two pieces of wood, hinged by brass at one end with a slotted bracket enabling it to be set open to that exact distance. The user could then march beside a man or group twirling the opened stick and measuring their exact step to ensure it was in line with regulation.

Before many men could register the pace-stick and its incongruity in this environment, broken beyond repair and very far from any parade ground, a strange sound escaped from the figure, causing it to jerk and tremor somewhat. It was a sound they were to hear again and many likened it to a cockerel being strangled at the beginning of its crow.

"What the fuck!" Men just gaped, some stopped suddenly.

There was a moment, a tiny stillness like the indefinable moment before a dawn. But this was not a bright dawn and finally the figure spoke words; or rather bawled them in a falsetto tone. *"GET THOSE RIFLES AT THE SHOULDER. I WILL INSPECT EVERY WEAPON ON THIS PARADE AND ANY THAT ARE NOT CLEAN WILL INCUR EXTRA RIFLE DRILL FOR THE OWNER."* His head moved around to take in the gathering throng. Then he added in lower but equally menacing tone. *"And that will be at the double!"*

Needless to say by the time the inspection was complete almost the whole battalion was in for extra drill. Little more than a glance at rifles attracted a very limited list of derisory comments; insufficient oil, far too much oil, rust, dirt. Those not detailed off would be on fatigue party to prepare the midday meal.

During the inspection there was a strange lack of officers on parade. Perhaps they were hiding behind some broken buildings or still ensconced in the best house in the village that would have been designated the 'Officers' Mess,' too afraid to venture out. Yes most officers were afraid of an RSM. But as the inspection was drawing to a close and names in every company for the extra parade, or perhaps names not on it, were taken; they began to gather at the periphery. As if reacting to the RSM's new regime, they quickly shuffled themselves into three ranks. The Commanding Officer of the Battalion took up his position three paces in front of the front rank which consisted of the 'field' officers, those holding the rank of major and some of the more senior captains such as the Quartermaster.

When the RSM spotted the officers, he curtailed his

inspection, leaving only a few men of the Headquarters Company to be done, who gratefully re-assembled their rifles under the eye of the Headquarters Sergeant-Major. The new RSM stalked with measured pace, probably of exactly twenty-eight inches, across towards the officers. Being small in stature the pace made him stretch a little which made men snigger at the comical appearance of it. He halted in front of the Commanding Officer, saluted and exchanged words for what seemed like several moments. Then he saluted with great emphasis and let out a screeched; "SAAR." He turned sharply right and sticking his chest even further forward he marched like clockwork to the side. After a few paces as was customary, he turned to face the parade and bawled; *"SAAR MAJORS, CARRY ON."*

"He's like a fucking puppet," commented Ben from within the ranks of Alpha Company.

"More like a muppet," adjoined jack.

"What's a muppet?" asked Ernest innocently.

"The mother of all puppets," suggested the Corporal.

"Exactly," said Jack.

Puppets, traditionally without a brain, dancing to their master's tune, were figures of fun. But there was a suspicion that the new RSM might have an actual brain; which made him an exceptionally dangerous puppet.

The war had a terrible momentum of its own. Sometimes that slowed to allow humanity to creep back into the souls of men, as supposedly when they were out of the line. If that had not happened men would have surely gone mad. Any changing of the balance, for individual gain or twisted corporate good could have a disastrous effect on the men at the bottom of the food chain.

The officers did join their companies and platoons eventually but the RSM had neatly usurped their normal duty of inspection, leaving them to listlessly address the men, telling them there was nothing they could tell them; before scurrying back to the Officers' Mess, probably for coffee.

After administering the extra rifle drill in such a manner that some men collapsed exhausted, the Battalion were allowed to crawl away with one question on their lips. Ernest expressed it. "Why the fuck…?"

"Cos he's an absolute fucking bastard, that's why." Jack profoundly voiced the knowledge that was in the heart of every man by then.

There was a period of administration which was set aside for uniform and equipment exchanges at the back of the Company Quartermaster Sergeant's wagon before the midday meal.

Other exchanges took place as well. "Ben let's fix us some extra rum. This is gonna get all fucked-up damn quick," said Jack.

"You got money for the CQMS?"

"Yea how else we gonna do the deal? So what you gonna chip in then?"

"Nothing else to spend it on is there?"

"Not unless you sneak out to the officers' brothel." Jack prodded Ben as they walked towards the CQMS's truck.

The rotund Colour Sergeant was at his post in front of the dropped canvas curtain that covered the goodies in the back of the wagon. He looked a little scrupulous as they approached and lost his face in the bills and invoices of his stock. There were sounds from within as the storeman picked out from boxes, the demanded items for the men in the queue.

Of course no money exchanged hands for the uniformed items though the CQMS would still need to account for the stock dispensed, to the Battalion Quartermaster's department. But when Jack and Ben reached the head of the queue a surreptitious hand went out from under the large stock sheets and money was passed into it; one shilling for one bottle. In this case two shillings.

"We'll be needing more of this, after that little lot this morning, colour," said Jack.

"Thought as much," responded the moody money grabbing NCO whose red crown above his three sergeant's stripes denoting the 'colour' sergeant rank seemed to shine more brightly that day. "I got a feeling the demand may go up all round."

They didn't get the rum straight there and then in daylight. Although the strictly controlled daily rum ration often was taken at the midday meal in line with the Naval practice when they were out of line. The 'extras' would need to wait until after last light when medical supplies were given out, foot inspections took place and the atmosphere was generally less vigilant. When forward in the trenches, it was sometimes even easier for the CQMS to get the 'extras' forward; perhaps via stretcher parties or the parcel post, which took packages, often from home, up to the trenches. Some men did sneak miniature bottles of alcohol through the parcel system, perhaps well wrapped by consenting parents or lovers, in thick socks, but most were confiscated, to feed the supply of extras. Besides jack did not want miniatures. He wanted a decent drink.

Ben had become used to that as well. As to the others they were content with complaining and moping and getting their legitimate share. The Corporal was under the influence of the Platoon Sergeant, still turned a blind eye but his loyalty to either side was questionable.

All loyalties would begin to shift. Regimes, previously anchored, would break loose.

The midday meal was taken under the watchful eye of the new RSM, carrying his useless pace-stick again, drawing out-of-earshot comments such as; "I could find a use for that pace-stick, up 'is fucking arse so far 'e could use the brass bits to fill 'is fucking teeth."

"Knock his fucking teeth out from behind you mean."

As if in response the RSM pacing the muddy road between companies, grouped around their cook sergeants' galleys, from which sounds of metal mess tins being filled and mugs and the occasional satisfied laugh emanated; let out a little impatient expletive, followed by a menacing growl. *"NOT FOR LONG, you'll soon be back in it!"* As if somehow they were going to be rewarded for enduring the extra rifle drill by an early return to the front.

That soon wiped away the laughter from those in earshot. Men miserably took their meal and bowed their heads, quickly returning to billets to shelter from the rain which had started again.

Thunder could be heard as well, but it was not the heavenly variety. Long-range artillery boomed and rolled, presaging something.

For the battalion it was training; section by section, platoon by platoon, gas drills, then finally combining the three rifle companies into a battalion simulated attack.

Rules of multiples dominated military formations, often it was threes, or the four battalion 'square' brigade. But at the heart of the army was the soldier and his companion or two; a two, sometimes three-man team. Sometimes they seemed welded together, such as the Lewis team. Sometimes they hung together for convenience, such as rum.

The next day brought another change. They were being 'thrown in' somewhere. No longer reserve, they were marching up to fill a gap. The pace-stick finally found a use as the RSM measured the pace of the leading troops. It was not Alpha Company but Charlie up front, always said to be the Old Man's favourite; perhaps because he always encouraged tail-enders and underdogs. With Alpha and

Bravo constantly competing in football and marksmanship, Charlie seemed content to bring up the rear.

The new RSM probably did notice this as he tapped and called out time: "Eft, ight, eft, ight. Keep up the pace there. No gaps between or within companies." He looked back down the men marching in three ranks. The road was met-alled and pot-holed in places but they could still march in formation; boots thumping the tarmac and breaking step over a hole; rifles and equipment banged and scuffled. Men coughed deeply. "SNCOs on the DOUBLE, keep your men up in line."

Some SNCOs liked being shouted at and goaded on with the men in earshot, as it gave them an excuse to do it to their charges.

On they rumbled in the rain; creaking, coughing and scuffling, some with the rifle slung over the left shoulder, its sling gripped, together with shoulder straps of a ramshackle array of equipment, by a hand which lay over the heart, as they had for the photograph.

It was a seven-mile march to their new area.

CHAPTER THREE

Another use for a trenching tool

Wet and tired they arrived at some holding area having been held up by the presence of two thousand German prisoners being marched through to the prisoner 'cage.' The Battalion stood bedraggled in Company groups waiting for news of billets or whether it would be straight up to the front. All the spirit and complaining had gone. What remained was merely a sullenness. Other logistic type outfits were there; horses, trucks and ambulances. There seemed a lot of ambulances. A six-gun artillery battery was parked half off the road with the outside wheels seeming stuck fast in mud creating a useless tilt which forbade any early deployment into an operational position.

They had been put on 'two hours' notice to move', which meant men could get out some food and settle a bit. Perhaps try to boil up some tea. Men grumbled into groups, sitting off the road, packs off; part of the indecisive mess of war.

"READY TO MOVE IN FIVE," came a sudden shout from the area where the battalion headquarters were assembled, near to a mud-spattered twelve-by-twelve tent that perhaps was some communications post. The battalion had radios though their working was often suspect.

"Move where? Why so quick, we're on two hours?" Men kicked over partly boiling tea with an expletive; "Fuck this battalion."

The officers were called into a huddle.

Men remained seated at the roadside, rifles resting on packs. Helmets were tilted back off heads and boots stretched out. New uniforms were already soaked and puttees mud-caked. Men had cursed the lack of new boots at the last billet. They were an absolute rarity. When the uppers broke free from soles some even had to bandage them up. The 'new army boot', was a myth that never became real. But good CQMSs did manage to procure some 'returned' pairs, from casualties no longer needing them, which came down the line eventually.

Surprisingly quickly the officers returned and fanned out back to their respective companies. The urgency about them planted a dread seed in some.

For Jack it was just another 'fuck up'. As far as they had been told by the Old Man they should have advanced about five miles by now, in the original plan.

"We collect a day's rations and ammunition; then we go forward," said the platoon commander who had gathered them all together.

"How far, sir?"

As if in reply a dull repetitive boom started, each explosion following before the other had reached its end. The guns were not far and the shells were not going over their heads. They were in support of another part of the battle. What battle?

"Not far, as you can hear."

"Rum coming up sir, keep out the wet?" Jack's usual question.

"Definitely not before we go up. We'll be in by last light."

Companies were already getting ammo from the back of a truck. The RSM was supervising that. The rations had not yet arrived.

"Not going nowhere without a couple of tins of something." moaned Ernest.

"You'll go when you are told." The Platoon Sergeant had heard the complaint.

"But Sarge I ain't got nothing!"

"That's because you eat what's in your pack even when there's food cooked for you, you lanky scrounger," said his corporal.

When things were 'fucked up', changes happened fast. But it seemed that no speed could be injected to make what had been promised, actually happen. So they were rushed off, without the resupply of rations mentioned by the platoon commander.

"It'll be up tomorrow, should have at least one days on you all," called the Sergeant as they were hurried into marching order.

"Make that one measly packet of biscuits," said someone.

Ernest had dropped into a black silence.

They hurried forward loaded with ammunition. Water-bottles had been replenished. They marched in file, or twos, not three ranks and soon the rough ground broke up the file as well.

Who was leading?

Alpha was in front this time. But they had pioneers guiding them. They smoked surreptitiously, coughing up phlegm which they left green and glistening in mouthfuls on the track side. The booming continued.

A small rise ended the track and they entered the trench system. The companies split. Alpha went forward, encouraged by the quality of the trench system they had entered. Saps and dugouts were plain and carefully revetted. Why were they empty?

"They've taken the bodies out of here then," said Ben.

"Ain't bin any bodies, nobody been here, engineers built these, only finished a few day ago," replied one of the pioneers.

"No nasty little surprises then, left by night visitors," the Corporal spoke.

"We bin here holding the fort."

"I thought we was about to attack, not defend," pointed out Ben.

The pioneer did not reply.

"Like always, all fucked-up," commented jack.

It was still hard daylight and they weren't making any effort to conceal the noise of boots scuffing and treading boards and equipment snagging and rubbing and curses and mumbled comments.

"Quieten down you men." The Platoon Commander was close behind the lead section, so they stopped talking, though the noise of equipment and steps made more noise than words.

They still moved quickly into the forward trench. It had almost everything, from fire and sentry steps, a decent bunker and newly dug latrine.

"This looks fit for a Royal Regiment, just need a four-poster in 'ere." The Corporal was impressed and sat down in the bunker to start his pipe going.

"No just us fuckers," said Jack.

The Lieutenant popped his head into the bunker. "Get your Lewis sited, Corporal, and make sure you get a good handover from the pioneers before they leave."

"Very well sir." The Lieutenant departed to do the same with the other sections, one to the left and one behind on the rising ground.

As they gingerly climbed a ladder, they could see the lie of the land. They were the end of the decent trench system. To their right the ground dropped away in a mass of broken wire and mud.

"We need a heavy machinegun up here not this pop-gun," was the first reaction of Alfred's number three, the young recruit named Peter.

"They gonna come through there tonight. Up to the Hun positions, up there." The pioneer pointed towards the low ridgeline to the east.

"Who is going to come through?" The Corporal took his pipe out of his mouth for a short time.

"Well it's gonna be most of the Brigade."

"Not our Brigade."

"No you're the reserve now."

The men listening in shook their heads. "We hear this from you, never hear nothing from our own people," complained an exasperated Peter.

"I know it cos I laid out the starting line, the jump off trench. Like as not they don't know it yet."

The pioneer was a sergeant. But his stripes were muddy and discoloured. His uniform was caked. He had several days of beard merging into a dark moustache. He grinned. This was his war. "But now I'm going back to the Corps area for redeployment, and hopefully a few nights rest."

"And leave us to the fucking battle, thanks Sarge." The Corporal was getting nervous.

"Done my job mate. Look at the trenches we dug for you. If you can't stay alive in them you didn't ought to be here anyway."

He disappeared quickly after that. And a Five-Nine shell burst in his wake just on the top of the trench they had used for access. The section were showered with wet mud.

Darkness drew on. The booming increased. There was some screeching of shells now as well.

"How far did 'e say that Hun ridge was?" Called the gunner Peter over his shoulder as he eased the Lewis forward, towards darkness before handing it gratefully to Alfred.

"He didn't," said Jack from the bunker.

"Mistake." The Corporal sucked on his pipe.

"Your mistake I think, pal."

"That black ridge seems to be getting closer anyway," said the gunner.

No one replied to that obvious statement.

But the next one brought immediate interest. "That barrage is beginning to creep."

"YOU SURE?" shouted the Corporal, as they all began to react.

"Yes, I'm sure," came the reply.

"Let's go and see the firework show then." Jack was the first out of the bunker, followed by Ben, the corporal and Ernest who was still in the doorway and Bert behind him.

A huge flash blinded them.

"HUN," screamed Peter. It was too close to get the gun going but Peter at the gunner's side fired his .303 straight into the face of one grey-uniformed attacker. Others were in the trench or on the firing step. There was screaming and firing in the trenches to their left. One came over a couple of yards to Ben's left. Images were blurred in the flashing lights which followed the blindness of the initial blast. A fury gave the adrenalin might. Ben had his rifle in his left hand but his right had hold of an entrenching spade which he suddenly clattered on the rifle approaching him. He was the quicker but the rifle was still discharged, into the trench wall. Ben's .303 was ready with a round in the chamber. He fired at the man to his left. He was left-handed. The Hun fell into the bottom of the trench.

Ben turned. Jack had bayoneted and shot another. They were big, heavy men, like huge grey rats. One screamed in the bottom of the trench, and tried to bring his rifle up as he had fallen there awkwardly. Ben brought the trenching tool down across the side of his face under the grey helmet, with a force borne of fear. He felt the sharp edge bite but he didn't look at the result, to see how much blood gushed out of the neck. He knew the head kind of jerked oddly. His eyes were almost closed, almost sightless from the flashes and all their ears were blocked by explosions. The Lewis team and the Corporal were fighting their own battle a few yards behind them with screams, gunfire, the bayonet and even grenades booming in the bunker which were to leave a terrible trail for them to discover.

Someone had got the Lewis firing. A parachute flare popped above them and blindness was ended for a bit. There was shouting and firing everywhere to the left and right. But no more Hun came over the top of the trench. Ben and Jack saw each other in the light above them, which was floating earthward and soon would be extinguished.

"Fucking hell." There was nothing more to be said.

The two grey lumps in the bottom of the trench were still and dead.

Ben's heart beat in his ears. He looked back at the gun team, there was only one man behind it, firing like a maniac, with flashes spurting from the barrel.

A wild figure was in the bottom of the trench, waving his rifle. "That bunker's a fucking mess." It was the Corporal.

"Where's Ernie and them?" Shouted Ben.

"That's what I mean, the bunker's a fucking mess."

"At least the gun's going... Is that Alfred?" asked Jack.

"Alfred's dead," came the response, between bursts which were calm and measured.

"What you firing at?" shouted the Corporal. It was a pointless question, firing was everywhere, it must have been at something, or perhaps nothing. The Corporal was afraid of another bunch of grey figures to finish them all off.

"Fucking Hun, moving down there to the right." The words were whipped away by the cacophony. Another flare went up. "Look."

"Our blokes supposed to be moving down there," screamed Ben.

"No, I can see em, it's Hun."

"I'm coming over." The Corporal had been paralysed but suddenly found his role. But he didn't go immediately, his feet had lead in them.

Ben and Jack shook with adrenalin and stood looking over the trench parapet. The flare burnt out.

There was a sudden movement behind them, followed by a shout; "Platoon commander!"

They would have shot him, but the silhouette of the helmet in the dying of the flare gave him away as he slid down the communications trench. "Looks like Hun taking advantage to have a go at us before the brigade down there could get their attack going," he panted breathlessly as he reached them. "Keep your positions here. Ward off the Hun if he comes again. Any casualties?"

"Yes... sir, half the section," the Corporal reported, as was his job, but his voice was desperate.

"Any of those wounded?"

"Don't know, yet."

"Get them back if they are."

He was gone, running with fear?

They daren't move, certainly not towards the bunker.

The night had only just begun.

"Stay alert, you people." The Corporal's voice was cracking. Eyes were the size of saucers. How could they not be alert? The gun had stopped. Was the little, formally silent recruit, still alive. Was he there? The Corporal now stumbled the few yards towards what had been the Lewis gun position. But he had to pass the bunker. "Some fucker's still alive in there." He cried out as he did so.

Ben and Jack held their position, searching ahead of them with eyes useless in the dark.

Flares were a double-edged weapon as everybody knew. They gave light but made silhouettes. The Old Man always favoured stealth and stillness, as movement even in the dark gave away positions. True, moving attackers could be caught like rats scuttling in the light of a flare, but defenders, even still ones, could be pinpointed by clever observation from positions at quite a distance and artillery retribution could then be brought.

It was always better to watch in the light of someone else's flare.

No more came.

"What a fuck-up." The Corporal, used Jack's normal expletive. "You alright, little Peter, where's the other two?" He was of course talking of the gunner and his number two.

The recruit was shaking uncontrollably. Unlike the gun that had sounded controlled. He couldn't fire it anymore in that state. "It was the grenade. They lobbed it over and it caught Alf and he just carried it down there, couldn't get rid of it. I think it caught on his kit." He indicated the bottom of the trench. Another lump could be seen, with the stillness of death. All Alfred could do was double over, while the grenade's explosion hollowed out most of the soft tissue of his entire body. But they were still to discover that.

"What happened to John?" The Corporal's voice wavered from high to low, like some maniac terrified of the answer.

"He's in the bunker. They tried to take the Lewis but I shot that one then another came and knifed Alf in the neck after the grenade had gone off, but then he collapsed. I think you shot him, Corp. I had to keep hold of the Lewis."

Of course he did.

"Can you hold the position and use the Lewis?"

"Of course, Corp," replied the recruit. His voice was steadier then. They steadied each other.

"I need to see what's occurring in the bunker right now."

No one offered help, there was no one to help. Eyes, such as they were, had to search out the results.

A match was lit by the Corporal mainly to find the hurricane lamp, unused so far inside the bunker. He had a fleeting glimpse of a scene of bodies, as if they were tailor's dummies thrown in random by some madman. One man moaned in the corner. "Is that you Ernie?"

"I can't move anything," came the reply.

"Are you bleeding?"

"No idea, can't feel anything."

Another match and after stepping over a man in the doorway, the hurricane lamp was found. "And John and Bert…?"

"Over there."

In the corner lay Bert with one Hun, alongside each other, like some lovers. Their soft tissue had taken most of the grenade. As had Alfred at the gun pit.

"I'll get you a stretcher Ern." The Corporal almost ran.

The platoon sergeant eventually brought a stretcher party with the Corporal.

They got Ernest out. He seemed to be paralysed, probably with a piece of grenade shrapnel in his spine. He would never walk again. They lifted him over the still grey lumps in the trench with difficulty. John the third member of the Lewis team was just a motionless lump, who had tried to block the bunker doorway and been shot, though it was not clear by whom.

The four men left in the section remained awake for the rest of the night although Ben fell asleep and slid down a couple of times onto the men he had killed.

The comfortable home created by the pioneers had become a pit of terror. The thought that the attackers had been watching its creation, gleefully waiting their moment, had not yet found words.

Sleep, wakefulness, rest and work took on new dimensions that night, bound together in an empty space between life and death.

CHAPTER FOUR
The April Fools

They heaved bodies over the parapet without looking at them. Death brings a numbness, in which everything seems worthless, including the casualties.

"This Arras is a total fool," said the Corporal, breaking a long silence.

"Yea an April Fool," commented Jack who always knew how to cap a comment. "Arras me 'arris… If Arras was an arsehole we are several miles up it, covered in utter shit."

"Oh yea, April the first, ain't it?" Ben looked at the trenching tool. "If my own brother had come over I'd have done for him as well." He picked up the tool and looked for the blood stains on it."

"Then called him an April Fool… You said you hadn't got a brother… or sister," responded Jack listlessly.

"So I ain't. Well if I had one I'd have done for him, as an April Fool."

"If he had a Hun uniform on," injected his corporal.

"Did we stop to identify the uniforms?" asked Jack. "Did we ask; are you really Hun, or just pretending? We need fucking rum, don't we Ben?"

"Course we do."

There was no rum. But they had heard from the Sergeant who paid an early morning visit along with the Platoon and

Company Commander, that there would be men to replace the casualties. They had not arrived and were probably on the way up from the logistic area. There would be no relief. They were the reserve battalion again.

They watched British soldiers picking amongst the debris to their front right. They watched an entire patrol of eight men cut down by machinegun fire from the Hun ridge pointed out by the pioneer sergeant, seemingly an age ago. The patrol tried to run but got caught in the wire and one after the other were killed. Blood leapt from their bodies at every hit.

"God, I bet the fucker behind the gun is enjoying that." It was only Jack who could comment on this slaughter of his own comrades like that. Deep down they all had bloodlust. It had been on display last night; a survival mechanism. But talking with it in such bravado, especially of their own men, was not natural to all.

It was after seeing the patrol shot that they first heard the cries of a casualty; somewhere out there. No one spoke of it at first.

The new men arrived with the Sergeant who also brought some rations and water. There were only three to replace the four who had become casualties. This was often the case. Replacements did not make up the numbers.

"You people get up on the parapet. We gonna eat and sleep. Who's a gunner among you?" None of them volunteered. The Corporal looked closely at them "Where you from?" He didn't see a badge he recognised and there was something about the body language of the group that made him take closer stock.

"Artists' Rifles," said one of them, who appeared bigger of stature than the rest.

Jack exploded. "Artists' fucking Rifles, what will they send next. And what sort of artists are you?"

"Musicians."

"Give 'em a chance jack, they must have been trained otherwise they wouldn't be here," pleaded the Corporal.

"So if you been training, you should all be able to man the Lewis and as the Corporal said who is going to do it?"

"Well I could I suppose," said the spokesman uncertainly.

"Well get up there and do it. The rest of you get up on the fire step. Don't get yourself spotted from that ridge to the East though, that's where the Hun is, so keep yourself down. We gonna get into these rations."

Peter the young recruit who had been firing the Lewis during the battle and may have saved the lives of the other three, gave up his post willingly. He was calm by this time and had loaded some Lewis ammunition into drum magazines. He avoided the place where Alfred had died as if it was consecrated ground. He passed up several of the heavy circular magazines to the new gunner. "What's your name?" he asked.

"Henry."

"There you are then Henry, looks like there'll be just the two of us now on the gun. Alfred our number one and John his mate were killed last night. Alfred's over there and we threw John out there as well." He pointed. "I'll be here if you need me." He took up a place in the bottom of the trench having secured several tins of food from the little stock that the Corporal left outside the bunker.

He was small in stature and the others had regarded him as a boy. But now he had become a man.

Jack and Ben got into the rum before taking food, downing a bottle between them.

"That's for the boys," said Jack as he lifted the small bottle in salutation, "the boys killed."

"And that's for Ernest," rejoined Ben, doing the same. "They were good people."

35

"The best, considering what we got now," replied his friend dismissively.

They sat outside the bunker with their backs to the trench wall. Then almost immediately fell asleep where they sat.

The sun had come out, a sort of tentative early spring sun but they were warmed by it.

The Corporal had found his pipe, from somewhere and began to stoke it up again. Then he put it aside to eat, straight from some tins of beef and processed cheese, followed by a whole packet of biscuits.

He ventured into the bunker and began to smoke. The pungency of the tobacco gradually tried to replace the intense smell of cordite that had caused death. He fell asleep before his pipe was finished, slumped exhausted against the back wall. There was light from outside which came through the low doorway. It was a cave-like construction with walls that had become greasy mud, wood supports, some splintered by grenade fragments. The roof was a little curved, supported again by beams, meanly constructed yet effective until the explosion came inside. Then it became an oven. Some bunkers had iron sheets supporting them. That wouldn't have helped either. The grenade might have brought the roof in.

The privates from the Artists' Rifles stood on the fire-step. They heard the crying. They saw the bodies over the trench parapet. They knew that the English ones would need to be recovered. That would be done at night. The German ones would be left.

"Someone out there is injured," said Marcus. He was a fair-haired, and tall recruit whose artistic calling was playing the cello. "Should we wake the Corporal and tell him about it?"

"Don't yet, he probably knows about him, " replied the other rifleman with him.

Still the sound preyed on their ears. It started to take on a voice, an English voice they thought, recognising certain words. Then they heard one distinct word; *'Please.'* The word came on a gust of breeze which came in an afternoon lull.

"He's asking for help. He must be conscious."

There were three of them facing directly towards the ridge and Henry was to the right by several yards past the bunker, from which snoring now emanated; manning the Lewis. He didn't respond to the conversation as he was out of earshot or ignored it.

"Of course he's conscious if he's crying."

"Well he may not have been before but now he said something."

They argued mildly amongst themselves, then fell into a brooding silence when no more sound came.

"We could have some food as well," suggested Marcus.

But they seemed reluctant to leave their posts.

They were looking through slots in the trench wall, not over the top. They were like small battlements with a kind of lid over them. But to the right some of these had been destroyed in the battle of the previous night, leaving gaps. It was difficult to fire rifles through the slots with a proper grip as when lying on a range. You could grip the butt and rest the barrel on the mud wall, but your traverse was limited.

With the Lewis gun, the pioneers had constructed a better position enabling the gunner to lie down and get a good line of sight. It was built up by sand-bags and beaten earth.

The section had two periscopes for use by a sentry or observer to get a better view. But still the overall design of the trench created a bit of a siege mentality. Men could hear but their view was limited.

Frustrated momentarily by this, one of the Artist Riflemen chose to get a better look over the part of the trench where the spyholes were broken. He had decided to get some food as they had previously discussed and was wandering a little along the fire-step towards the bunker and taking a good look while he went.

Perhaps the quiet of the afternoon had lulled them while the sleep of the others deepened with snoring. At least it sounded so, though who knew of the dreams they were experiencing.

Suddenly the Artist Rifleman dropped to the bottom of the trench with a single cry. Then he started screaming. Meanwhile a low thump might have been detected. Blood spurted from his neck. He clutched at it with his head at a strange angle.

"Sniper," shouted Marcus, the cello player, who was nearest and he dropped to the wounded man's aid. He got covered in blood quickly as he tried to cradle the head. But then reached into the man's uniform and fumblingly extracted his field dressing from a top pocket. With shaking hands he tore it open and started wrapping it around the man's neck.

Jack had awoken and sat listlessly watching. His tunic was open at the neck, helmet pushed back. He sprawled somewhat, the rifle and web equipment at the side on the trench floor. "Now you got a problem there, coz you need to stop that blood but the tighter you put on the dressing, the more likely you are to strangle the poor fucker." He burped loudly and then showed dirty teeth in a dark stubble face.

Ben leapt up. Something touched him and made him act. "We need medics." They hadn't had any the night before, but now they could save somebody. He scrambled over the injured man and ran into the communications trench shouting; "CASUALTY, we got a casualty, need medic."

After a few minutes he ran back, stooping and sliding. Then he crouched at the man's feet. He had stopped screaming but not stopped bleeding. "Medic on the way," he breathed.

They had been isolated in their battle and now seemed isolated in their need for help; completely alone. But behind them was the platoon sergeant and the platoon commander and further back in what had seemed a good trench system the Company Headquarters and further back the rest of the Battalion. These had been friends before and the Battalion had been one. But now...

A man with a Red Cross armband did arrive. They did not know him. Perhaps he was new to the Battalion. He looked at the blood-soaked dressing, completely blood-soaked and the man cradling the head who was also a mess. He looked at the casualty whose head was at a strange angle. He did not say that the one holding his head might have killed him, that the bullet might have severed the spinal cord through the movement of the neck. He did say simply; "He's dead..."

The Corporal emerged, suddenly awake from the bunker and looked down silently. "Sniper got 'im," explained Ben.

The gunner Peter who had given his Lewis to Henry was awake. He shook with emotional pain at the sight of the dead man. He had another battle to fight within himself.

These battles were only just beginning.

"Well it seems this is a fucking unlucky trench, don't it?" said Jack. "But a man's got to eat and right now, I'm hungry. Coming Ben?"

"Let's get him back first," replied Ben.

"Suit yourself." Jack shrugged and disappeared into the bunker.

There was no question among the others. Bodies of friendly dead were entrenched and preserved in lime at battalion or further back. A padre conducted a service in the presence of some officers and others perhaps. Names would be noted and the burial site marked, as well as an accurate grid reference recorded. There was no reason to think that if the area was subsequently lost, the site would not be respected by the enemy.

The grave could be destroyed by artillery fire or other action but its positional notification would at least be known. No one knew what else to do to respect those who had died; though respect for the dead and for the living was not high on every soldier's daily routine.

Ben, the medic and the cello player, heaved the dead rifleman back down the trenches in an undignified manner. They returned to a grim silence and headed to the bunker where Ben looked for food for both of them. They hardly looked at each other. The Corporal and Jack with Henry back behind the Lewis, held the section trench. But the men were now down to six.

After a while they dropped to the normal single sentry and it was Peter again behind the Lewis. In an awkward way the others squeezed into the bunker together.

"Artists' fucking Rifles," ejected Jack after a swig of rum. He hardly concealed his drinking now. "Musicians, did you say?"

"Yes," said Henry. "I play the trombone and he... that was... did the violin and Marcus there is a cellist, very good one too."

"Trom-fucking-bones, violins, a cello. Well I suppose you could frighten the Hun. If we could get you some instruments we could have a concert eh?" The Corporal was back on his pipe. "Then they would know we was definitely mad."

"So how's that going to frighten them?" asked Ben.

The Corporal looked into his pipe. "Just talking Ben."

They fell to their own tasks avoiding eyes, no longer in the 'pals pairs' of before.

Henry made a comment into the fuggy atmosphere of smoke, rum, boots and the soldier's creature comforts. "There is a man out there in no-man's land, lying injured. We heard him this morning, did you know Corp?"

"How many men d'yer think there are out there, who are not yet dead?"

"This one is English, he's crying and pleading for help," said Marcus the cellist. "I was telling Ben about it when we went back with…"

"Oh don't you know his name. And what's your name mister cello player?" asked jack.

"Marcus."

"Fuck me, Marcus and Henry and the nameless dead. Well let's just call you Cello.

Henry and Marcus looked at each other. "We don't know the name of the one who was killed. We only met the other day," Henry said.

"Oh, but you two know each other well don't you."

"Artists stick together. We don't really know each other too well, just talked about our work."

"Work is it, work?!" Jack scoffed.

"Yes work," said Henry confidently.

"Not real work though."

"It is artistic work. We use our brains and hands… But mostly our hearts."

"Doesn't seem important now though does it?" asked Ben.

"It's very important to keep focused on what we do in the real world," said Marcus.

There was a moment's silence as men shuffled about eating or drinking. But Jack continued to look at Marcus and Henry with open contempt. He sat back and lit a smoke. "Well you people better realise that you are in the *real* world here. It's war and people get killed as you have just seen. So give up thoughts of your world. This is the only one now." He sat back in a peaceful manner. "Now I'm gonna smoke and have a bit of drink, take a shit and sleep. That's our world, until the Hun comes again eh Ben."

Ben nodded turning his face away. He had shaved and cleaned his rifle.

Marcus looked like a boy, with blond hair and a face that hardly had hair on it. He ignored the face of jack but turned to the Corporal. "So what are we gonna do about that man in No Man's Land then Corp, crying for help?"

The Corporal shot a look at Jack. "Probably be dead by morning." He sniffed, as if that was a reason for regret rather than indifference.

"Probably another April Fool, what d'you think Ben?" Jack opened his mouth laughing in a cackle and coughing. His teeth were not good.

"Well if we can't hear him in the morning we'll know that it was!"

CHAPTER FIVE
A patrol is planned

They were awake for the dawn stand too. They were awake listening. It was not the time for talking. Private pain was beginning to creep into their hearts but it was out of reach of expression. Sleep had dulled the adrenalin of the night before last but now they had to go on living, though some wanted that more than others. They shuffled past each other with eyes down.

Every man should be at his post for stand too. Every man should be alert with his weapon already cleaned and fully ready for action. They faced the enemy, standing along the trench taking care this time not to be seen, while NCOs and the Platoon Commander came behind them to inspect and question. Very little eye contact was made. No one could see what the other was thinking in these brief exchanges.

As the Lieutenant and Sergeant stood outside the bunker surveying the backs of the men the crying came again so distinctly it could be heard by everyone. *"Please... please... help."* It floated on the morning air, which was clear and quiet; like a voice in waiting. It came across more like an accusation than a plea.

"Good heavens," exclaimed the officer. "Who is that, do we know? Is he one of yours Corporal?"

"No sir, all our casualties accounted for 'cept a couple of dead over the parapet."

"He sounds very close though."

"Don't think he is sir, sound plays tricks, one moment he sounds close, the next a long way away. When there is no bombardment and no other sound, y'know."

The crying came again. This time it was just a desperate sort of sobbing which fell upon the listeners ears.

"Well are you going to get him?" the Lieutenant asked sharply, obviously disturbed by the voice, twitching his head from side to side.

The Corporal spoke. The others remained silent as if they had no knowledge of what was being spoken about. "Well sir, like I said we have no idea where he is; one moment he is close, then far away."

"Could be a stomach wound sir. So his head is close to the ground and you can't get a proper direction on him," volunteered the Sergeant.

"Yes, you may be right. Well Corporal this is not good. He might be there for days."

"I don't think so sir."

The all looked at one another. For an instant some eyes met. Questions of a deeper nature formed themselves in the echo of the darts. Perhaps he had been left out on purpose, forgotten deliberately. Who had the courage to go out and look for him after they had witnessed a patrol being slaughtered?

War will always have its dirty underside.

"Well we are not in the business of just leaving a man out there to die, especially one of our own. I want patrols out to find him, this evening please."

"Very good sir... Sir, is there any news about... the offensive."

"It's delayed, apparently the French are in an awful mess, and it won't involve us any way, all happening over there to the East. Our orders are to hold here... and wait."

"Thank you, sir."

"Right, well we'd better be off… Don't forget, tonight, get that chap back!"

"Sir…we down to six men now you know," said the Corporal.

But the officer glared and left. They stood down. Single reinforcements were not always forthcoming. All extra men were needed for the push, not reserve units.

"Get that chap back!" Jack mimicked the officer's accent. "Apparently the French are in an awful mess." Then he changed to a voice of bitterness; "that's it, always blame some other fucker…one of the first rules of war."

"Right you men. I want someone looking for this man all day. Use the periscopes and get a bead on him as soon as you hear him again," the Corporal ordered his men. His leadership was rejuvenated after his talk with the Platoon Commander and Sergeant.

But Jack appeared to be heading for the bottle again. "Breakfast Ben?" He lifted it.

"No I'll take first stint with Henry, get these periscopes set up."

"We can't use the periscopes in that part of the trench." Marcus indicated the place where the other Artists' Rifleman had been killed by a sniper. No one dared use that piece of trench.

It wasn't long before they heard the crying again. Ben was looking through one of the periscopes. He saw a land-scape of mud, in small spaces. The periscope magnified a small circular area which could then be moved and tra-versed; rushing over the ground then focusing on another little circle of mud. He heard the crying then looked through the periscope at the place where he had heard it and saw nothing. But the periphery of hidden undulations were magnified, leaving their contents to the imagination.

Craters where there might be life, half submerged in a pool of water and blood, a soldier unable to move; a soldier like them, like those who had been remorselessly killed by them and by the enemy.

But who was the killer when the adrenalin smashed your arm holding a sharp entrenching tool down onto a man's neck; when you didn't even think, before shooting? Ben brought the periscope close to the trench and surveyed the dead Germans. The ones he had killed. They were just lumps. He didn't look for their faces.

The crying became unbearable to listen to as the day wore on with soldiers' tasks. So they didn't speak about it, as if they weren't listening to it.

There had been a barrage, which had changed the face of the place where the periscope ranged and traversed.

It was quiet; a quiet afternoon where men waited. They waited for an action, a promised action. They waited unseen by any periscope. Many were in underground bunkers, to the right, the east; waiting for a word, an order. To attack.

Ben came back onto periscope duty later with Marcus, the Cellist.

Ben tipped the periscope up towards the ridge. That's where the enemy were. He worked along it carefully, noting some bits of wire. The Hun that had attacked them had crawled through their wire, under the cover of the barrage. Some had been cut, leaving a repair job which so far had been unaddressed. The ridge ahead looked lifeless. Sometimes you knew where the Hun was. Sometimes you knew when a shell would come over.

Something made him feel the Hun was not there.

Looking through the periscope made him feel calm. Then he heard the crying, crying for a mother. Marcus had gone to get something to eat. "Why don't you get back up here on the other periscope Marcus and look at this." He wanted someone else to listen with him, not look. The sound touched a heart that he didn't know was there any longer.

Marcus was getting used to his periscope. He brushed a long lock of blond hair away from his face and tilted his helmet back as he put his eye to it and lifted the top over the parapet, where the mud was hard. It waved about a bit and then he knelt down on the fire step. He was tall with long hands, so he tried bracing the long barrel of the scope against the trench wall.

Ben noticed something about his movement. A good footballer never puts a foot wrong or out of place. A fast runner runs gracefully, keeping his head still. "Do you mind if we call you Cello?" He asked.

"No, of course not," said the young man in a steady voice.

"Not that we know anything about the cello."

"That doesn't matter."

They surveyed the ground.

"How did you come to join us as reinforcements?"

"I don't know. We were brought up to the logistic area and then told we were coming here, to the Worcesters."

"Why do you say it like that?"

"Nothing…Except."

"Except what?"

Marcus was looking. The crying came and he looked far to the right. His height made him look further over beyond where the Lewis had its zone of observation. He was suddenly still. Then he lifted one foot onto the step, in line with the other knee. "I think I see him."

"Where?" Ben showed excitement too.

"Over beyond the Lewis gun. Who is over there anyway?"

"You mean, who, from our side?"

"Yes."

"I don't know. I think that is where they are waiting to do the attack."

"What are they waiting for?"

"I don't know. What can you see anyway?"

"It's confused. There is so much wire over there and its going downhill, not flat ground."

"Nowhere's flat is it when you look through these things."

"No, but I can see something, looks like it may be a helmet."

"Is it moving?"

"Not really."

The sun was beginning to drop behind them. Evening was coming. "Corp, you awake?" called Ben.

A muffled grunt came from the bunker.

"Bring a compass if you got one. We might have a bead on this voice."

"Coming." The voice held exasperation not excitement, as if a sleep had been disturbed. But he did bring the compass and grimaced when he heard the moaning of the casualty. "You got him?" He asked Marcus, too casually.

"Can't tell, but it could be."

"Take a bearing then... You do know how to take a bearing don't you?"

"Yes I do."

Henry and Peter had taken up positions on the Lewis gun. "We have all been trained to take a bearing," pointed out Henry.

"And have you been trained to use those things, hanging around your neck?" asked the Corporal, pointing to the haversacks that held their gas respirators.

"Oh yes," replied Henry without conviction.

"That's good, coz we'll probably need 'em tonight," gloated Jack as he emerged from the bunker.

"Yes, take a bearing and that's where we are going, and we could meet some gas lying in those craters," agreed the Corporal.

"Hun could throw some more over at us as well," said Jack.

"Don't know whether they still up there on that ridge," said Ben. "It looks sort of empty."

"That's what they hoping for, to get the attack going." The Corporal sucked on his pipe. "You got that bearing yet, Mister Cello?"

"Yes I got it."

"And what is the bearing?"

"Its around zero three zero degrees."

"Right that's our direction then," said the Corporal decisively.

But he seemed to be speaking in a vacuum, nobody moved. Nobody showed an enthusiasm for the decision. Then Jack said, "Why don't those people over that side send a patrol out? Why does it have to be us? With only six men how can we do it and hold this trench."

"We're nearest."

"Are we? Where is everybody else. In fact, where *is* everybody?"

"There are a lot of people in the logistic area, just hanging around," said Henry, looking back from his position at the Lewis.

"Seems like everybody's waiting for something," said Ben.

"We're not waiting, we're acting." The Corporal tried again to change the mindset. But he had no help, no Old Man to come down from the battalion headquarters; bring the men together and encourage them to get behind the cause.

They were uncertain if there was a cause now.

CHAPTER SIX
An instant of change

They waited for last light. Then they waited some more. The patrol was to include: Henry, Cello who had taken the bearing, Jack, Ben and the Corporal. They had to stop the crying, the unbearable sound. They wanted to get to its source, just get there. Then they would know what to do.

Eventually deep into the night after some reinforcements from another platoon had finally, wordlessly arrived to hold the trench, with Peter; and they had heard that word of their patrol had gone out to neighbouring sub-units; they set off. Leaving the trench system was like leaving home, cutting off. They moved in single file, feeling their way to and then through the gap in the wire in front of their trenches. Each man became an island of privacy; in the dark, alone, struggling to see the man in front, ignoring the man behind.

No one had visited to update them, or wish them good luck; something the Old Man might have done. In fact under him they would have already been out dominating No Man's Land. Now they didn't know what was out there, in front of them or behind, to the side. They were going alone.

Ben held suspicions that the Hun had departed. There was less night activity than usual which might have added weight to this feeling.

But the crying came intermittently, in between the night noises. Everyone thought that he must be dying. Nobody voiced that. They just struggled on hopelessly, around huge moon bright puddles, over shallow craters, avoiding large ones.

Every mission has a mental possibility for each man; success, failure, hope, disaster, even under the worst of circumstances. So did this one. No one questioned it outwardly. But mentally it seemed like a defeat. Why did they have to go? There would have been no victory in the bravado of waiting for the death of the casualty but just going was in a way an admission of failure, though it was an action. Jack even voiced the remote possibility that somehow this was a Hun trick, using some kind of electric loud speaker left in No Man's Land.

If that was the case, they had to do something, take action, to smash whatever machinery was the cause. It had been April the first, which added to the notion that they were all fools.

Any snagged equipment as they slid out of their trench and moved along the bearing, was yanked in an exasperated way. The only words were curses. There was noise, but nobody cared. There was light from flares, nobody cared. The Hun might have been there, in his place, listening, waiting for another lunge at them. Did anybody care about that? Death was a bayonet thrust or a desperate chop with an entrenching tool away. The new recruits brought no new life. They had brought the death of one of their own to continue the jinx of the previous night. Deaths were often the responsibility of those who had died. Sympathy was not part of action on the battlefield.

They moved through wire, old trenches and debris. The Corporal had the compass and blundered on in front without turning or stopping, which lost those behind him.

Every soldier in No Man's Land at night without a sense of purpose was lost, as though at sea in a very small boat.

Finally they did stop, the Corporal stopped to listen. They seemed to have gone some distance. They went into a circle just as some guns opened up.

"That's Hun Five-Nines isn't it?" whispered Ben.

"Why you whispering? Probably gas, so we best get these fucking things ready." Jack dragged his gas mask haversack round to the front of his body with difficulty as it always got tangled up with all the other equipment that hung on them. He turned to the men of the Artist's Rifles. "Can you get these on at all?"

"Yes we can," said Henry, a little too hastily. But they didn't move to secure their gas masks.

A light show started with flares and booms and then, adding to the sense of loneliness, explosions close by; too close.

Preparations for gas had been a training aspect of 1917; the third year of the war, along with new masks which actually could be worn more than once.

"Can't hear that fucker any more, can anybody?" asked the Corporal.

"Can't hear nothing except them guns." Ben looked at the faces of the others, flashing on and off in the explosions and flares.

Someone panicked and pulled his gas mask out with a yell as an explosion seemed to come too close. They all reacted then, fumbling and cursing like snarling animals.

Finally they had them on and crouched like a pack of newly met aliens, afraid to look at each other and afraid to turn away. The loneliness of having the gas masks on was like being in solitary confinement. That's how men described it. They just sat on the ground and waited.

Time diminished the bombardment. Perhaps it was just an exploratory one.

Someone had to do something.

The Corporal eventually gingerly removed his mask. Slowly they all followed. Usually it took several minutes in the breeze for gas to dissipate. It had been more than that.

"Let's move on then," said the Corporal.

"Move on where Corp?" asked Cello. He appeared enthusiastic and engaged. Perhaps he was the new leader.

"Well, on your bearing."

They turned away from each other, back towards an individual mental silence. Instead of single file they moved into a sort of line-abreast formation.

The bearing was difficult to follow. The sound of the casualty seemed to have disappeared. Suddenly they breasted a small earth bank and came into a shallow crater. A flash revealed water and something in the dancing shadows of the alternate light and dark. Perhaps it was movement.

"Something there?" The Corporal raised his voice a little wildly, questioning the unknown, the shadows. Of course there were bodies, lying in No Man's Land, but this…something beyond death perhaps. So they stopped and crouched. The pool of water became a moon in the next flash, a source of light and on its far bank something did move. It may have been just rats, or one rat dragging something made big in the shadow.

Ben knew the stillness of death, having spent the day with the grey lumps in the trench next to him. This did not have the stillness of death. Then the moon disappeared.

It was a crater of some proportions, which would have made it difficult to have seen anything inside it from their trench, even with the periscope. But perhaps the helmet; the reflections of the false moon; anything was possible in the land between life and death that was No Man's Land.

They paused and began silently to question what, beyond anything they could fathom, was here; sharing this space. A dread, beyond fear, rose in them, as the false moon faded to black and the night reclaimed the pit. They stared into it, a kind of hell. What lay there?

"Who are you?" Again the Corporal questioned in a voice high with a new emotion. The mouth usually comforted with a pipe could quiver easily.

No sound came, no answer.

A voice that had called for help would have had joy in the prospect of receiving it. But anything in this pit was long beyond joy. The patrol were loath to advance, loath to step into the water; yet to tiptoe around it was not the act of a soldier, at least not an upstanding one.

So it was Jack who took the first step. He was a leader. The Corporal was something of a reluctant one. His Corporal's stripes could not be seen in the dark. The strength of personality was the test which raised up leaders in the darkness and uncertainty of the battlefield, whatever the content of their character or the badges on their arm. "Oh fuck this shit, let's just get this over with." With that Jack stepped forward.

The others were behind, the tall Cello was almost alongside Jack and as they splashed through the water, only ankle deep. On the other side of the pool a grey lump came up, a face turned upwards from the mud; a terrible face without half of its covering, a moving skull. A hand came up, perhaps pleading. But it was too late; firing from the hip, Jack shot the lump then reloaded another round into the chamber with a ratchetting of the cocking lever and fired again. The face subsided back into the mud without an accusation. The body, for it was obvious now that it had been a body, convulsed and was then still.

Cello saw the helmet; the British helmet. Something inside him was touched. His heart suddenly cried for him. He heard his own voice. "Why have you shot him? He moved. He was alive, one of ours. *Why?*"

They had all reached the other side of the pool of water. The bombardment was slowing, flashes of light were longer spaced. They dropped to one knee, rifles pointing.

One rifle did not point. Cello just held his rifle down, already it didn't seem part of him.

They became still, on guard against the body, against the chance of it rising up against them. They now had to confirm the events that had happened in a moment of action. That moment; the shots fired, the noise they made; would create other consequences, perhaps for their safety. They might be attacked by a nearby patrol, from either side.

Rational action, reaction, consequences; such things were often impossible for a soldier. He had to live in an adrenalin moment.

How was he then to be judged or make a judgement?

They had bayonets fixed, seventeen inches of steel on their rifles. Moving at night in single file without stabbing the man in front was not easy. Rifles were often cradled in the crook of the left arm. Turning around might then be the cause of an accident. But now they had a chance for a long armed exploration of the lump in the mud.

They advanced very slowly. "Stick him then, just to make sure." The Corporal had gone back to speaking in a high and quivering voice. But no one knew whether it was a ghastly joke he was making.

"Just prod 'im," said Ben.

"He is or was a casualty, not an enemy," Cello had seemed to grow in stature during the night. His voice was steady.

"Oh you know that do you, very know-all suddenly ain't we, Mister Cello?"

"I'm not a know it all. But I do know what is right."

All this was whispered. But then suddenly Jack broke into a laugh, a high forced laugh at the top of his breath. "Ha ha ha, oh right, what is right. You know what is *right* do you? This war is *right* is it? What we doing here is *right* is it?"

"We can choose to do what is right regardless of the situation we are in."

The lump in the mud waited patiently for them to decide his fate. Before they had heard crying and pleading, now he lay motionless, silent, inviting anything. Seemingly angered by this, Jack advanced the few paces towards it and in a classic lunge and with an exasperated grunt stuck the bayonet into the middle and highest point. It was a quick in and out penetration, probably only a few inches. He did not want the embarrassment of the point being stuck inside the casualty's body.

"Awww!" Cello reacted as though he had suffered the stabbing, diverting attention away from the lump which reacted as a felt-filled sack used for bayonet practice might have done. In his turn of anger, Cello cast down his rifle which before had hung listlessly from his hand.

"He is fucking dead. He is totally and completely dead, you silly fucker," said Jack.

The others were incapable of speech or had nothing to say. They remained still.

"We best be getting back," announced the Corporal after some time, as if they had gone out for an evening stroll in a dark wood and should now go back for their supper which would be getting cold.

They all paused, not knowing which way or where to turn. Then slowly stood up. But Cello, leaving his rifle where he had thrown it, approached the casualty and bent towards him. He put out a hand and very lightly touched the man who tipped and as if balancing on the edge of some moment of private endeavour, gave up and slowly turned over, settling into a more comfortable prone position in his mud bed. Cello almost jumped back. Then after a moment's shocking stillness they all took half a pace forward and looked.

It was as if the mud had eaten the casualty. It had certainly drained the blood from his face which shone like the finest vellum paper crumpled over bone, with its dark sightless sockets of eyes seeking the moon above; not accusing them. Mud had engulfed at least two limbs. Where were they? What remained of the body was so small. But he had moved. Had he therefore been alive?

Then suddenly as if remotely taunting them, there came a low cry, more a gasp, surely from the same original casualty, not close, not within the arc of the patrol movement that had brought them here; but on the wind of a moon that did now suddenly present itself again. Had this mud man summoned it; the moon and the cry, as if they were comrades about to enter another life, or the afterlife.

Men often spoke of experiences of the void between life and death such as seeing and speaking to men who had been killed the day before. Some men would enter the realms of death instantly, accepting it. Some refused to go there even though the body they had inhabited had ceased to function.

The patrol just dropped their heads; as if a football match long overdue its final whistle had just yielded another goal against them. But Cello lifted his head and turned it this way and that as if sniffing out the source of the sound. But they were not animals. Their powers were limited. They could not even bring to bear those they did have; of speech and movement. Only Cello did move. He stepped further away from his rifle, away from the apparition in the mud. "Well that gives you the answer doesn't it on our casualty – he is still out there, out here."

"Not for much longer he won't be. We've done what we can. This patrol ends here." The Corporal had suddenly taken back the leadership. Perhaps because he finally knew how to take his men down a path that they wanted to go and still satisfy his mission. The man, the real casualty, would probably not survive the night anyway. So the platoon commander would not hear him at stand too the next morning. His voice had been so low anyway.

Dawn would soon be approaching.

They had come together into a sort of circle but with Cello standing apart, on his own. "For me it doesn't end." He said.

They seemed to notice then that he did not have his rifle.

"Pick up your weapon," said the Corporal in a slow deliberate voice.

"Come on Marcus, no sense in carrying on like that is there," said Henry. It was the first time he had spoken.

"Yes Cello, this is over for us," added Ben.

"And if you don't come with us, that's you deserting," said Jack simply.

"How can I be deserting. I want to carry on with the mission. I want to find this man."

"And I have said we are finished," said the Corporal. "So you are disobeying orders and you have thrown away your rifle, so that's another offence."

"A very serious one," added Jack.

"It's not an offence, for me it is the right thing to do."

"You don't have that ability, to think what is right and wrong. You obey orders. You pick up your rifle and come with us. That is your order. That is what you must obey. If not then you will have to suffer the consequences." The pipe-smoking Corporal whose mouth had quivered and demeanour had seemed weak, suddenly found strength.

But Cello seemed the stronger one even though he had no military backing for it. "We had a mission; or did we? What was the mission? Was it to rescue a casualty, or end his life because of the burden that his crying, his voice accusing us, had put on us? To remove that burden, we have shot a man. Now we can return with our consciences clear... You can return, *not me*. You speak of orders. We had been given an order, bring him back. But...we didn't even have a stretcher."

"We are not fucking stretcher-bearers," said Jack.

"But our mission was to rescue the casualty."

The others were silent.

"Our mission was to find him," said the Corporal.

"No, you remember what the officer said, 'bring that man back.' Those were his final words. Is that not true Corp?" asked Cello.

"Yes but..."

"So you in fact are the one disobeying orders."

"I am the one who makes the decisions. I have made one."

"Yes, you have made one, perhaps a wrong one."

But Cello was on his own, against the others, only one of whom, apart from the Corporal, seemed to have a voice, the others were bending. Their bodies had no resistance. So they could not stand with Cello.

"That's not for you to judge. Your duty is to obey orders, the last order... mine."

They had forgotten every rule of military discipline and were standing in a huddle, not guarding themselves, or each other, not ready to fight. So an explosion from afar reminded them of where they were and slowly they sank, to the mud. "Come on men, let's get out of here," urged the Corporal. His duty was also to look after his men.

They turned their backs on Cello. He had put himself beyond the boundary of being worthy of looking after.

The Corporal turned a final time. "Are you coming then, private... what is your name again?"

"It's Harris, that's my name," said Cello.

"Well Private Harris. I'm ordering you to pick up your

rifle and come with us. If you do not you will be not only disobeying an order… You have already cast aside your rifle and you know how serious an offence that is… And you are in effect going awol, so that is the offence of desertion as well."

"No, that's not what I'm doing is it. I'm still on the mission to find that casualty and bring him to safety." Cello stood with the strength of a man possessing free will.

"You don't just wander around in No Man's Land conducting your own mission," scoffed Jack. "You are a soldier, although I know to you that means nothing… does it? To us it means obeying orders and doing what you're told."

"When it suits you," suggested Cello.

"Well it suits us right now. So you better make up your mind."

"My mind is made up." Cello stood his ground as if guarding the grizzly half man in the mud.

"If your mind is made up then you will have to face the consequences." The Corporal turned away again and he took the other men with him, willingly or reluctantly. They didn't verbally identify themselves on either side. Their bodies however moved as though they had no choice.

Cello was standing still as the others splashed back through the water. There was a slight pause midway and Ben turned, came back to where Cello's rifle was and picked it up gingerly. He looked at Cello and their eyes met across the darkness.

When passing weapons from one soldier to another the bolt should always be opened to 'prove' its condition; whether ready to fire or not. This was a special circumstance. This weapon was not proved. They were taking control of the .303 to help prove that Cello had cast it away.

He seemed happy to let it go. The moment was sealed.

CHAPTER SEVEN
Alone

Cello was alone, but suddenly not lonely. He sat down near the body, which had attracted such revulsion and fear but now was his only companion. He thought about water, as his mouth was very dry. He was cold as well. He had some water in his bottle, but no blanket or great coat. The great coat had not been available to the men. As it was spring, they had just rain capes. But these had been left in the trench. When it rained he would get even colder. Wet did not matter, but being cold and wet without something to cover your body took away your spirit even quicker.

It wasn't raining now, so water had to be taken from his bottle. That was the only good thing about rain. You could drink it while it ran down your face. It had been cleaned by the clouds, filtered. So you could fill your bottle with it also, without chemical cleaners.

He felt light; no rifle, no bayonet either. How was he to defend himself?

Did the man sharing this space with him have any weapons on him, under him. Cello looked at the body, covered in mud, as if he had bathed in it.

The water carrier, a steel bottle with a capacity of one pint and a half, covered in green or brown hessian held on the belt by a web carrier, was difficult to extract, especially when the canvas webbing was wet. It was little more than half full. It did not provide the correct amount of water for a fully-grown man in a very physical environment for a day. So Cello sipped it, tasting the chemical purification. It calmed him though, so he was able to think rationally about his rifle. He had never fired it at a man, not stabbed a man with the bayonet. So he concluded that if he needed to use any weapon to defend himself he would probably not be able to do it. If that led to him being killed, then let that come.

He had already gone beyond his threshold of courage. He was now in the high plain of free will which required him to make decisions, not just go over the top when the whistle blew.

Replacing the cork stopper with a steady hand, he sat with head bowed. Now he could think and make a plan. The crying was no longer there. But where had it come from. It must have been further out. They had hugged a line from the trenches almost parallel with their own lines where men waited to attack; so it was told, in underground bunkers. But he had to go out further, where they had searched through periscopes, over folds in the ground, folds where you could hide, when the sun came up. He didn't know whether to fear or welcome that. Would he be able to search then? He had no periscope. But being closer to the casualty perhaps he wouldn't need one.

He had no compass either. The moon of before and stars were clouded over. There was a dull thunder from afar; the anger of the guns; from the German side. That would be his bearing and star for guidance; through the wilderness.

He looked for a better place to sit, where his back could be supported. He found a steeper bank a little to the left and as he moved there he put his arms out gingerly to control something; his cello. Right there; he held his beloved cello.

He had wanted to bring it out with him to France. After all it was a travelling cello, brought for the reason of taking it around to places that a normal instrument in its huge awkward box could not be taken. Thus it folded down into a manageable carrying case. But in the end he left it for his mother to look after. He regretted that now and wished he could play a lament to the man here.

So he began to mime one. It started with a very low moan. The strings trembled with the weight of the bow applied suddenly with a hand and wrist carving the music out. The music was created by the hands. He had not composed music but often thought he should. Now all he could do was imagine... and mime.

He had to get his cello. If he ever got out of this, that's what he would do.

But for now he hefted the imaginary music; the low shaking lament; a moan that could express better than any words, a feeling; his feeling. But then any music was also beyond the human feeling. It came from the earth and passed the living by, leaving them breathless and taken out of themselves, leaving them with a memory of things they didn't know they knew and an understanding of things that they might know in the future, from the earth. A low frequency cuts the air but is often unheard by humans; an elephant talking from afar, a thousand cellos talking. If only all the rifles could be replaced by cellos. He thought of this, of the sound they would make. They would shake the world then; out of this terrible stupidity. They could make a gigantic fart as the soldier's expression of this war.

But now as a solo cello he could only make a threnody; some Greek word for lament, he remembered from a somewhat arrogant teacher.

He stopped and slowly turned his ear to listening. Slowly, as if in reply to the playing, the crying came again, on the night breeze. Or was it his imagination? Was it music from the earth to overlay the things that had happened here? To calm this broken piece of the world so that it might recover from the devastations of humans, who knew no better.

Except they knew music. He knew music.

He lifted his body, as if helped by an unseen hand.

The sound had been all around, but he had to go further out and explore the folds and craters that could not be seen through a periscope.

His uniform felt cold and unfamiliar. His equipment hung heavy. It was on a tired body and perhaps he needed sleep, though he had nothing to bring a shred of comfort; no covering, nothing on which to lay the head; only the cold earth to lie on. He had to become a friend of this earth.

He moved across the crater threshold and began to wander towards the guns, towards the German side. After a while he suddenly dropped into a small dyke or ditch. It held no water but he was amazed to find some long grass growing in the bottom. He lay down and within a very few minutes was asleep.

He awoke when it was almost dawn. He was shivering and hungry. The night had given a sort of cloak for the world under which his imagination could flourish with silent music. Now reality came with the grey light, with questions to be answered and decisions to be made.

The casualty Jack had shot; was he real? Had he really been alive? Cello thought about going back to check on him in daylight. But moving would be difficult. This ditch could save his life or preserve it for a few more hours until he could find the real casualty, which had become his casualty. Perhaps when dusk came again. He needed to stay very still. His section of soldiers would be standing too, looking out for him. Looking through periscopes to spot him. His .303 would have already been handed in and checked against his name. Each rifle was numbered and the holder's number recorded by the Company Quartermaster Sergeant. Word may have even reached the RSM that he had thrown away his rifle and deserted. News of misdemeanours always travelled fast. Good news did not travel. Wheels were being put in place to get him Court Martialled, if he returned; if he returned alive. As a casualty the only reason he would be kept alive would be to face his Court Martial.

Remembering a packet of biscuits in his ammo pouch he rolled slowly, stiffly, to try to retrieve it. It was on the same side as the water bottle. He got both out.

Breakfast was taken as the dawn broke, wedged into his ditch, which was in some ways almost more comfortable than the trenches. He could remain lying, didn't have to stand too, or clean his rifle ready for inspection.

He thought of his purpose. The real casualty might also be awake. Though he may not be alive. He might have had biscuits and water two days ago; not any more. Or perhaps, mortally wounded he could not reach them. Cello would need to save something for him, perhaps one biscuit and a mouthful of water might be enough to keep him alive.

But where was he?

The sun did not warm as there was a chill undercutting it. Perhaps the sun would win later. Early April was always an unknown. Here, as in England, it could be winter, spring and summer in the same day.

The rain would come, the April showers. They might come, not as showers, something heavier, reaching back to winter, not forward.

He dozed as the sun rose.

A boom awoke him.

God, gas! It must be. How would he survive? Chlorine and mustard crept into the trenches staying at ground level because it was heavier than air. How would he survive in this trench? He fumbled and yanked at the gas mask pouch. He got it out. Helmet had to come off to get the mask on with its snout, sticking out like a pig's nose. By now he was sweating and his arms had been flailing about above the ditch like a mad man. They would have seen him surely.

There is a point beyond caring. Walls of belief break and then you are in a new territory. A man does not know how many territories he can inhabit, short of death or complete madness.

Cello lay in the ditch with his chest rising and receding, breathing into a rubber space, smelling the rubber and old musty canvas like something dragged from a suitcase of clothing that had fallen into the ocean. His eye pieces rapidly fogged up. He would see nothing. He heard the booming continue. But no shrieking of the shells coming down close. There was no indication of where they were landing. Perhaps the gas would not come. The gas usually kept close to where the shells did burst, moving sluggishly from there. Unless there was a wind in which case it was driven along. Cello's vision was nothing. He could only go on sound. He looked up. He was lying on his back. Was it time to give up? How many casualties did give up? Without bothering to call out for help, to cry for their mothers. Without doing anything. Just close your eyes and breath your last, deep breaths, deeeep... His chest rose. It was nothing, his chest. It did not stick out, the medics who examined him when he first joined, commented on his apparent lack of strength.

They did not know the strength in his hands to carve music.

The booming seemed to lessen. Or was it his imagining. Still nothing shook the ground nearby. Perhaps he would be spared. Could he remove the mask? He raised his hand carefully to see if it had any traces of gas. How would he see traces of gas? Were there any on the grass?

Not being able to see made men frustrated and wanting to remove the masks, perhaps prematurely. Cello did so carefully. Without its horrible stale smell the fresh air was almost a delight. Though as always the air was tinged with the ever present smell of war; of death and earth mixed with the broken things driven into it. So he breathed and did not choke.

Suddenly he heard, perhaps very close, the real casualty, his casualty, the one he was going to find and take care of. He heard not a cry or a call for help, but more of a talking, perhaps to himself. Something like; "Oh god I'm going to die here."

"No you will not," Cello replied from his trench in a hoarse loud whisper where the sound of his voice surprised him.

Then came silence.

CHAPTER EIGHT

Minds in the mud

The earth was battered and bruised. Once there had been rolling green fields with small streams bubbling from little indented pockets in the ground, feeding farmers' fields; providing drink for cattle and water for farms and their inhabitants. They gently meandered down towards larger waterways and thence to rivers and through towns. A stream would have fed the ditch in which Cello now lay, taking water, essential life; to other land, livestock and human activity.

Streams couldn't move now. Their source was blasted to mud puddles. Their tender spouts forced down into oblivion and filth. If the water was able to emerge at all it became instantly vile; mixed with the residue of gas, the remains of bodies and the poisonous gun powder of war. Even the rats would get ill from it and pass disease around.

As Cello turned towards the certainty of the sound of the voice, he had a sense of a small re-entrant ahead, towards the enemy, but across the lie of the ground. On the map it would have been probably only one contour of ten feet in height, going in a tight U shape, almost a V. The water source, if it had one, would be to his right front. Beyond that the ground rose above the first ten-foot contour towards the enemy.

The question he had to ask himself was; could the enemy see into the bottom of the re-entrant?

The day was as clear now as it would get. The sun as high as it would get, just behind him. He could not risk a move now and if he called to the casualty he might be heard from his own trenches, only maybe two or three hundred yards away, as the casualty had been heard. He would need to attract his attention in another way, or wait until dusk and move then.

It should be wait, but his impatience might get the better of him.

He looked at the wall of his ditch, inches away from his face. They used crawl trenches to move between section positions and when there was no proper trench system. This ditch would probably contour round towards the head of the re-entrant. He could use it as a crawl trench to get near the casualty. He had to turn around first though. He couldn't crawl feet first.

He managed to carefully set a screen of grass clods, gouged from the ditch bottom, on top of the wall towards the enemy. When it was done he twisted without breathing, delving deeper into the soil and sides of the ditch and eventually was lying the other way around. He breathed again, lying still for many moments, waiting perhaps for a shout of recognition or a stream of machinegun fire; from either side. He was now the enemy of both.

Nothing came.

He started to move along the ditch. It was a canal, man-made, a very small canal. Or he had suddenly become a huge giant. But the sides gave him no room to move. In some places the sides were of stone and he could claw his way along knowing that he could stay under the top and not be seen. In some places the sides were destroyed.

The line of the ditch might be visible to the German

trenches. It would have stood out as a solid line on the landscape where nothing else was intact and unbroken.

Cello breathed heavily with the effort, or more with nerves. He stopped every few yards, his chest heaving. The noise he made seemed to bark like a dog in a lonely street of empty houses, except it was more of a scraping. But when he stopped he could hear no other sound. So he wondered if the war had stopped for him. He almost wanted a sign to tell him what was occurring instead of this unwarlike silence which made all things possible in his imagination. It even made music possible. Music floating over No Man's Land, guilty music; rendered by soldiers who had laid down their weapons together and taken up... cellos, trombones, trumpets. Maybe the dead would rise up to the sound and march towards each other. On meeting they would sit together in No Man's Land and raise a glass, a glass of dark brown beer. Laughter would be heard drifting with the music in and out of time.

That was the joy that music making brought. Could it ever be brought again? Could people from different cultures ever again share the same music; make the same music together?

He was sweating. It dripped into his eyes. Perhaps he was crying. But he knew the strong salt taste of sweat, over that of tears. He wanted to cry, but his work was too hard to allow that luxury. His helmet needed separating from his forehead where it had become welded.

He rested and dozed.

The sun had been warm but dulled in intensity eventually as the early spring day was drawing towards late afternoon. He was very hungry and thirsty. Another nibble at a biscuit and sip of water was called for. It would be a tiny ritual to break the madness of that day.

He scraped on desperately. There was a rhythm now about

his movement. He had become well practiced at doing it. And he must have made… He had no idea. It seemed like hundreds of yards. Probably about seventy. Just a few more yards before…

Then he did stop for water and biscuits… half a biscuit. He also urinated, turning to try to get into a position to do it without soaking his uniform. Not that he was in a position to care.

He looked forward towards perhaps the last ten or twenty yards to take him to where the casualty might be. The way was blocked he saw. He knew it was a decomposing body. He hadn't seen many so far in the ditch, which he had decided was a leat, rather than a ditch. He had been smelling the body for some time. He knew this was not his casualty. The smell indicated some time since death.

He had to turn the body to get past which released an overpowering smell and a mass of maggots. Crawling through them he comforted himself with the thought that they had come to live because of this man's death. They represented life, however loathsome. He could even eat them as well.

He thought of the two or three biscuits left in his pouch, then he looked at the mass of white squirming life that he was now moving through. But somehow their movement, a sort of wriggly celebration of death and their food from the rotten stomach and bowels of this man, repulsed him too much. He decided to look for worms instead. So he quickly brushed the maggots off as he worked his way past the body, trying to smell earth instead of death.

Suddenly he dug both his hands into the soft floor of the ditch where it was a little cleaner beyond the body. He bent his face close to the earth and dripped into it. Now these must be tears. He wanted its comfort, its closeness, just a clean piece of earth.

71

He had not forgotten about his casualty but suddenly a voice brought him nearer. "I can hear you, oh god I can hear you."

Cello's face suddenly burned with shock. The voice was very close. It was not a loud voice. It was almost a voice comforting him, in his loneliness. He didn't breathe or move. His helmet suddenly tipped forward into the soil. The back of his head, now naked, his blonde, boyish, hair that usually seemed to stay clean, pricked and scalded with anticipation. Perhaps something loomed over him, ready to bring down a terminating blow on him. "Yes, I am here," he heard himself murmur. Then a little louder, *"I'm here!"* There was now a strength in his voice.

That strength was perhaps his last gasp. In the night he had felt energy. Now he felt a terrible weight upon him, as if death if it came now was better than sleep. He had found his casualty. But like a runner who collapses feet from the tape after the race of his life, he could not cross the finishing line.

He had found his clean bit of earth and he breathed a wholesome breath, one cool breath told him what had made him; not dust as in a funeral elegy; 'We are dust and unto dust we shall return'; but the clays that gave life from the earth, the earth that fed all life. Our mother's mother's mother, going back and back, down through ages. Was this a tiny speck in the earth, this war? Could not he Cello, Marcus; to whom the earth had given a gift, the gift of music making; not be stronger than this tiny speck on the earth that was this war.

He didn't know what to do now. Darkness was falling. He had spent hours in this trench or ditch or leat, whatever it was. Now it was time to go and meet his fate.

The bricks in the wall had given way to mostly solid earth, some stone and some gaps. He struggled with new

72

energy towards the next gap and without thinking or worrying, breached it and rolled out of the ditch. He came to rest in a mud pool. There, looking at him was his casualty.

"I knew you would come," gasped the man.

"*I* would come."

"Someone! You are someone." He spoke with shallow breaths.

"Yes." Cello had never walked into a public house to meet someone, that he could recall. But suddenly absurdly he thought of that. A friend had been waiting for him.

The man was lying in the mud with his legs spread apart. They were immobile. Immediately that much was obvious to Cello. He was not covered in mud, but blood, even though he had been lying in mud for at least two days. He must be so cold, with trench-foot setting in, frozen! Immediately Cello noticed on his arm a set of sergeant's stripes. They had been almost pulled off and were hanging in tatters. On his collar were the regimental badges of the regiment Cello had joined. This man was part of the same battalion.

Cello wanted to drag him out of the mud. That was his first thought. Get him out of the mud!

"I need to get you out of there. Get you dry."

"My legs'll never work again," he said. He was crying.

"I'll get you out… Sarge," said Cello.

"Not much good to me, they'll probably Court Martial me now."

"Well actually that's what they are going to do to me as well. But let me try to get you out of this mud hole." He moved towards the Sergeant, still conscious of the possibility of being seen, so he crouched and sort of stumbled like a baby learning to walk but only on one leg.

But it was now getting dark so movement was safer. The Sergeant's stripes ripped as they were, seemed to shine, with light from the white coloured braiding. That was the intention, so that all junior ranks could see them. It was not thought that the enemy could also see them and snipers pick them off, as well as officers and others with rank.

"Do you think we can be seen from the Hun trenches?" Cello heard himself asking.

"There's quite a lip over there and a bunker on top, so I think we are in a blind spot here," he said, adding; "Are you a medic then?"

"Why do you ask?"

"No weapon."

Cello had arrived at the side of the Sergeant and even in the gathering gloom he could see some terrible wounds. The right foot was almost torn off and around the lower leg and hanging boot was blackened tissue and a protruding bone. There were fractures in both legs which rested at twisted angles. They had many other holes in them as well. He had tried to apply a kind of tourniquet to the right leg with one of his puttees twisted with a bayonet scabbard.

"I'm not a medic. I just threw away my rifle."

"Oh well, I've got one you could use if you need to defend us." He gestured into the mud and Cello noticed that his hand was also completely lacerated. "Not much good to me anymore." He lay back again. He spoke in a hollow whisper, breathing a lot behind the words. Getting them out was an effort. "Number 13216 Sergeant John Thomas Wall at your service."

"*My service,* you're the sergeant I should be serving you, rescuing you. You're the important one! Now let me help you."

"Well you see my stripes hanging in there but I don't have anything else to prove who I am. They made us leave everything behind including the ID discs."

Cello had got his hands under the sergeant's shoulders. He hated the thought that he had been lying in the mud for… nearly three days perhaps. He began to drag. Then stopped. "Why did that happen, we were told always to wear your ID discs at all times?"

"Sometimes when there is a high possibility of capture they make you leave everything, so the Hun don't ID you. Not right but it happens. Ahhhhh. Keep going. It hurts, but keep goin'. Can't feel my feet, but somehow they still hurt."

Desperately Cello dragged him slipping on the mud but making the first steps towards a piece of dry-ish bank. Once there they both collapsed, Cello with exhaustion and the Sergeant in pain. He could not speak from it. But their touch and physical contact had done something, established something between them.

After his breathing had become better Cello asked. "What happened Sarge?"

The Sergeant's breathing did not get better. "Call me John, please. Can we talk about something else."

"Do you want some water and biscuit?"

"I would like that," said John Thomas Wall, at the top of a deep breath of expectation.

Cello pulled out his crumpled packet of Huntley and Palmers. There were three occupants of the packet. He offered a whole one.

It was taken and eaten almost in a flash. Then the sergeant searched for the water, his face showing sudden interest; the first real interest. The face was smooth and almost bloodless. Just as the face of the first casualty they had found. Cello felt a sudden need for medical help. But there was no medical help, so he had to give it himself. There was hardly any water. He held the bottle and put his hand under the sergeant's head; who gulped then reached forward as the bottle was gently taken from him. "Got to keep some for later," Cello said, straightening the man's helmet.

"Later, yes… Will there be a *later?*"

"Let's hope; I'm going to get you back."

"Back, back where?"

"Back to get some help."

"You sound like a medic. But where is back? I thought everyone was moving forward, to attack."

"Supposed to be, perhaps they will pick you up as they go forward."

"Except they never do that, the dressing stations coming up behind are supposed to pick up casualties but they will be more concerned with casualties from the assault coming back. I'll be gone by then."

"Well I'll take you myself before the assault starts."

"You going to carry me then. But where, coz we both outcasts now aren't we."

"I shall take you to a German med centre then," said Cello.

John Thomas Wall managed a slow and painful laugh, "Aha-aha-aha that will guarantee you a Court Martial and a charge of desertion, if you ever get back."

"I think I got one coming anyway. But what about you?"

"I was told to take some men into a bunker when we were caught in a bombardment a couple of days ago and went to the small bunker just over there. When we came out the rest of the patrol was gone and then we got caught in another shell burst which gave me this and the other men ran off saying they were going to testify against me that I had deserted."

"But you didn't, you were told to take cover."

"Sometimes taking cover is as good as running away, as far as some people are concerned."

"I have heard about the RSM, he might have that thought mightn't he."

"Yes, and he gives his attitude to others. They take it up because they want to become like him, they want his power."

John Thomas suddenly became listless and exhausted with the talking. He lay back.

"That's why we have to go to the Huns." Cello stared out away from the sergeant, across the muddy re-entrant and towards his side of no-man's land, which was no longer his side. Any temporary home that the army had given him as they brought him into this war had been snatched away.

CHAPTER NINE

Witnesses

Cello had got Sergeant John Thomas Wall onto his shoulders. Quite a light man, he could be carried for some hours during the night on and off, struggling towards the occasional flash from the Hun side, where a bombardment had begun to land. They seemed strangely free of worries about this though, despite moving towards it. Cello had tied one of his puttees onto the Sergeant's right foot to try to keep the foot in place, but the blood loss and infection setting in, made it inevitable that the foot would be lost. The main worry was how they would get through the wire.

At last exhaustion overtook caution and both slept where they collapsed. They awoke well before dawn. Hunger almost doubled Cello as he lay. But Sergeant Wall did not seem to be hungry. He was still listless and his shallow breathing seemed quicker and lighter. The bombardment boomed on, like a careless thunderstorm.

They took turns in taking sips of water. But denied themselves biscuit. They did try to eat some grass they came across, caressing it against their faces almost lovingly, then chewed it to get some juice. There seemed only grit and mud in it. But by touch Cello found some tiny shoots which did have some juice. It unlocked their sandpit mouths and gave them a tiny bit of saliva. They were becoming mad with a sort of closeness and terrible abandonment, like a pair of lovers, light-headed through lack of food, sleep and water and in sergeant wall's case his loss of blood and injuries.

Cello's thoughts turned to the night before last, when he had been with the other casualty and had imagined playing his cello. "What did you do before the war?" he asked.

"I was a boy. I've been in the army five years. I am twenty-two now so I joined at seventeen."

"Oh, well you were a young man, man enough to join the army."

"Just wanted to get away from the farm really, hated it… Now I just wish I could get back there."

"A farm, that sounds marvellous." Cello spoke in a sort of exhausted whisper his voice cracking regularly.

Their conversation was punctured by long pauses as each summoned the strength to reply.

"It was, now I look at this land, it was all good farming land, but it's ghastly now, absolutely contaminated with all the war shit. Take years to make it back to farmland," John Thomas sobbed.

Cello remained silent, sympathising in the emotional moment. Then he said. "I am a cellist. That is what I was training to do before the war, well… and during… up until last year when I joined the Artists' Rifles."

He was expecting some derision as he had got in the trench. But none came. "Ah I wondered about the badge," was all sergeant Wall said. Then a thought was expressed. "Cellist! Would you play it here?"

"That's exactly what I would do and I did it night before last, well in my imagination."

"What did you play?"

"Well you know the cello is a great instrument for showing sadness. I played a lament for the soldier we had just killed."

"So I'm a farmer and you're a cellist out here waiting for the dawn, playing, farming, far away from all this."

"Yes far away from all this. But still on this land."

"Yes still on this land. It could be beautiful. It was beautiful."

"Will it ever be again?"

They were lying on an exposed slope. It was gradually rising up towards the enemy. To the right it seemed to drop away, very gradually. They sensed rather than saw it in the darkness before the dawn. Cello put his hand down on the cold earth and tried to pick a piece of it up. He felt something move under his fingers. He pawed at it uncertainly without interest. Then he felt its shape. It was a worm. "Hey Sarge I got a worm." He moved his hand across it in the dark and rolled it, then picked the whole thing up and brought it carefully up to his face. It was longer than he thought, perhaps five inches and quite fat.

"You eat it, I'm not really partial to worm for breakfast, never been a fish, or a fisherman for that matter."

"Oh come on Sarge, its food, of a sort."

"As I said you eat it."

"If I eat half will you have the other half?"

"I might." But the Sergeant's head was turned away in disinterest and bent upwards with pain.

Cello put the worm to his nose. It smelt of earth. Then to his mouth and in and screwing his eyes, bit into it. It tasted smooth and gritty and there was a bitterness about it. He swallowed though and then tried to spit the bitterness and grit. "God, I think that worm may have been gassed. Do you still not want it?"

"No, eat the rest."

Cello threw it. "I don't think so."

"As I said, everything on this land has been contaminated with the war."

They both lay back flat and began to laugh in a sobbing way that might also have passed for crying.

"I wish it would rain now. I would just lie here with my mouth open." Cello's mouth was open anyway and his breathing was shallow like Sergeant Wall's.

The light strengthened and more earth became visible. It was undulating. There was no real cover. They could see more to the east, where the sun was supposed to be rising.

Suddenly the bombardment stopped. Smoke remained.

They could put their heads up and look. There was something small standing up, some way across the ground.

"There is going to be an attack, now that the bombardment has stopped," said Sergeant Wall. "You can play them into battle… with your cello."

"No that's not what I would do… Sarge is that a gate over there?"

"Gate??"

"Yes… That thing over there, like a gate sticking up, on its own, with no fence, a farm gate, as if between fields."

"In between fields."

"Yea as in a farm."

"A farm." Sergeant Wall sounded incredulous, as if everything that had gone before in their conversation had not happened, had not been said.

"A battlefield…This is a battlefield, not a farm," he said as if far away, as if slipping.

And suddenly the strength had gone from Cello's fingers which he used to play, pretend to play, his cello. Was it a pretence? Was his whole life before, a pretence? The playing and the practise, driving towards an art-form. Driving towards something that kept moving away, further away with each practice, each performance.

You must improve. In order to play… Bach or…

That first night he had such strength; in order to play a

lament for a dead man. Now he had a living man to protect, to share with, to play for. But it was slipping from him. All the hours, days, years of practise were leaving him, unravelling, passing out of his mind, his hands, as if the war was taking everything.

What about his heart? Was it beating?

He supported himself on his elbow. His eyes were very deep and looking at them you wouldn't know whether there was sight in them. This time he looked beyond the thing, the gate or whatever it was and further away was a kind of crawling. Not like the worms of which he had found one. But these were still inhabitants of the earth, the mud, mud men, moving and crawling.

The attack, just as the Sergeant had said, was beginning.

His helmet was on but on a tilt, as if he was a Don Quixote, looking quizzically back to something he believed in and should have been a part of, but wasn't. It had become a mystery. Was he the mystery or was the battle, the mystery? The values of the cello that he had brought to the war; were they real? Or was this, his now predicament; real?

Now he focused back on the gate thing. Something hung on it. "There is something on that gate Sarge." He whispered with a small dread creeping on his voice.

But the Sergeant had swivelled round while Cello was in his reverie. He had drawn a little fresh strength. "It's not a gate, it's a wheel and that's a man on it, crucified!"

"Crucified!"

"Yes, crucified. They do it, the Hun I mean, as a punishment. Normally it's to a cart and when it goes along everyone can see him. But in this case they must have just left him."

"But he would have been shot, or got blown up."

"Or just starved to death," added the Sergeant in a stronger tone. "One way or another you gonna die."

He was scarecrow-like. "How long would you say…?"

They were beginning to catch some scent on the stronger morning air.

The Sergeant sank back. He couldn't speak at present.

Sergeant Wall's words hit Cello. Yes this was a sort of warning, this wheel, or gate, gateway to battle and crucified on it a body, a warning that 'one way or another you're gonna die'. Were these the remnants of a man who wouldn't go forward. He was therefore not allowed to go back. He was a gateway to the battle. Go forward because if you don't, 'you gonna die anyway'.

It had often been told that if you don't go forward in an attack when ordered, when the whistle blew; you would get a bullet from behind. Was that what the Sergeant was referring to. Who would deliver that bullet? Would it be an officer, or a sergeant or an RSM perhaps, or a general, with a twisted idea of discipline… Not so twisted, this was the reality. Someone would do it, because those harsh disciplinarians always won in the end. The harshness was the right way; at school, the flogging. Boys were flogged into a bitter hateful compliance, from behind. Here some would be shot so that the others would comply, with a bitter fear, because the discipline was right.

How then can it be a glorious thing to go into battle? From somewhere inside, Cello held, as did all boys, a thought of the glories of war. What glories now? Where were the glories in front of him in this show? Men moved like thin caterpillars across a blasted land. Cello could see it was a broken land on which they advanced. The maggots of the dead man he had crawled through were here wriggling gleefully to their death, disappearing, some down holes like craters full of wire and mud and gas, to greet other dead men there.

Somewhere behind, instead of the casualty collectors would be those shooting soldiers who refused to go forward.

Perhaps they would be together; the shooters and the casualty clearers, separating the injured from the malingerers. Some would be cowering in holes saying "Please shoot my leg, so that I can be picked up by a stretcher bearer." And the officer shooting would say, "No I must kill you so that the others will still go forward." But the man might argue, "They have already gone, no one would see you shooting my leg, please I beg you sir, shoot my leg." But if the casualty clearing people were there, they would say; *"No, you would not be a real casualty then, shoot him in the head sir!"*

So while the man cried and begged for mercy the officer would coldly shoot him in the head. It would be obvious to all that it was not an enemy shot. But then who would find out, who would know, except the stretcher bearer, who would leave him to be collected with the other dead, or to rot more likely, into the mud. Then no one would be any the wiser. So many bodies lay there rotting, unknown, unlooked for, uncared for, uncared about.

Better then to be like the Hun, crucified, not killed, as a punishment. At least he was here for all to see. He would get picked up by someone, eventually.

Cello was very still, fixated by the images in front of him. His mind running over these things.

But Sergeant John Thomas Wall was more awake. "Well once that little show is over, we might be able to get ourselves picked up by our own medics… Might!" He suddenly had an innocent hope about him, a desire to get back what he had lost. He had seen a ship that might rescue them stuck in an ocean.

Cello turned to look at him and saw a face hardly recognisable even from the night before. It was a sallow and flat face. The eyes did not challenge and nose did not protrude. Everything had sunk back into the darkness. The light did not want to see him.

"But Sarge they may shoot us as deserters and malingerers," Cello said after a long pause.

"The medics won't, but an officer would question you as you don't have no weapon… Everything comes back down to basics in the army, you ain't a soldier if you haven't got one of these." His rifle was slung. Cello had carried them both.

They lay on their sides, exhaustedly watching. Cello was buoyed up by the Sergeant's sudden urge of hope. Perhaps after all everything would be alright. Instead of going to the Germans, who crucified men on wagon wheels; they would be able to go back to their own side, without being shot.

"Should we move down there Sarge?"

They considered the question, not able to raise up more than to elbow height. But somehow they could have stood and wandered over there. No Man's Land had been compromised. It was no longer a place of secrets and creeping, where each side watched the other. A new No Man's Land would be formed.

Some obscene desire made them want to get closer to the body hanging on the wheel. They couldn't go past him and down towards the battle or advance, or whatever it was, without paying a compliment to him, acknowledging his presence. He was after all a fellow soldier and was no longer a threat. Something about his predicament, akin to their own, created a fellowship.

"Let's take a closer look at our Hun friend," said Sergeant Wall voicing the thought.

Moving now took a great effort. They were very weak and Cello's spirit had dried to a tiny thing, like a fragment of muddied biscuit, or a dead worm withered by the morning sun. His hair was strands of mud instead of straws of blonde. His youth had gone.

Sergeant Wall's maturity and strength had carried him

through his days in the open mud. He was three years of war senior to Cello and two years in actual age. His youth had long since gone and been replaced by some hardening of character but his English faith had endured. Now this had ruptured badly and was leaking away. What did he have left to keep him alive?

Still they moved together in a kind of dragging motion, an elbow and knee crawl with Cello supporting. Sergeant Wall's breathing became more quick and he coughed suddenly, deeply. "You can do it John," said Cello, sensing a deterioration in his casualty.

"Finally you calling me by my name mister Cello."

"You're not calling me by mine."

"No but Cello has something about it, a mastery. I'm sure you are a master. I mean if you were a top marksman I might call you rifle!"

"In music they call it maestro and I'm nowhere near that yet."

"Fancy name, means the same."

"Yes, it is Italian for master actually."

"Like I said, fancy name, still a great thing to be."

They began to reach some small craters in which they separated, negotiating banks and broken trench walls. Cello could get on his hands and knees, but Sergeant Wall could not and lay crying with pain, before struggling on again dragging himself using his hands and elbows. His cries, Cello noted were not as they had been when they were heard from the trenches. These were more frustrated by his inability to move forward. When they had heard them before they were more desperate. Cello was happy with this. His presence had bought another human spirit which had prolonged the Sergeant's life, he felt.

So Cello stayed close to his Sergeant, to try to help him over places which might cause pain. Moving on his own gave Cello a tiny bit of renewed strength. "We're nearly there John I think, shall I carry you again?"

Sergeant Wall was breathless but had a little colour back in him. "Maybe if you crawl I can ride on your back."

"Play horsey, horsey, like I did with my little brother."

"Yes something like that… Is your brother out here as well."

"No he…He died when he was young."

"Oh sorry to hear that."

"Thanks, yes, I'm all my parents have got now…"

"Hard for them."

They piggy-backed forward, almost laughing at some moments in a half-crazed way. Cello couldn't tell how he got renewed energy. Perhaps their combined remnants of energy carried them. They mounted the edge of a small crater and were suddenly almost abreast of the man on the wheel. Then Cello saw something that made his heart give a small jump. "John, there's some of his gear there on the ground, might have some food and water in it."

"Cello, you little beauty, go and get it then." Sergeant Wall had collapsed off Cello's back and was lying facing away from him. His words came out in a strange croak. He was very still.

"Wait for me John." The Sergeant could hardly do anything else. Cello's hunger and desire got the better of him and he half limped, half crawled towards the wheel.

CHAPTER TEN

Death and a meeting

Cello couldn't wait. He struggled towards the scarecrow apparition hanging on the wheel. He daren't look properly at him but did notice the wire thongs that seemed to be biting one arm almost in half as they lashed him to the spokes. The body was more whole than they thought, not blown apart by bullets. His head was bowed in surrender to death with a dried blood-coloured face. His equipment seemed to have been left carelessly on the ground tantalising him, as he certainly couldn't reach it. There was a small pack and a belt with a water bottle and ammunition pouch. Cello's first thought was of boobytraps. Many of the German units were experts at this. Cello eyed the equipment suspiciously. Under it was uninterrupted mud. There was no mound which might conceal a grenade with the pin already removed and ready to explode once the equipment was disturbed.

Nevertheless he tried not to disturb it but gently started to open the small pack. He was hungry beyond reason. So he threw away any caution, like a coat discarded in winter. Had any boobytrap exploded it would only kill him, which under the circumstances would not be a loss to the world at that moment.

His persistence was eventually rewarded with a packet

of biscuits, not Huntley & Palmers, but the German version. They were very hard, but also very tasty to Cello. He couldn't resist eating one.

The water bottle was harder. He found it difficult to get out of its pouch without moving the belt. But he was desperate and eventually managed to extract it, though the belt did move.

He drank some there and then and looked around. A noise came from the battle, where previously there had been darkness and the thunder of the bombardment. The noise was thinner now, a noise of men. There were few actual gunshots as the men did not seem to be moving against the Hun, who may have departed. Perhaps that was reflected in some voices of joy as the attack went forward. There would hardly be any casualties or any men cowering in terror ready to be shot, thought Cello. So he granted himself a moment of peaceful watching before taking up the journey back to his Sergeant.

On approaching his companion, he noticed that the Sergeant had not moved, at all. Nothing about him had moved. He put this thought out of his mind as he shuffled over, grunting a little. "John, look we have water and more biscuits. This should be enough for us until we get rescued."

It was an admission that perhaps moving down to the battle area was beyond them. Cello didn't notice that his voice, even after the water and biscuit, had become dry with a kind of rattle of complete exhaustion. He did notice that John did not respond in any slight or tiny way.

"John, John, wake up, I've got more breakfast for us!" He shook the Sergeant's shoulder, gently at first, then a bit harder. As he did so the Sergeant rolled onto his back and his lifeless face looked up at Cello. It was a calm and warm face of a man who bore no grudges. The black exhaustion had somehow gone, now that the pain had also left him.

A terrible sad guilt hit Cello. He had held his brother after death. It was not unfamiliar to him. But this man needed him and he wasn't there at the moment of death. Cello laid his head on John Thomas's chest. Perhaps he had known it was his end, that was why he turned away. Talking had been a big effort for him. He had turned away for a moment of peace, something he hadn't known for almost three years of war.

"I'm not leaving you John," said Cello. "You were left before, now I will stay with you." He knew that would not be possible and that Sergeant Wall who was still warm now, would soon leave him and begin the process of decay. He began to look for the Sergeant's details or anything including his ID. Then finding nothing he remembered that he had said that he had been told to leave everything behind in case they got captured. Cello felt strange at this.

In those moments Cello knew nothing for certain, except that the man, John Thomas Wall, who knew only about being a soldier and had risen to a sergeant in five short years, was dead. There was a terrible thought within him that the Sergeant, who had given his life loyally to the cause of this war and suffered three years of it, had now lost his life because the people who he trusted to look after him, had actually killed him. They hadn't shot him, but had broken him, actually broken his heart. Of course his blood loss had been extreme and the heart needs blood, but when there is little blood, adrenalin takes over to make us do desperate things and survive, fuelled by will. Sergeant Wall had had his will, as well as his ID discs taken away, perhaps by an injustice.

The face had become innocent again. Now perhaps he finally was at rest. A man who had given all his adult life to a cause in which he had no say, no voice, but believed in, through a sort of duty, had lost the only thing he had left to give. Those he had fought for and with and who might have readily accused him, now had lost a true soldier, a true servant. They would never know his real value.

Real value! Reality. What was it now? Cello's eyes were full of mist and grit. He looked over Sergeant Wall's body at the events of the assault or whatever it was. He was no longer interested. Or he couldn't focus. It was a blurry world in front of him now. There were shouts and voices. There were explosions. But not like a mine or anything earth-shaking. It was weak and weedy, like an orchestra unsure of their instruments.

Cello did not smoke. The Sergeant had not mentioned cigarettes, so perhaps he did not either. Men who were dying were often happy to go if they had a smoke in their mouths. It did dull the pain somewhat they said, especially the strong ones like Woodbines. "Give us a 'Bine mate?" was a familiar request. Cello wished now that perhaps he did smoke. There was no one to ask for a 'Bine from.

He was alone again.

Not for long.

"Guten morgen freund." A German voice wishing the man on the wheel a good morning.

Cello could do nothing. He looked over his shoulder.

They were yards away. Shuffling through the mud and earth, over the blind crest just adjacent to the man on the wheel; four soldiers, now stopped, with their rifles levelled at him. Slowly Cello raised his hands.

"What doing Tommy?" The accent was thick but the English was good.

"Looking after my friend."

"Your friend is dead I think."

"Still I must look after him."

"But why; you are his brother?" Only one spoke. The others were just grey menaces with their helmets, covered to cut out the shine, dirty tunics and leather belts, unlike the British webbing equipment. Cello noticed the difference now although he hadn't noticed it when trying to get the water and biscuits out of the equipment of the man on the gate.

"No… He was just my… friend."

"Well this was our friend." He half-turned towards the man on the wheel.

"So why is he like that?" Asked Cello.

The Germans looked at each other then they sort of shrugged.

Cello did not feel that should be pursued. It was as it was, the war was out of the hand of soldiers. "I don't have a rifle," he said. "All I want now is to look after this man."

"The man has his rifle."

"You can have it."

The Germans slightly lowered their Mauser rifles as Cello had not made a move to take up Sergeant Wall's Lee–Enfield.

"We should take you prisoner."

"Why not just take the rifle?"

This almost convinced them. Trophies are prized by soldiers and give evidence of a victory. Any dead men should be deprived of their weapons.

"How will you take care of him as he is dead?"

"Dead men should not be left on the battlefield. They have to be collected."

"Is that your job?"

"Yes… yes, it is."

"So you are a medic, where is your Red Cross armband?"

"I don't have it but look at the badge, different from his. This is my medic's badge. There are some stories that your snipers target men with red cross arm-bands. So we don't wear them when we go into No Man's Land." Cello sweated as he lied. The Artists' Rifles badge was nothing like the medics badge.

They shuffled a bit but it was clear that at least two of the men were becoming impatient.

They paused, then the speaker said; "We will take the rifle."

Cello withdrew it carefully from alongside Sergeant Wall's body, keeping his hand well away from the trigger guard. He turned it and took hold of the barrel. The Germans seemed to relax a little. They came closer and the English speaking one took it, looking all the while at Cello. He had a slightly lopsided grin on his face and Cello had the notion that his own helmet was on also in a lopsided way. He must have looked ridiculously exhausted and broken, without weapon and without a cause.

"I know you are not a medic," said the German. "What are you Tommy?"

"I am a cellist..."

The look on the man's face became a sort of pitying laugh, then puzzlement. "What is this cellist?"

"I play the cello." Cello brought his arms slowly across his front and began to mime.

The men burst in laughter. "Ah cello. Yes, music, very good."

Cello began to laugh as well. But it was croaking laugh. One of them took out a small package of tobacco and papers. He cradled his Mauser and rolled a cigarette. "Zigarette?"

"No," replied Cello but then he thought he should have accepted. But they shrugged with indifference. Two smoked and the rest just looked. Behind Cello voices could be heard. They looked beyond him, spectating the attack, unworried about it.

"Well are you going to join your side then with your dead friend?"

"I suppose... I have carried him before now I will carry him again."

"Yes carry him over there and let him join the attack." They all laughed again. "Soon it will be over and it will be back to..."

"Back to... stalemate..."added Cello.

The German left his zigarette dangling in a turned down mouth, cradled his Mauser in the left elbow and moved his right hand this way then the other like an imaginary wave breaking lazily on a beach. They did not understand the word 'stalemate', but they did understand the war.

"Das ist der krieg."

Cello nodded slowly. "Ja, das ist der krieg," he said demonstrating a pathetic schoolboy knowledge of German. He felt drawn to the men in a way. Perhaps becoming a prisoner would be a way out of his situation.

Probably not! But they didn't seem to pose a threat, unlike his own side. Still there were those behind, to whom he would be turned over; the scowling Military Policemen and the bastard RSMs, or the German equivalent of them; those who had put the man on the wheel and killed his Sergeant.

'Das ist der krieg' was an excuse for everything; for leaving men rotting in No Man's Land; for shooting casualties.

What he could do was to look after one man, one dead man. These men wouldn't take him, not Sergeant John Thomas Wall. They would leave him to rot like garbage which soon begins to smell and attract flies. He was a stranger yesterday, now a friend for life. He didn't have a life any longer, but Cello would ensure that Sergeant Wall had a friend. You don't leave friends rotting in No Man's Land, or anywhere.

"But I will try to find a medical aid post I suppose," commented Cello in a voice cracking like sand driven onto rocks in the desert.

"That won't really help you, or him." They didn't seem in a hurry to leave and even sat down in a small circle completely oblivious to any danger from shellfire or being seen from the trenches at their backs now.

"Are there any German medical aid posts nearby?" asked Cello suddenly, his eyes flaring with a sharp red point of life. They had been deep and black but suddenly the lids opened.

"Ha ha Tommy you very strange. I think you want to change sides don't you? Yes you will find one somewhere over there." He indicated the direction in which the attack seemed to be heading, though it had more or less petered out now. Men did not pour into that plain of No Man's Land any longer.

The men still sat there. And now Cello looked at them as well. Decisions had been made and future plans pondered. Now the question remained who would act first and what action would they take?

Cello knew he would have to act. He was their prisoner. He was theirs to let go, if they chose that.

"Thank you… I had better go… with my friend."

The English speaker waved a hand, perhaps in surprise. But one of the others started to laugh and raised his Mauser, mockingly hopefully. Cello's back began to burn as he turned it on them. He was not showing weakness which could be eliminated without a thought. If they shot him in the back, they would also be showing weakness.

Dead men are heavier than live ones, who can have small wings and air in their lungs to lift themselves even with the gravest of injuries. Cello struggled to lift Sergeant Wall then the effort suddenly bore him forward a few staggering over-balancing steps. The Germans all started to laugh, a wheezy sort of hissing. "Good luck Tommy…Tommy the cello, heh heh; give your Sergeant a good burial, when you finally realise he is dead. Heh, heh."

Cello knew he would not get shot from behind, perhaps because he had become a figure of fun. So having regained his dizzy balance, he struggled onward, like a man or indeed a clown, resolute in his cause, self-belief giving him strength. He marched forward carrying his sergeant across his shoulders, with an overemphasised lifting of the knee.

CHAPTER ELEVEN

Choosing sides

He stopped and closed Sergeant Wall's eyes and to rest a little. He didn't have to go up or down hill. He contoured across a couple of hundred yards before he would need to descend. The ground changed as he went. There was more mud and wire; the real No Man's Land of battles fought with no winner. His veins were bursting and his breath was frozen into a pumping heart.

Cello sensed he was approaching a scorched earth, smouldering with an incomplete conflagration. There were distant sounds of groaning and crying but nowhere was there evidence of medical aid, or the friendly troops who had so recently traversed this useless piece of land. As he stood and surveyed the area a screeching started and rounds started landing almost immediately. Soil flew up and the ground did start to shake. He had brought Sergeant Wall to the boundary of hell, where he shouldn't have been.

He turned and again without breathing the smoke and metal stench, started to climb the hill behind him towards the unknown. His burden was not heavy, or he himself was dying. But physically somehow he went into another plain. He knew what he was doing. He didn't go back towards the German on the wheel. He went straight up towards the crest of the hill and possible safety, perceived safety.

A collapse came soon, but it wasn't total. He drew heavily on the water in his bottle, not bothering to save anything. This had to be the last lap. At the crest, the end would be in sight.

But some crests are almost impossible to reach; so many of them are false. So many journeys are never ending. But Cello staggered on, higher and higher, further and further away from the shelling.

He began to reach empty trenches almost unprotected by wire. Just a few strands and coils did not impede his journey. He managed to pick his way through it, suspecting a Mauser or machinegun would take him and his burden out of existence at any moment. But he had become a fool and so foolishly he blundered on.

He stopped at one trench to search for food and water. He did not fear boobytraps as with the man on the wheel. He had met the enemy and somehow trusted them. They had sent him here. There was nothing in the trench, not even a smell of excreta. He left Sergeant Wall on the top as he couldn't climb down with him. Perhaps in a bunker, in his own vault, Sergeant Wall should be laid to rest and the door blocked with a boulder, if there had been such an item.

Cello explored the network, desperate, at least for water. He found none. He did find some wrapping and empty tins in one corner, piled as if after a tidy-up. The Hun was disciplined. They all knew that. He rummaged deeper among the rubbish. Something caught him in the chest, a photograph, not torn, though crumpled carelessly, as if from a pocket. It was a girl, laughing. Looking at the camera with head thrown back. She half sat on grass. It must have been summer as her arms were naked. Why had the owner of the picture thrown it away? He looked further, no letter. He could not have read it anyway.

Cello crouched, with his back against the trench wall.

His equipment hurt him, rubbed him. He smelt himself and knew he was foul and he needed to urinate and defecate. Suddenly the march he was making with his Sergeant was... He opened his hand and looked at it. It began to shake. It was not his hand. It was a bow hand. He tried to stop it shaking, to make it strong so that it could still hold a bow, which could attack the strings and create... music. He looked at the photograph in the other hand. His mouth had sand sticking to its roof and sides. He tried to run his tongue over his teeth but didn't feel them. The tongue had lost its taste. The teeth were like rocks sticking out of the sand.

What is this? He asked himself.

He closed his eyes and the left hand let the photo fall.

If only it would rain he might be able to drink. When you wanted water it was nowhere.

His head hummed as though an engine were approaching.

Perhaps a tank would crush his Sergeant. He scrambled and fell upwards, dizzyingly. Back he went to find his charge and lay thankfully beside him... The Sergeant had no need of water but suddenly he remembered that he had given John nearly a full water bottle after taking some into his own bottle. Was he mad? No he had found him dead so where...

Oh god, a full bottle.

Had he left the bottle as he picked the Sergeant up after they were disturbed by the Hun patrol?

He fumbled for John's bottle, on his belt. It shook with a little weight. Cello drank, though somewhat guiltily. Why should he not take water when this man had no longer a need for it. Perhaps soon he would have no need of it either. Then he slipped down beside the dead man, who was becoming unfamiliarly cold and rigid.

"John... John," he said. *"Don't leave me John."*

He was on top of the trenches on a beaten earth bank from which he could look down, but not right into the valley from where they had come. In the far distance was a line on the horizon. He thought of the periscopes, watching him. Perhaps he should wave. His thoughts trembled, uncoherent in his mind. As he lifted Sergeant Wall and settled him somehow across his shoulders Cello looked at his right hand. It trembled again. He shook it. Then he turned away from the line on the horizon, turned to take a sniper's bullet in the back.

Snipers were seen sometimes in the trenches, special groups of which there were some in each battalion. They came and took up a position especially selected within the trench complex, perhaps slightly to the side, in a hide of sand-bags or a wooden structure. Rifles were the .303 Lee–Enfield, but with a telescopic sight. The rifle often had its own hessian camouflage to cut down any glare or sheen of oil, making them look like the branch of a tree. Triggers were often set on a very light pressure to prevent movement during a long trigger pull. Accuracy was everything. Stillness, patience, breathing and calmness, were also the tools of the sniper; in contrast to the rushing, screaming adrenalin of the sweating line soldier as he rushed towards death, desperately yanking his trigger.

Cello knew nothing of the sniper's art. But he knew that in the little section he had come from, there were no snipers. Its chaos gave him confidence that none would have taken up position there since he left.

So he ignored his safety. He faced a new direction and a hardening of his decision to choose the 'enemy'.

A familiar scent suddenly caught his face like a claw: death.

The trench system did not seem to be too much damaged by bombardment. So how would this have occurred?

It wasn't Sergeant Wall, whose odour had become familiar to Cello.

There was a breeze in Cello's face coming from higher ground now in front of him. That was where the death was.

Cello staggered onward, pace by pace. He had nowhere else to go and he knew that death was his domain now. John Thomas Wall had died in his care. He, the cello player soldier, could have died at the hands of his enemy. His own unit had threatened him with death through desertion and he had seen how they had all complied with the killing of one of their own, a casualty, stabbed with a bayonet.

One of their own: a body lying in mud. Sergeant Wall was one of their own but now just an unfamiliar body who could not resist, not fight, not complain about death. He had obeyed orders, been injured and called for help. Deserting him; 'killing' him, if that was what they had done, had shown something of them; at least for the moment, for that moment. Or was it a great conspiracy, the leaving of John Thomas Wall to die, like the making of a sacrifice, to satisfy the bloodlust of the shooters coming behind, like the man on the wheel, like Jack shooting the casualty.

Then came a very familiar sound; shovels on soil.

Cello sank to his knees. Then he dropped the Sergeant off his shoulders to his right. The body took Cello's helmet off, catching it under the belted equipment, now devoid of ammunition, water and any useful thing.

Cello, a boy again with dirty blond hair, did not try to retrieve the helmet, just as he had tried not to retrieve the rifle which he had cast down, He lowered his head and listened as he could, without looking. Even when adrenalin has taken away the power of movement it still allows perfect hearing. Only the breathing interrupts that, though Cello's breathing had become shallow and quick.

The digging continued. Then voices. With voices you can

detect mood, sense threat, or joy. The digging of a grave, perhaps a mass one, was not a subject for joy. The voices accompanied movement and action. Hard work of the most unpleasant kind does not encourage much comment, only direction, probably by a Non-Commissioned Officer.

Bodies were dragged, heaved and landed. Soil was shovelled.

Was this the place for the burial of John Thomas Wall.

Why was this seemingly large burial so close to the front?

Or was it a large burial?

The bombardment that had gone before the battle may have been very accurate. The trenches had been cleared. But then they hadn't been badly damaged, so how had a lot of people been killed?

How many?

One more to be buried.

The thought that the burial could finish for the lack of more bodies spurred Cello. He was beyond fear. He had practiced action in plain sight of his enemy. They had already discovered him. Now he had to reveal himself for the first time to his enemy. He had to do it for the sake of his friend; John Thomas Wall.

Cello stood up, without his helmet, to look for the grave to bury his friend.

CHAPTER TWELVE
The burial party

There were some trees over to the right. The sound came from there. Cello could perhaps approach unseen.

No; any sneaking up would get him shot. Just then he did not want that. He wanted to give his Sergeant a burial. He pulled his helmet up his arm with the strap around to hold it, then heaved the Sergeant up and over his shoulder, perhaps for one last carry.

"I've got one more," he called, forcing the words out through the desert that was the inside of his mouth and lips ravaged by wind and dirt. They were split, bloodied, dried then split again like the torn opening of a paper bag. The words caused the lips pain which he did not notice.

He saw some flashes of white moving as he approached. Then trundling forward, he finally turned the corner of the line of trees and came upon the burial party.

There were only three of them and two had large white aprons with red crosses the length and breadth of the apron which ran chest to knees and went around the body. They wore gloves as well and masks. Their hands were for bodies, not rifles.

One grey uniformed, soft capped, slightly portly NCO stood to one side, without mask but with Mauser. He had a leather belt with tiny pouches, not designed for carrying supplies for a patrol of any duration. He might have been a gamekeeper out on his estate with his shooters, or bringing in the bodies of the birds that had been shot, after a good day's sport.

They hadn't heard the croaking that Cello's voice made. But when the two white-aproned ones saw him come from beyond the trees, they stopped and dropped their hands to the side, having just deposited a body into the pit. The gamekeeper turned. His Mauser was slung, not ready for use. He did not struggle to make it ready. He did remove the cigarette from his lips and after a moment opened his small, pursed up lips into a smile, showing a hint of dirty teeth.

Cello stopped. "One more…" He pointed to the grave.

The smile broadened. A hand pointed to the pit. All three were motionless.

Cello went forward. He seemed to have forgotten that he was empty of energy, empty of every sip of adrenalin. His mouth was not even dry and eager for drink. Water could perhaps not be forced down at this stage. He was nothing. Only his burden was something, something that needed the earth for its sustenance.

He reached the lip of the pit. It was like a trench, made wide to accommodate bodies lying across it, as opposed to along it as they would do when sleeping during a pause in their fighting. They had no fight left to do. The earth would take them without a battle for territory. The earth was mother, father, bed and blanket, a place to rest.

His knees gave way and Cello dropped onto them. He sagged one shoulder and his burden slid down onto the ground, but it was bent into an angle and Cello needed to straighten his Sergeant out before committing to the earth.

"You have not been dead long John, have you, not as long perhaps as these that are to be your companions." It was a whisper that only the Sergeant could hear. "Let's straighten you." He turned John Thomas Wall onto his back and pulled his legs straight, then his shoulders. He turned him again so that he was facing downwards, on the edge of the pit. Then with a roll and a shove he sent the body down the three feet to the trench floor where a convenient space had been left for him. He almost succeeded in making him end up facing upwards towards the sky and his freedom.

Cello's job was done.

He didn't want to look down. He missed his Sergeant immediately. He missed his cello. He stood and slowly turned.

The gamekeeper had unslung his Mauser and it was pointing at Cello whose spirit finally let him collapse and black out.

CHAPTER THIRTEEN
The guest

They splashed water on him and he revived. But he was obviously in need of some assistance. The two men in aprons lifted him while the rifle of the gamekeeper remained trained and unwavering. They did not speak. Cello had heard their voices already, probably expressing disgust at their job. But Cello did not screw his face up at the bodies, one of them was so close and familiar to him. He had even felt John Thomas Wall's penis as he lifted him, trying not to touch his injured legs by putting his hands further up. Post death stiffness had not set in there.

having lifted Cello out of his feint the two men sat him down again to watch the filling in of the grave. Cello had been right to make a move when he did. Their work was almost done. Feet, bodies and finally faces were blanketed over, comforted by a brown shroud. Earth; the soldier's friend had accepted them. Grotesque injuries were hidden. What did their injuries matter now, death had come to end the pain and they were being laid to final rest.

It may not be a final resting place.

The Sergeant did not have the terrible injuries of some in the trench that he shared. So how had he died? The burial party did not question the reasons for death, which obviously had already occurred, they were merely a burying party.

Geographically the site would be easy to find should there need to be an exhumation for reburial. The gamekeeper no doubt knew his land. He would be marking it on a map for future reference. But what could be done to protect the sacred ground. How sacred was it?

Once the soil had been deposited and filled to a mound they searched for something to mark it. Of stones there were few. There would be no permanent memorial, not yet. They did find a few stones to put around the mound and sticks were placed on top, not in a crucifix but in some kind of prearranged sign.

Then they turned their attention to Cello. He stood on the gamekeeper's bidding. He could not speak but made a sign of drinking. One of the white-aproned ones drew a bottle from somewhere and passed it to him. They had already used some to revive him. Cello's hand shook without control. He managed to get the bottle to his mouth and water passed down unnoticed at first.

It did refuel him enough to move his feet, listlessly, shuffling along. He did not bother to replace his helmet. It was out of his hands now; his future.

His captors did not press him to move quicker. They were unhurried.

They were at some rounded hill top on which life, rather than bodies, carried on. A trench here and there, wire entanglements through which to find a path, craters to negotiate. It was nothing like a front line, or was it?

Men looked up from their huddled business. What occupied soldiers did not change from one army to another. A different language, uniforms and weapons and perhaps mood made the difference. The work still included digging, daily life and construction perhaps of a 'jump off' trench. Perhaps they were planning a counter attack.

The battle of Arras, founded in such optimism, starting

with a great advance and the taking of prisoners, would end in another stalemate – probably, with these men going forward, in retaliation.

There was carefree eating and drinking. There was no bombardment.

Cello did not take in the safety of the scene. He was a prisoner. But somehow he felt safe – or he felt nothing.

They arrived behind the occupied trenches at some tented area. Cello was not aware of the red crosses which were on the roof. He was aware of lying down, or been put into a lying position with a firm hand, though not an oppressive one. There was murmuring and he was left to drift in and out of sleep. Time moved out of reach, along with the responsibility to do something.

Then a confident voice, a female voice, of care and nursing and something like motherhood, said; "Can you sit up young man." It was not a question. It cut through fog and fatigue and Cello knew he had to obey. He struggled but rose shakily. The English was good but broken and heavy. There was a white coat; unusually clean.

"You brought in a casualty, to bury," said the white coat.

"Someone needed to look after him," Cello said, or he heard himself saying. He subsided back to a lying position.

"He was another body. Are you a relative?" asked the medic.

"No."

"You, yourself are not injured though."

"No."

The white coat stood there. It did not have a red cross on it. Cello was troubled by this. He wanted the red cross.

"Could I have… have some water and perhaps food," he managed to say.

The coat moved and thought about the question. "Our food is not plentiful… But I can see that you need something. I suppose you can be our guest for a short time."

"Thank you."

They waited. The white coat waited. Cello could not see the face clearly. His vision was not clear. His hand was not still. He took his eyes off the white coat and they drifted up to the tent ceiling. It had a wooden frame and the canvas in between was drooping. He began to feel unsafe. He was not in a reinforced bunker underground. Soldiers spoke of the Hun being in such underground bunkers, way underground. He could not be safe from a bombardment here.

The white coat moved after some murmuring.

There were other, real casualties to attend.

His treatment changed. What was Cello doing here? He didn't need treatment. There was food. It came to others and then to him, grudgingly. The white coat was elsewhere. She was needed. All Cello needed was food. There was meat, of a sort and potatoes and cabbage, delivered by an orderly. He was in uniform, not medical uniform. His eyes were surly. He had probably spat in it, or worse.

There was water, clean and fresh, as from a river. He thought of a river, water flowing over rocks, cold and quick. Cello had bathed, paddled, in one. He had been with his young brother.

Something had happened. Something terrible. An accident.

He couldn't think of a river.

As a cellist he could make amends and make his mother proud and end her grief. The brother was no longer there. His family had been… broken.

The silent years were filled with cello practice, which was a healing of all that. But now that world too was broken… utterly. Who could mend it?

Maybe the cello again? It seemed an impossible task; a dream, especially with a shaking, uncontrollable bow hand.

After the meal and enough to drink, for the moment, Cello

drifted towards sleep. He knew it could not be a long one. He would envy his Sergeant's long sleep, without dreams. Real sleep was a luxury in the trenches, so rarely achieved. It was also feared, lest death should prevent an awakening.

He did dream. He was in a garden, playing his cello. It was a sort of party, a garden party. Characters inhabited the grass, running to explore the edges of the lawn, where bushes bowed over bare patches, littered with pine cones. These images were clear but individual characters were dim and fleeting. They were impressions rather than real; Sergeant Wall, Ben from his section, the Corporal, playing a sort of hide and seek like children.

He knew they would come back, maybe more white coats would come, to take him. The gamekeeper. Prisoner and escort, *'ATTENSUN!!'* Music played to escort him away. They were laughing! Would John Thomas Wall be laughing? He tried to look, but he was dragged away from his cello. The laughing and the shaking hand.

CHAPTER FOURTEEN

The earth

He awoke. It must have been morning, the hours of sleep had seemed moments; to more murmuring in the background of his consciousness. Then a shout from outside, a shout of panic. A bombardment?

Why had they put this field hospital here, without cover? Was it all a dream?

A crashing literally lifted the bunk he was lying on. But it came down again.

"GEH RAUS, RAUS, RAUS!"

"PUT THIS ON." The white coat was beside him again, why him, who wasn't injured?

ANOTHER CRASH. Instruments and tables spilled this time. Cello's bunk tilted but didn't lift.

She held out one of the white aprons with a red cross on it.

"Can you run, English?"

"I can try."

"Yes you better do it."

In the confusion he managed to get out. He saw some knocked over water jerrycan spilling. Water could not be wasted like that. Water bottle, bottle, anything.

He turned back to the tumbling chaos where colours were merged, casualties had been thrown from bunks their wounds broken open afresh so red stood like a broken signal, a tattered flag. They screamed as well. Glass slid together and broke. Some bottles were not broken. He caught one up and came back to the jerrycan, still dribbling. He filled the glass bottle. It was probably a urine bottle. He hadn't thought to drain it first.

Another crash. Earth flew up. A scream. "MEDIZIN."

Someone had seen his Red Cross apron.

Cello stood. Eyes looked at him from yards away. The crashing stopped, only in his mind though.

Back again to the chaos of the tent. BANDAGES! Near where the breaking glass had been there were some. He gathered himself. Instead of holding the bottle he drank from it.

"RAUS!" Someone was in his face. Did they think he was German? People were running in panic.

He ran out before the face realised he was the English 'guest'.

The man who had summoned him lay half out of a trench. What of his legs? Sergeant Wall again, his legs riddled. But no it was an arm blown under him, that had taken a hit of shrapnel. Cello pulled him up into a sitting position in the shallow trench. The arm was spurting blood.

He put the man's hand on the spurt indicating to grip tight. It didn't stop the bleeding. He took the arm back, lifted it. He pulled some of the man's sleeve, hanging in tatters. It came off easily. He wrapped it into a ball and put it into the crook of the raised arm.

The bombardment continued. But they didn't notice. They could have been blown apart at any moment.

Cello sat there intent on his work. He tied the bandage as tightly as he could, round as many times as possible, then looped to the head to hold the arm up trapped so hard that the bleeding should stop. It slowed. He let the man drink.

They got down in the trench. Down to the earth.

Yes he could have run, but that might be running into the bombardment.

The earth, the earth. Its arms will shield you better than your legs can carry you.

It will catch the shrapnel in its soft spraying hand.

Stay safe in my coolness, it says; while the bombardment screeches overhead.

They are not under the earth, the earth is fighting with them, trying to spit against the explosions.

Cello's inner ear began to compose music to the sound of the earth? The blows of the bombardment would be a crash of bow on strings? Notes from a low grip. His hand would need to be like a hammer in one moment and a surgeon's knife the next. The earth had no hand in creating the bombardment. It cried against it. The earth hurts. It would cry with a long moan, vibrating strings, then a high-pitched crash again, then a low rumbling. The earth bleeds. Its streams cannot run free, like veins; they bog and bulge with mud that festers in the poison of war. Strings tremor low, like the complaining water, then high to a screech as the bombardment crashes again, and again.

Oh earth, brown like an old cello, brown and pitted but still alive, ready to throw against the bombardment: to throw up in defence of the blows it was taking.

Let it stop? Or will you take us into you, oh earth? You don't deserve this. We have caused your pain and you are defending us.

Cello pushed the casualty's head down further into the depths of the trench. Some soil pattered over them like grateful rain. Thank you earth! Gently cover us.

The bandaged arm was gradually turning pink. Blood was coming. Perhaps he could use the man's bayonet as a tourniquet.

The hail was soft earth, not hard shrapnel.

The sound was not like a cello. It was the music of hell. That was where they were. The crashing, the last whine as the shells in an instant ripped through the air towards the earth, the patter of earth thrown up.

Those guns had a terrible anger. Every crash was an insane repetition of some monstrous vendetta. Music? Never. WAR IS A MONSTER THAT DEVOURS every good thing belching out a choking miasma.

The casualty collector – him.

What's your job Tommy, not a medic are you? What are you?

I'm a cellist. He had said.

Here they would Have said; Raus, Raus, dirty English in our hospital.

Some would. But the white-coated woman?

The conductor of an orchestra controls the music.

There was no conductor. The artillery bombardment just flew down irresponsibly; careless of where it hit: lazy, irresponsible destruction.

Cello, saw this and his heart began to rebel. Why should this happen, in such an indiscriminate way. War was never tidy. Death happened and no one took responsibility.

It was not the anger that gave him strength. The music, gave him strength, the music he must make.

The man looked at him. Soon he would speak. But what did it matter? WHO IS THE ENEMY IN WAR? Who was his enemy?

He looked at the man and raised his eyes, meaning: how are you? But the man just dropped his head.

Where was this man's weapon?

When you give a soldier a rifle and more weapons, it makes them more vulnerable to a shameful failure. When someone doesn't have a weapon they can have naked bravery.

Should he run now? Run screaming to his own side hoping that they wouldn't shoot him as he made his dash; dressed in his absurd white apron with its red cross.

No he would not run. At least not that way, not yet.

CHAPTER FIFTEEN
Those in need of help

The bombardment had come from his side, his English side. When would he be blamed for that if he stayed. The looks he received in the hospital, would be more than looks.

But the closeness of this casualty. The trust he had put. They were on an island in this inferno where the looks were different. Whoever the man next to you is, he becomes your best friend.

So who was the enemy here?

Why should enemies not get help from each other, give help? Why should they have a personal vendetta to settle?

Revenge was different. Shoot my friend and I will want to shoot you.

The trenches created hate. A sniper's bullet delivered it: a precision weapon, unlike the artillery of the bombardment, but both created hate, a sort of unfocused indistinct hate. "I am English," he said as another crash hit the earth. He said it from under his fall of dirty blond hair as he checked the man's bandage. His face had not been washed, just wiped by a bandage, wet from the water he had drunk. But the face of the injured man looked directly at him, ignoring others who moved around them and ignoring the hell of the moment of destruction.

Then he grinned. "English? You are English!" Then he laughed.

Did he believe Cello?

In battle things are said and done which are beyond humanity. The moment controls everything, though nothing is controlled. Humanity can go to its depth and bring a terror; or a touch from a heart with a feeling like blood returning, like wounds being inexplicably healed; can melt hate away.

Now the bombardment faded and what was left were the cries of the humans damaged by the inhuman, unconducted artillery.

Cello listened to the silence, blistered by cries. Had the bombardment moved on or ceased. The silence made him feel the cries more. It took him back to the cries of John Thomas Wall. They had sounded demented at times, close to death. But when he found the Sergeant, he seemed far from death, despite two days of lying in a mud hole.

So why had he died?

A shaft hurt Cello's heart.

That made up his mind. He lifted his head to look for more casualties. Maybe he could get to them and do something. He had nothing to give, no more bandages, only a small amount of water in the bottle.

But the silence now seemed filled. The voices of children suddenly came from his inner ear. The cries were those of happiness not pain, a relief from the crashing.

Was another artillery shell waiting in the clouds to fall?

A tiny screech answered him; YES.

He buried his head in dirty earth hands; OH GOD not more. The silence was better. Give us back the silence and the cries of children.

God answered him. But it was not total silence.

A small hiss came to him. Then the cries were suddenly more alarmed, much more urgent.

He looked up. He had to look up. A shell was buried. It had not exploded.

It was too close to the wreckage of the tented hospital, far too close.

There was no thought in Cello, no decision, no words in his inner ear. He gathered up the casualty; *"COME, COME, RUN!"*

They ran, away from the hissing thing. HUH HUH, KEEP RUNNING. They grunted as they went.

Others took up their example and loosed their bonds of paralysis. They exploded like rats whose hiding place had just been revealed. They had been hiding in tiny pockets of earth or behind wooden crates of supplies.

But Cello and his charge did not see them go. They were over the first small lip of the ridge and looking for suitable cover. A shallow trench system was revealed. They went into it looking for safety and collapsed down again in a type of communications line. There were telephone wires running along it.

Arms and legs and bodies were together, beating hearts and beating breath, stinking with anxiety, exploding out in each other's face. The casualty had teeth, yellow from tobacco, some were broken. Cello tried to keep the man's arm still and still bandaged. But it seemed to all start unravelling as they hit the ground. They had run for their lives. So what was one arm when they had preserved life, for the moment.

The moment!

Everything was a moment; a life and the living of it. But Cello did not have time to think or plan the next one because soon others joined them in the trench. They could not have been alone for more than a moment.

There were cries and expletives which fell deaf to Cello, though the shouting voices searched him for understanding. He nodded hopefully and dumbly. They became more strident.

Were there casualties here? Did they need help?

The soldier cellist checked his casualty, set the arm more comfortably. If that were possible.

Then he stood up.

They were in a line of men. The white-coated doctor, if she had been a doctor, was not there. They were in tatters. There were no fighting soldiers here. There were no game-keepers. These were logistic people. If the English came now over the ridge, they could walk through this line and kill them all, scythe them down. Except he, the soldier cellist, had a kind of flag that might stop them.

It had a double meaning, this flag; a red cross; two slashes of blood on white. It could mean fight and cut through the white, like a crusader. But everybody knew it for something else.

"Medizin." A strangling cry from further down the line. A hand raised. The hospital had gone. He, Cello, was the hospital for this moment. He could do nothing but respond. To ignore would have cast suspicion on him. He was in that sense a prisoner. But he didn't think this. He didn't have time to think. He waded down the line, past the prone or sitting bodies, past the suspicious, past the frightened and the indifferent. Some looked at him sullenly, soon with a kind of comfort, a trustiness. None raised a hand against him.

He moved purposefully onward and came to this casu-alty, who seemed strangely bent over, doubled almost. He was retching and some blood was coming up in his coughs.

There had been talk. There was always rumour, but this was more than rumour, of a terrible illness sweeping the world; a flu sickness. Soldiers confined to barracks or their trench have no knowledge of the rest of the world. Nor do they care unless they are affected. In some cases soldiers were affected.

This could be such a case.

Cello had another bandage, somehow. He knelt beside the man and wrapped it into a pad which he handed over. He extracted the man's water bottle and after the man had momentarily paused in his coughing, he handed it to him. The man drank and then sunk back against the trench wall.

Cello knew he should not breathe near the man. He instinctively knew that. So he stood up again.

The hissing had stopped. Silence had fallen.

Slowly, Cello, the burier of his friend, the hospital patient, then the part-time medic and now the survivor; moved back towards the wrecked tent.

Of course he was not the only survivor. Others had mostly run in the other direction. They slunk back under the example of the English casualty, a now gaunt and slightly leaning young figure, in large white apron, with a striking red cross, but without helmet. It had been lost somewhere in the destroyed hospital, which was a good thing. Had Cello hung onto it, for his own safety, he would be instantly recognisable.

But personal safety had been long since placed into abeyance.

For the sake of those in need of help.

There were a lot of those now. Cello was not one of them. He had somehow regained some strength.

The doctor directed operations. To get the main tentage back up. Cello was mystified again. The underground hospitals, the bunkers dug deep; so deep that no bombardment could reach them; why was this hospital so vulnerable? Why wasn't it concealed? Why did it seem so close to the front, on the front for no real soldiers guarded it? A hospital, at least should be much further back.

This one had been further back. There had been attacks that had depleted the resources of the Germans both on the front line and towards the rear.

A hospital could not retreat quickly. Casualties under treatment cannot be moved. This was perhaps a hospital for the brave; a brave doctor treating people near the front.

The woman doctor surveyed the wreckage. It wasn't completely wrecked. It was as if a mighty wind had swept through it, turning things upside down, breaking bottles. There had been no direct hit so the hospital had not disappeared into a crater.

Setting to, the men and one woman began to bring the hospital back to shape.

Cello just imitated what others were doing, helping. Blown down tents can be repaired with rope. Canvas and wood beds can be bandaged like men. But it was soon clear to Cello that enthusiasm to rebuild was lacking.

They should be further back.

But the men being treated finally began to become familiar to Cello as well as the fresh ones from the bombardment. Some had stayed in the wreckage. Some had run for cover, those that had legs.

Blood and bandages and hanging faces soon showed Cello he was not in the right place. He would not lie down again on one of the beds here. He did not deserve a bed here.

He was not one of those in need of help anymore.

Cello caught the eye of the doctor. Evening was approaching. Under cover of darkness he could move. He went outside under the partial protection of the doctor. She indicated the West. No sun was setting. There would be rain in the night.

Then Cello did begin to run.

CHAPTER SIXTEEN

The return

The day grew on and the earth under Cello became unknown, uncared about. He hid in craters. As night approached he got up and strode over it. He thought at one point that he should write to his mother. As if sitting down right now, he could do it. Men did. Some were always writing letters, especially out of the front line, but even in the trenches in the middle of a everything, they wrote; saying they were, 'alright here,' no one back home was to worry. Parcels were sent; chocolate, fags, writing paper, socks. Mothers were like factories supplying every form of comfort.

His cello would be needed. That's what he would ask his mother to send. Why had he not brought it? He deeply regretted that now. Perhaps at the time he thought he would not be able to carry it. Now the things he needed had reduced almost to nothing. But that one thing was needed.

Please send my cello. Everything else is alright here really. We are in good heart and I have met some pals (they are Germans who decided not to shoot me or take me prisoner when I took a stroll over to their side). Strike that out, amend the sheet music. Play the tune; the tune that everybody else was playing. They didn't want to upset anxious families at home. So phrases like 'we are in good heart' and 'everything is alright here', were regularly used. The censors probably liked them anyway.

This was the tune that everybody played to.

No, play the real tune.

That was the job of an artist. Be truthful!

Cello's eyes were darker than night. They had retreated into his head. Nothing else had retreated.

It had started to rain, hitting the rubberised surface of his apron, running down and streaming onto his puttees.

He needed to stop and consider his plan. He couldn't just walk into his own lines. He would be shot. The apron was probably already shining like a moon in the darkness, a walking moon; so obvious it was laughable. It was swishing noisily as well. They would wake each other in the trenches and start shooting at him and laughing as they did.

Perhaps he was too obvious. That might be his saviour; brazen and free, unafraid.

Yes unafraid. But still he crouched down to remove the apron. When it was light he might replace it. That would be the time to be bold, to show that he was unarmed and alone and therefore no threat to anyone.

The Germans he had met did not see him as a threat, more a strange Englishman who knew nothing about 'Das Krieg'. Probably an insane deserter that his comrades were happy to be rid of.

When he crouched he was still in the open. He didn't find the ditch again. He didn't search for it. He found a small crater which smelt of death and sat in it.

The smell bothered him not at all. Getting his cello bothered him; nothing else.

He was going in the direction of his instinct, unburdened by his Sergeant. The gradient of the ground was negligible, which bothered him a little. The route away from his previous trenches had been uphill. There was a wind in his face which gave him a sort of direction. He would head into it.

But should he sleep? There was no decision making like that in the trenches. You slept because you were exhausted not because you had decided to. You slept because no duty called, no order needed obeying.

He did feel free. Why not just fuck off then? Try to move between lines until he came to an end of it, an end of the battle lines. There he could find peace and beautiful farmland, untouched by all this. There must be an end. Was it in France or Belgium?

Or was there some monstrous ungod sealing the end to keep everybody fighting. Was it the Canadians, who had done well at fighting? Now they had taken up the role of; Guardian of the gate of battle.

He wrapped himself in the apron and lay on the ground.

A patrol might find him and stick a bayonet in him, like Jack had done, *'just to make sure'*.

He just laid his head on earth. He had nothing except his uniform and boots and this bloody apron. He was lucky he had his boots. Some casualties removed them or had them removed along with the leg attached to them. Had he not kept his on he would not have been able to run.

Some men did run, without boots, feet or lower legs. They ran on torn stumps of legs. Cello hadn't seen this. He had seen a horse hit while they waited in the logistic area, the hit was in the back and crippled the animal's back legs but it dragged itself around in circles on its front legs screaming horribly, until someone shot it.

Injured horses were not taken to hospital and treated. They were just dispatched, however small the injury. If they couldn't walk and move on their own they were no good. Moving their bodies afterwards was difficult because of the sheer weight. The carts and other horses all had jobs.

In some ways men also became animals, impossible to save when terribly injured, so killing them was the only thing to do. It happened, not just to the 'casualty' they had found. That was wrong, he had decided. It led to his 'desertion'. Who would agree it was wrong. Such is war. *'Das ist der krieg.'*

Then he had met his Sergeant.

It had stopped raining. He had drunk a little of the rain. He dozed and woke and re-dozed.

Thoughts drifted. In the trenches exhaustion brought deep sleep wherever the head could be laid. At other times thoughts and fears, noises and rummaging rats kept the head full and awake. Out in No Man's Land rats did not congress but scurried aimlessly and meeting them was a surprise unless they were having business with a corpse. Cello was not aware of corpses in his vicinity, except the smell ever lingering.

He also smelt rain and mud and something of himself, something of his fear.

It was not a fear of the enemy, or battle, or even death.

The fear was beyond, where humanity existed somewhere at the end of the line where the trenches ran out and farmland began again, and music inhabited the villages and the voices of children were raised, though not of the children who had died. When his hand was not shaking, he would be able to play his cello. His hand had power in it again. Music was power. It was more powerful than war. Though nobody here knew that.

His fear was that his world was no longer there. There was nothing beyond these trenches. They went on for ever and ever.

There was another fear, of what he might face; injustice.

John Thomas Wall seemed to die from shame. He did not rail against the injustice, if there was any, in the situation he might have faced. In his mind he already faced the shame, which might have been worse.

Cello did not feel that. In stronger moments when a little plug of anger caught at the back of his throat he wanted the injustice so that he could challenge it. There was no shame in what he had done. He had given a decent burial to a dead man…

Who he failed to keep alive. Failed…

He had failed? But why should he take the failure upon himself. Was this whole war not a failure? It wasn't his failure.

The rebellion came from music. He knew that. But music was dying in his mind; that was why he needed his cello so.

John Thomas Wall had been a soldier for five years, a regular of the line, proud and the making of pride in his dress uniform no doubt. Any potential rebellion had been drilled out of him, especially in his rising to sergeant, the responsibility which seemed to sit heavily. But then he had greeted Cello in a strange manner; "Sergeant John Thomas Wall at your service," for a sergeant.

He was the one in need of service… help.

So the greeting was an admission of his service, to whomever. His first thought, I'm here to serve.

His failure to provide service was a cause of shame.

Cello drifted in and out of dozing. His knees at one point began to shake and he could not really feel his feet. He thought of standing and trying to shake them back to life. It was not cold enough for trench foot, of which they had been warned in the training, another failure. If men's feet succumbed – it was your own fault.

A breeze moved his hair. Dawn must be approaching.

Dawn was decision time.

He waited for the grey dull light and began to shake from head to foot.

Who was doing that? No bombardment crossed over him. No attack was imminent.

The world was waiting for him; Marcus Harris, the apprentice master cello player and failed soldier, to stand up.

He did not fear standing and walking to his own side.

Still he did fear injustice.

Suddenly he wanted to stand up to try and stop the shaking in his body. He did so but then sat down again. It was stand too time. Every soldier would be pointing their rifles out into No Man's Land. That would virtually guarantee him being shot.

A challenge from a Corporal. Who's that out there? Who the fuck is it? That would be enough to set some recruit off with his shaking finger to loose one away.

I thought you wanted him gone Corp.

Well now he has gone, silly bugger and what the fuck was 'e wearing!

Wait a bit, have you got 'im or just winged 'im?

It would then be a turkey shoot. He would be wallowing, struggling and bobbing. That would excite. Yes the bobbing about would attract and encourage, there might even be cheering.

First man to make him stay down.

Take his fucking head off, the silly fucker.

Perhaps then he would place his hands above his head and start screaming. No no, it's me Private Harris. He would start to run, where, away or towards them in the desperate hope that they might come to their senses and stop.

Cease firing?

Would they?

Finish him you buggers, finish him, someone would shout.

Who would know whether he was German or French or some streak of nothing, not human.

He would run this way and that, perhaps being hit several times but not going down, still with the arms up, or outstretched, pleading, running to his mother. And with each fresh hit there would be a fresh scream accompanying his refusal to go down and surrender to death.

Until finally a head shot would bring a whoop whoop as his head burst like a pineapple.

Why a pineapple?

His mother's not gonna recognise him now. See that fucking head go, like a pineapple.

Pineapple. Who even had seen that? Did they have pineapples in the trenches. Never. You could get them the size of heads perhaps. It had stiff leaves sticking out of the fruit at the top, like a mad man's hair. Pineapple chunks came in cans. They never saw them here in the trenches.

Here in the trenches! Suddenly a sense of responsibility seized Cello. Yes it was his responsibility to go back, right now. Now that he was close and he had done his duty with his Sergeant. What was left.

Face the music!

Ha ha yes. He was in a state of mad hilarity in his shaking heart, face the music and create the music and take the injustice, when it came.

Instead of a rat, an absurdly small mouse came into his vision, came near his face. This mouse was lucky as rats generally disposed of mice very rapidly. This one was tiny, a sort of field mouse who lived on tiny grass seeds and other micro plant life instead of rotting flesh. It knew how to survive and keep out of the way of the larger rodents, the very much larger rodents.

The mouse did not see him, Cello, as a threat to its life and so rummaged carelessly searching for his elusive food. Searching among the million cells of plant life in a square yard of soil. Did that plant life survive the devastation it had been subjected to? The worm he and the Sergeant had partly eaten, the shit of that worm, the blood of that worm, these were part of those million cells. The bodies of men were not.

So with the courage of this mouse he must go and meet his destiny.

He stood again and this time was not shaking. The dawn had hardened a lot more, though there was no sun. There was a silence above and beyond Cello. The battlefield was waiting for his moment. This was his moment. So he began to walk slowly, very slowly towards his own line. He knew where his own line was. He walked over the mud through wire and a few shallow craters. He walked across them as if they weren't there.

Fear had fallen away though he kept himself tense with a strange passion which would have normally shaken his hand, shaken him into the music he played. Now it merely tensed his body to await the first bullet.

Instead, after stumbling into more solid wire, a loud voice came, a calm English one. "Halt who goes there?"

He did so. He raised his arms.

He had made his return.

CHAPTER SEVENTEEN
Back to the regiment

Cello's disorientation prevented any feeling of home coming, despite the English voice. Was this his regiment, the regiment he had joined seemingly a few days before and left? *"Private Harris."* His speech sounded strange as it does when unpractised. It had been unused except when he had been whispering to his Sergeant, John Thomas Wall, for... two days. It seemed an eternity. His voice came out low.

"Speak up man. What regiment?"

He gave it

There was a pause

"Advance, Private Harris."

Cello could not advance. The barbed wire was well concealed but thick around his feet and the mound which he thought was a mud bank was in fact the wire in front of the trench. Any German attackers would be lured by a well-concealed trench behind the bank which, once plunged into would hold your legs, the upper body ready for the concealed machinegun.

"Path to your right. Move right, keep your hands high," he was commanded.

Cello found the path. It dropped down, then up and there was a bank up to the trench. The voice had come from higher than he had thought. They had probably seen him from way back.

He relaxed a bit. But it was not the time for relaxing. "Just stay right there where you are." He was in the pit just outside the trench. He looked straight ahead and saw an aperture with the small barrel of a Lewis gun pointing through it and behind it the thick cooling shroud; then part of a face. The sand-bags surrounding the opening were mud brown and caked with mud in between the sides of the bags making the wall look very solid, like sandstone.

He didn't know how long he would wait or what he should do. The feeling of stupidity about the white apron was gone at any rate. The orders given indicated an acceptance that at least he was a soldier, of sorts.

"Turn around!" What. He froze. *"Turn around you soldier."* Yes he was a soldier. This was someone else's voice, a Corporal perhaps.

Cello turned slowly around on the spot where he stood, keeping his hands in the air. Someone might have come with some ghastly German grenade in the back of their apron, a stick grenade with the handle conveniently sticking out ready to pull and throw. He didn't have such a weapon. He had nothing and anyone looking could see that.

He faced again the small opening and waited. No question about his apron came, no comment or laughter, only silence. Then a voice; "Private Harris, advance."

He advanced until the Lewis was pointing at his chest. "Look to the left."

Cello looked. A few yards away was a hole where the dip disappeared. "Take the steps!"

He turned and walked or stumbled towards the steps. Down below the base of the trench they went, until a gap in the sand-bag trench wall was revealed by the extraction of a tightly coiled bunch of barbed wire. Cello scrambled through.

As if it had been waiting, the rain chose that moment

to deluge down onto the scene inside the trench. Unlike the supposed order of the sentry position and the intricate entrance into the trench system, this was chaotic and unordered. Three men lay asleep in the bottom of the trench within a few yards of the doorway. They were covered with groundsheet capes and could have been dead bodies. They did not move as the rain started, though one hand did draw its cape further up the face and helmet. Another prone figure lay on the fire-step some yards along, perilously teetering on the edge over which one leg hung. Two men huddled over a stuttering little cooker, trying to boil a mess tin of water. They looked up with a sort of scowl. Everything was covered in earth which was now rapidly taking on the sheen of mud with an exhausted, bedraggled look.

Cello waited in the rain. The sentry who had called him in, continued to look out. Cello was not his responsibility any more but a Corporal standing behind the sentry, moved into Cello's lowered vision. He advanced to within a few inches of Cello's face then moved his head backwards before jutting it forward. "So *Private Harris*, can you explain, what you are, were, doing out there; a special mission was it? Lost were we? Or… And where if you could enlighten us, is your rifle and your equipment?"

The regimental badges stood out. Cello was home, with his people and comrades in arms.

"I found Sergeant John Thomas Wall," said Cello. "I went out to find him. Well I didn't know that. I… we went to find a casualty and found him. But he died. I made sure that he was buried." He stood with head bowed, completely bowed, as if defeated; not home with friends.

The Corporal was fixated on the rifle. "Where is it then… your rifle?"

"Well I couldn't exactly have carried Sergeant Wall while carrying *it* could I?" He spoke to the ground, his head still bowed. But something was rising within him though not yet raising his head. He needed water and food.

"Company and platoon then? Come on?"

"Alpha, number three."

"Ahh." The Corporal acted as though he had extracted some vital piece of intelligence. "Now we know."

"Not exactly keeping it secret."

"What was that," demanded the Corporal?

"I'm not trying to keep it a secret, I said," replied Cello.

"No well you had better not do that, don't have any secrets around here." The Corporal puffed his chest out.

The two men trying to boil water looked up. They had a vacant sort of look and didn't react to the apron, or to anything. They were pre-occupied. The water was refusing to boil.

Something was in the Corporal's eyes, a tiny pinpoint of nervousness. His men were not reacting to him taking control of the situation with this man in the apron, this extra-ordinary soldier who was not a soldier like him, that much was obvious. But there was still a strange power to him, which he the Corporal would have liked to have himself, but he didn't. His soldiers lounged around in a disinterested way.

Cello was not finished yet, despite his seemingly resigned posture. "Don't you want to know about Sergeant Wall?" His voice was steadier than he could have imagined. "And could I have some food and water." Then he did raise his head and looked directly at the Corporal. He brought his dark eyes, pushed deep into his skull by fatigue, to bear. In fact they met the Corporal's eyes.

The meeting of eyes of two men cannot be monitored by a third party. It is a very private meeting, however long or short. In this meeting Cello saw the flicker of uncertainty in the Corporal's eyes. That gave him hope.

"You will need to wait, wait for the Sergeant. He will say, what food and water you can have… If you can have it."

So that was it. The Corporal hung his head, not his place to even give a drink. Cello looked beyond the head and he could see equipment lying around the trench. There were water bottles there. "… So could I have just a sip of water then?" he pressed.

The rain had been a bit of a cloud-burst but had now settled into a monotonous heavy drizzle, of the sort that could not be caught in a mug placed under the crease of a cape to drain into. It was all brown mud water. So the Corporal would need to physically give him a bottle. His soldiers seemed very loath to offer any of theirs.

"Don't move, stay just where you are."

Cello did move, as the Corporal turned away perhaps to extract his own water bottle, he sat slowly down and put his head in his hands. It was not a motion of resignation but a bodily need for rest, rest in relative safety. He could not avoid the scene around him. The looks became more insistent. Eventually a soldier's curiosity has to be satisfied. "So where did you get that fucking stupid apron then?" The water had finally boiled and the two non-sleepers were sipping their tea.

"It's a German medics apron."

"Of course it is, silly question."

Cello's desire overcame him. "Could I perhaps, have a sip of tea."

"Come and join us mate, Looks like you need it."

Cello went to where the two were half-sitting against the back wall of the trench, against some revetting. He crouched and took an offered steaming enamel mug. "Thank you." The first sip gave him some life back. But it may have been the simple generosity as well as the actual tea that did it. He could not hold the mug. Its heat was not much but the shaking caught him again and he feared he might spill it.

"Give us it here mate," said one of the men. Gently he took the mug and held it for Cello to drink.

Cello dropped his useless shaking hands and surrendered, taking a longer draw on the mug. "Take it… its yours," he said, motioning the mug back to its owner. His mouth and throat warmed.

"You're alright mate, take it as you want."

"Thanks." Cello held the mug gratefully.

Cello was gaunt. Three days had seen his body lose some of its fat, lean though it had been before. They looked easily into each other's eyes and found a sort of patience as well as a little humour.

Both the men began a ghastly smirk. "Fuckin' German medics apron… You look a fucking idiot, you know that."

Cello too couldn't help but smile. "Yes I do."

The Corporal was eyeing them by this time. Then he approached. "Alpha Company is it?… Deserter ain't yur?"

"He's no harm Corp, let the lad have some tea."

"Water you asked for, here it is." He waved a bottle at Cello.

"But with this weather, tea would give him…"

"Not sure the RSM would even allow water, leave alone tea."

"Couldn't we just smuggle him back, you know. At least he came back on his own." The soldier who had given Cello the tea looked pleadingly at the Corporal.

"Smuggle him back, smuggle him back, past his Sergeant-Major, his Sergeants, Corporals? They going to let him go back without saying nothing?"

"Sergeant John Thomas Wall, do any of you know him," asked Cello interrupting? Even a Sergeant, had seen injustice, or the threat of injustice, despite being a casualty. So what hope for him.

"John Thomas Wall… What Company?" asked one of the men.

That startled Cello. "I didn't even ask him that," he regretted.

"You were with him. You buried him. You didn't know what company he came from." The Corporal was astonished.

"It was not important, we were alive and we sort of celebrated that, until…"

"How did he die?" The men who shared the tea were more curious about him than the Corporal.

"Died of his injuries." Cello's head was bowed, to avoid the curious eyes. But the fact that they were curious, perhaps suspicious gave him hope. "But he was in the regiment." That fact he did know.

"We are going back for some rest," said the Corporal as if mention of the regiment had brought him to his senses. "You couldn't be smuggled back to whatever trench you came from." He had joined in the sharing of tea. "Back there you will get some new kit and… meet the RSM."

That meeting had to be done but no one relished it.

CHAPTER EIGHTEEN
Going back to rest

The rain was intermittent but hopelessly heavy when it came. Men woke soaked from the trench floor to seek some shelter but they found none and stayed propped miserably against the trench wall, trying to imitate the tea drinkers. The man on the step slept on, his cape soaked and glistening as brown water ran off it.

A sergeant decreed that Cello should be 'held'.

Where would he go? Back to the German side. There was no 'holding'. He didn't have the inclination to run. But he would have liked some warmth as he became very cold in the rain. There was no bunker as such but a kind of indented shelter. The trench had a latrine in a wood-lined slot, no bigger than a man with nowhere to put feet, and just a wooden bar to sit over, supported by sand-bags. You could fall in. Perhaps the builders had a sense of humour. Falling backwards into the stinking hole full of blue, eye-watering disinfectant was perhaps another way to die.

But as they went back there was a need for 'holding'. Military police had been called for but they were some-where in the rear areas, investigating whatever crime might be committed there. Perhaps a bottle of whisky stolen from the Officers' mess. Or guarding whatever was to be guarded from desperate civilians who clung to life there and sought to steal anything.

At the front everything was down to NCOs and those soldiers who might be designated as guards to men under punishment. Working parties they were called. 'Work' could constitute anything from bringing up supplies which would be a good scam, as it might involve nicking something extra for the rucksack; to tying a man onto a wagon wheel; the punishment that Cello had witnessed with his Sergeant; or clearing rotting bodies from a trench. That was joyless work, but it had to be done.

So Cello was guarded by men whose opinion on his guilt was not sought, who were not briefed of the possibility of his guilt. But by the implication of his coming through the trench wall without a weapon and seemingly without a story; had demonstrated that some sort of guilt must exist.

It was the tea-drinkers, one of whom had been like a Samaritan to Cello. They had to watch and be with him every step of the withdrawal. In a bit of a cruel twist the Corporal did not allow the removal of the apron. He was thus signalled out, for derision if nothing else.

The relief in line has to be controlled well by NCOs, otherwise it becomes a rush to the rear. You are not allowed to leave your trench until relieved and even then you may wait at an assembly point, bitterly complaining about the danger of being caught there in a bombardment. Routes should have been laid and marked by tape which has a shine about it at night. But sometimes it is broken or lost or trodden into the mud. Men, in files; blindly dragging back; thinking only of food, rest, dry clothes and a bit of peace; are lost and wandering and bump together into groups which curse and grow and turn to chaos.

The routes taken are not the same as men might be used to, in their journeys around the front line on working parties and messenger duties. The relieving unit must not get mixed with the one going back. Another chaos would result from this. Hence the tape on a pre-planned route.

But plans invariably go wrong. One small delay some-where may affect the whole operation.

On this night streams of men went missing or became entangled with others. Companies got muddled and ended up missing their times for passing through rendezvous points. Cello's apron shone in the night and as he waited with his escorts at one track junction to join up with the rest of his new company; Alpha Company, his original unit, passed through. They were more orderly and seemed to be moving more smoothly. They moved in file, in pairs.

Cello waited disconsolately in his section group. He was chilled and beyond shivering, just listless, the body allow-ing the cold and rain to just go through it. He attracted the sniggering attention of passers. However exhausted, sol-diers' humour will always draw some sneer but when his own section with Jack and Ben passed they did more than snigger.

It gave reason to stop. "What... It's that fucker Cello. Look that silly fucker. What the fuck does he think he's doing?"

"Keep going, don't stop you fuckers. Keep going." There came an immediate rebuke from NCOs. But a group rap-idly formed. "Sarge, look that deserter. You gonna charge him?"

"Deserter?"

"Yes, like we told you, from that patrol."

Men shuffled off the track, glad of a temporary diversion of interest. A sergeant came up from further down the line, their platoon Sergeant with the youthful face and blond moustache. His face lit up like a beacon in the night. "Ah, so there you are."

Cello looked ahead of him, not at the Sergeant. The noises and movement of the night, might take this away from him perhaps, this moment. The men, the mud and the movement, equipment piled on backs and strapped around and around the bodies until they thought nothing more could be set on them. But they did weigh more stuff on them. Then on top of everything came the brown respirator haversack, the gas mask. It should be on the front, sitting across the chest, like a nosebag on a horse, but not for food.

Men were locked into this task of carrying, of dragging their loads back, not the sometimes-neat bundles they started with. These were dumped together and humped by exhausted and sometimes-bandaged bodies.

But Cello had nothing, nothing at all to carry, not even a gas mask. That set him apart. It made men stop and take note. So the moment could not be lost. He was different from them. If gas came they would watch him die from the relative safety of their own masks.

"Well what do you have to say for yourself… eh? *Deserter!*"

'Deserter.' The word was whipped away by the night but it turned eyes momentarily. Most of them were dull and without due regard. They only had thought for the end of the journey.

Cello's head remained bowed but he did mutter something.

"What did you say eh, what?"

"He said he isn't a deserter Sarge," said one of the escorts.

"Oh he isn't and what would you know, you his friend now are you?"

"No we are just taking him back to rest."

"Taking him back… to rest. Won't be much rest for him where 'es going. Feet won't touch the ground. I say feet won't touch the ground; not when the RSM gets to see 'im anyway."

The conversation was shouted above some din from artillery that had started. Though no one seemed very bothered by it. It wasn't very close or the din would have been deafening.

"You hear that Mister Cello," added Jack who had taken up a place next to the Sergeant, pointing and gibing. They were sitting now and easing loads off backs. The rain didn't bother them as they knew there would be fresh clothes where they were going. They leaned back and the two groups looked at each other across the track junction.

Then an officer came wandering up out of the night. "Come on you men, get up, no time for shilly-shallying, get along."

So they all joined up together and after a conversation between the two platoon sergeants, Cello got handed over, like a commodity. The two escorts, the original tea drinkers, did seem a little regretful at this. Particularly when the new Sergeant grabbed Cello by the arm and dragged him up, then turned him over to Jack. Then he hesitated. "No you shouldn't go with your section." He waited a few moments by the track and another small file of men appeared through the night. "Here number three section. This man is a deserter and you are going to be his escorts back."

He thrust Cello at them. They were a tightly packed little unit. One man carried a Lewis gun over his shoulder, which he took down and prodded Cello into their midst with it before they trudged on without a word.

Cello had almost to stumble along to keep up with them. The pace was set by the Lewis gunner who was tall and being close to him, Cello could see he was wearing a leather jerkin. These items were prized and usually only procured by the strongest characters in the section as there weren't enough for each man. There was never enough of the attractive items of equipment; only the very basic and unwieldy items were plentiful. His boots were probably comfortable and solidly leather as well.

Boots were a constant source of discussion and envy. Some officers had riding boots with breeches above them. This precluded the need for the long puttees which were both a curse and a god send. New recruits struggled over their entanglement when trying to put them on. But they made very good bandages. Once properly on, men often did not remove them for days, or the boots below them. A tight seal around the ankle was necessary to keep the feet dry. But once that individual haven was breached and a foot or feet were wet, drying them out was almost impossible, while the whole thing of puttee and boot was assembled.

Cello looked down at the man's boots. They were solid, general issue ones. Every man was supposed to get two pairs when he started training but their solid leather soles and metal studs supposedly to make them withstand every-thing, made them no good for keeping out trench foot when the cheap leather became soaked and the stitching finally gave way. So brown leather handmade boots of the finest quality were the ones men craved, but few could get hold of. The 'cardboard' leather of the general issue ones was the fall-back. They went white after repeated soaking and part drying and dubbin could never be procured. Solid looking on the parade ground when newish, they rotted on men's feet quickly in the mud of the trenches.

No army is ever happy with its boots. Army authorities inevitably took the cheap, mass-produced option.

As with everything else, they endured.

"What you looking at?" asked the Lewis gunner as they marched along.

"Your jacket."

"It's a lot better than yours."

"Mine's not a jacket."

"Not arf it's not. Not even close to a jacket... So what the fuck is it?"

"German Red Cross apron."

"Ahh, well the Hun does make some good stuff, but I don't think that apron is one of them."

It was quite difficult to conduct an in-depth conversation in the circumstances but the gunner seemed willing to try.

"Where did you procure it then, a Hun trench?"

"Hospital."

"Of course, it would be a hospital – What are they like, Hun hospitals?"

Cello needed a moment to consider this. "They treated me," he said simply.

"So I would hope," said the gunner.

Cello looked at him and knew by his words that he had in him a natural compassion which had not been destroyed by their situation.

"But I'm fit now," said Cello. Their conversation came in a sort of marching rhythm.

"Yes and you got nothing to carry, so do you want the Lewis."

"Well I..."

"Go on Mister Deserter. It'll make you feel better."

It did.

Cello did feel a little privileged. Gunners usually never give up their machineguns. They guard them like children and look after them in the same way.

"Thank you," said Cello after a few moments of walking.

The man smiled down at him. He was taller, which was unusual as Cello had the height advantage over almost everyone he knew.

When they reached the end of that section of their journey however the Sergeant took charge again. "What are you doing giving that deserter a weapon? He threw away his rifle. Why you giving him another one, a more powerful one?"

"Maybees he had reason to throw it away," said the gunner.

The sergeant went close to the gunner and looked up into his face. He could not be dominant though over someone so tall. He could not use his voice to reach the man's height. So he shied away from the confrontation, but then snatched the Lewis from Cello. "Maybe you are not fit to carry this either," he said to the gunner. Then in the dim light, he noticed the Lewis gun badge on his sleeve. And with that the man just took it off him without a word. The rest of the section looked on approvingly. They knew who should carry it.

The ground became less pockmarked. Some grass appeared. They couldn't see it at night. The track on which they marched was still a mud path. At the next rendezvous there was a larger group and the battalion seemed to be reforming into its component sub-units.

"Alpha Company over 'ere." A shout greeted the marchers. Men huddled towards other grey figures who steamed with sweat and recent rain and moved with the rattle of carried war detritus.

It had become war rubbish. The enthusiasm for battle was gone.

Then there was another sound. Sealed food boxes were sprung open and the insulated lids removed. A heavenly smell exuded. Well it was heaven enough for that moment.

"Line up in platoons."

But the gaggle could not be forced into that. They were of one mind. "Just fucking serve it up."

"Come on," Shouted those unfortunate enough to be at the periphery of the gang.

Dead men cannot be fed. But their numbers were never

known until after the sub-unit chefs had prepared the food. Some quartermasters regretted the subsequent grabbing of double rations by some. Those serving it, soldiers on working parties, storemen or some with walking injuries, could be easily intimidated, especially by tall, badged gunners.

Cello also was lent a mess tin and spoon by the gunner.

He sat and slowly ate. He didn't see the buildings that stood waiting for them just off the track.

CHAPTER NINETEEN
A letter

With a full belly a soldier will sleep anywhere. This night there was a degree of luxury few could have imagined. A school had given up its pupils. Education, like cello playing, was a forgotten art in the war zone and the children had been returned to whatever homes still existed or to move far away to relatives or refuge, if there was any, or to live out towards peace; If such a thing was to ever come again. At first it would have given the children joy. Then boredom would have set in, and a strangeness without the aid of school to move their lives forward. The occasional dose of terror was also present as bombardments came close, then went away, then came back. The search for survival and peace from the shells finally created an enmity against the war which became life, with nothing outside it.

For soldiers there was new life; taken first in sleep, where all are equal, with uniform discarded and some weird underwear or even pyjamas dragged out of blanket roles, amazingly. "Just kept 'em for this moment, bin treasuring 'em since me mum sent 'em," said one small man, pulling out the striped set seemingly in pristine condition.

"How did you keep them so dry?" asked Cello.

"Being careful, that's 'ow. My mum always told me, look after your stuff. She always kept a tidy house, everything neat and tidy, polished every week, no dust. I've got to write to her about some more stuff I need as well."

That brought Cello back to his goal, back to music that was somewhere in his mind; in the movement of his hands and arms and in the way of thinking. It was a fall-back in his mind, a final rampart of hope. So suddenly he was given a lifeline of thought. He had to write a letter. "Yes I need to write to get something from home as well. Any chance…?"

They were ready for bed but the man in pyjamas looked at Cello who was dressed in stained underwear having removed his apron and his uniform. "I got a bluey from where Q left 'em at the door, didn't you see 'em?"

"Oh no I didn't."

"You better get there or theys all be gone." He pronounced 'gone', in a Worcester way, 'gorrn', which reminded Cello of John Thomas Wall. He had been a Worcester man, a Worcester countryman. Perhaps this man was a Worcester countryman. Perhaps he knew the Sergeant. But Cello did not have the confidence to ask.

Cello staggered out from between beds nearly tripping over the Lewis, discarded on the floor among a mass of equipment littering the amazingly well polished boards. He looked towards the door where a small table stood, like a sentry for another world, clean and intact and in order, as if messages and notices should be left there undisturbed.

There were some blue papers on the table. As Cello approached, the door opened and Ben, his colleague from another life came through. Had he wanted to write a letter as well and didn't have any blue forms in his room?

The 'bluey', called as such because of its colour, was a mass-produced letter form. Words went on one side, the address on the other. It was folded along some dotted lines and then it was handed in un-licked so that the words could be read and approved by whoever did that and without the requirement for a stamp, they were sent to wherever the address directed.

"Well Cello you got yourself sorted out then," said Ben.

"Yes I got a bed here… You?"

"I'm next door, great place ain't it. It's like being in a hotel."

"Yes we might have a good night's sleep at last."

"Until parade in the morning."

"Yes I've not got anything for that parade."

"Anything?"

"Equipment, nothing," said Cello.

"You can get yourself kitted out," said Ben looking regretful. He was wearing braces over a shirt and trousers without puttees; having finally removed them.

"I hope so… I need to write a letter first. I need to get my cello." His eyes dropped to the table. "Did you come for a letter?"

"No… I came to look for you."

"Me!"

"Without jack, y'know." Ben looked down at the floor.

"Yes, he's a bit…"

They were hesitant, as if they had something new to explore. Without weapons or uniform they were different people. But they couldn't forget where they were. With John Thomas Wall, Cello had been able to forget, for some hours.

Here they couldn't. They merely turned away from each other. Turned away from what might have been in their minds.

"But you are back and in one piece."

"Yes I'm in one piece…" Cello wanted to talk about the 'deserter,' label and whether Ben agreed with it. But they didn't manage to reach that level of communication. So they turned to their tasks. Cello to the scattered 'blueys', on the table. He picked one up and waved it towards Ben. "I need to write my letter."

"Yes you need to…" Ben looked a little sheepish. He had nothing to do himself, so he left.

Cello stopped for a moment considering the meeting, his head down, with hair falling over his face. It hadn't been washed yet but the rain which had taken out some of the mud had dried and left it a little limp. His deep dark eyes were a little clearer. But he turned to a more pressing task. A letter had to be written. He might get a pencil from someone.

Dear Mother

Mother I need my cello. I know you are anxious to keep it safe but I find myself yearning to play something in the times that I have to myself. I know it will draw attention and it is not a soldier's thing to do. But as at now my playing is something I need that will take my mind off being a soldier.

I'm sorry that you have not received a letter for some days and will probably be wondering about me. I am really alright here. We are behind the lines at present in a school which is very comfortable. But the comfortable things cannot last for long and soon we will return no doubt to the front.

I hope you are well and father of course. Please pass my best wishes to him and for his work. I hope all is well.

England is so far away from here. It is a world away. But we hope that this cannot last for ever. All I can do for now is hang onto my music and the thought that I will return to it. It is the most important thing in my life.

Your ever loving, Marcus.

He could not write any more, the blue paper was completely full of words and they were closely written ones. He did not put Xs on the paper as most soldiers did. They displayed the emotion that they didn't speak about to their fellow soldiers. They had wives and many had children already, waiting patiently, not really understanding why their fathers should be away.

Letters, if they weren't for wives and fiancées, were for mothers, or at least someone, generally a woman, who might send socks. But a cello. Who would send that, who would look after the parcel containing it?

Cello the player, the musician, who understood the emotions that the cello induced, but did not write a kiss to his mother, fell asleep on his bare but clean mattress, already becoming infested with lice from a discarded uniform and from his army blanket just covering his body.

Early in the morning the letters were taken by the Company Quartermaster Sergeant, the Colour Sergeant who brought up the food and the fresh uniforms and the weapons and the ammunition and the rum and took away the written letters. He was the link with humanity. Except that the Old Man had been above him in that respect. The Old Man was a very different human. Some wondered whether the new RSM was human.

CHAPTER TWENTY

An awaited meeting

A parade had become part of the new RSMs routine. Those at the front hardly ever saw him in the trenches but the parade was how he re-exerted himself, giving the impression that all the while he had been at the headquarters organising something important for the Battalion. Which was strange to contemplate as the Battalion Commander did come to the front line quite often, either on his own or with his radio operator and a batman soldier, or with another officer, perhaps the Battalion Second in Command who took notes about such things as the need for more leather jerkins.

The more discerning of the soldiers noticed that the Colonel had become less relaxed since the death the Old Man. He mourned with them, but death was so regular that mourning could not be indulged upon or change the course of the next day's mission. And if a congratulatory message about the performance of the Battalion on that mission came from on high, deaths and mourning could be conveniently laid aside. Yet still the Colonel didn't lose the cloud above him.

Was it all worth it after all, his face seemed to say?

Humanity must be continued; or an excuse for it.

Some men, voiced it. There were always voices on parades, undervoices, undertones, as they were forming up; like the voices of football players that could not be heard by specta-tors. "That Old Man was humane, but I don't know about this fucker." He pronounced the 'e'.

"Do you mean humane or human?"

"The same ain't it?"

"No it's not the same." More voices were raised in the section. On a point of education voices were always raised, with one wanting to show more knowledge than another.

"But I make you right," pointed out one wiseman. "Coz I think you meant human and I got a feeling that this one ain't human."

The original speaker stood mouth open. "Yea," he said uncertainly.

"You mean no."

"Yea, he ain't human absolutely."

"But the Old Man was humane as well, and there ain't too many of those people around here in this war."

They formed into platoons, loosely. Though the RSM's screeched version of the word *"BATTALION,"* as if a chicken was being strangled, made them sharpen up their three-rank dressing.

He had their attention. He was rather gleeful and hardly concealed this. *"Something exciting for us today, you'll see. Come on, come on. Sar majors lets be having your reports please."*

The normal parade routine was that platoons form up into companies and then march into a position on the des-ignated parade ground, indicated by man markers placed out before, whether it is a village square of mud or a road junction or a farm field. RSMs did not usually present themselves for this but kept a discreet distance. As officers did, usually in whatever house had been designated as the Officers' Mess. So the men were the full responsibility of the designated senior non-commissioned officers until the time came for them to be handed upwards, to the RSM, thence to officers.

But this RSM always made his presence felt. He was there watching, gloating at some misdemeanour of formation. This caused the Company Sergeant-Majors to bawl some poor unfortunate soldier out all the louder.

The RSM could hardly wait. The Sargeant-Majors reported to him one after the other; *"Alpha, twenty casualties SIR!"*

"Bravo fifteen casualties and three reported sick this morning SIR!"

"BRAVO YOUR CASUALTY LIST GROWS WITH SICKNESS LET ME SEE SICK BAY RECORDS AFTER THIS PARADE. I WANT REASONS, NOT EXCUSES."

"Very well sir," replied the Sergeant-Major in question, somewhat weakly.

Other sub-units on parade, the rifle companies and elements of headquarters and support, reported and shuffled into stillness and expectation. Despite the universal dislike of the RSM there was a fascination for what he might do next and the announcement of *'something exciting',* brought expectation.

He didn't keep the parade waiting. *"Now that we are all assembled I want to bring one man to your attention. He is… was, a soldier. But he has chosen a different road… It is a member of Alpha. HE IS HERE IS HE NOT SAR-MAJOR?"*

"YES, SIR."

"GOOD GOOD, NOT ON THE SICK LIST… NOT BECOME A SUDDEN CASUALTY. BUT HE WILL BE IN A WORSE CONDITION SOON… BECAUSE HE IS A DESERTER."

He put a sudden spitting emphasis on the word. It was a disgusting word for him. Or he made it seem such. Though no one knew what was in the RSM's mind. How much was, for him, a display or a play for his audience. He needed an audience. No one knew how he was when on his own.

But after the pause, Cello was to find out.

"So let's be having you then... Private Harris, lets be having you right out here, in front of the whole battalion. You're famous... Ain't you? Don't suppose they've ever seen a real... deserter. We don't see many of them; thankfully."

There was a movement in the ranks of Alpha and eventually Cello did appear. He appeared not like a soldier on parade with polished boots and stamping them, but with some slow movements. He was without a rifle unlike all the others. He was dressed in a fresh uniform and looked alert. He had a cap on so there was no way of telling whether his hair was clean. But they had all had baths, such were the facilities of the school where they had found billets.

He did march forward towards the RSM. That was where the private meeting took place. Cello was not afraid and that would impress the hearts of some men, the lack of fear, the lack of shaking. It was a dignified lack of shaking.

The RSM's quiet voice had a menace about it. But Cello somehow drew and neutralised it. The watchers did not witness any penetration of the words into his body.

But there was to come a summary punishment which the RSM conceived to humiliate.

"You have disgraced the uniform you are wearing. Clearly you don't want it any more. Go to the side of the parade and remove it... Dismiss."

It was a simple instruction. One that was heard by some but not all. But all watched as Cello did turn right, pause and march off. The pause did not include a salute as there was no officer on parade and there was no emphasis on parade ground moves again.

They watched as he proceeded to the edge of the parade and removed his uniform in a simple manner as if about to get into bed. White underwear and the keen breeze, though there was no rain, would have made him cold and his skin would begin to pimple. But after placing his uniform on the ground he stood back to attention, loosely, some would have thought insolently; looking up and out, way beyond the RSM, showing that he was still not afraid.

CHAPTER TWENTY-ONE
Due process

The Military Police were the agents of the RSM; a sort of secret police who worked under his command. No one else seemed to control them, not at battalion level. They often came from a higher formation supposedly, not commanded by the RSM, but they always reacted to his word as they reacted to the word of any officer, the senior they were the more emphasis was placed on that reaction. The red top puppets, as the soldiers saw them because of their red caps, headed by the RSM, seemed to have an assumed chain of command but no visible puppeteer.

The Commanding Officer was the figurehead to whom due deference was given, or usually over-given, especially in the case of the RSM. But there was a higher ideal that existed and everybody in authority gave it the nod. If anybody asked what it was, they would be told that it was 'due process', and it had to be followed. Authority nodded, of course; 'due process' was necessary.

The MPs came and removed Cello's uniform and after the parade during which not an instant of attention was paid to him, he was marched away, barefooted.

Soldiers do not control their own lives. So they have to accept what happens to others. Just as the German soldiers had accepted the fate of their comrade tied to the gate, which Cello and Sergeant Wall had encountered. The men of Alpha Company marched off the parade to their routine. They wanted an easy two days before they had to return. Training and resupply of equipment and whatever else had to be done would be fitted around sleeping and eating and perhaps time to play cards, write and receive letters and parcels from home. These were what the soldiers anticipated. They would do anything to preserve those things. They would certainly forget Cello.

Ostensibly at least.

The sections regathered in their billets after the parade. They smoked and lounged on beds while doing so. Breakfast had been taken and the next thing was to be some training before the midday meal at which there might be rum.

The navy took their issue of rum before the midday or lunch meal, at sea. This did not always make for a safe afternoon shift for those men who had managed to procure an extra tot or two; taken, sometimes, in fact usually, in a 'oner'. Young sailors under twenty were not supposed to take the tot. That rule was hardly ever enforced.

Of course the army followed the tradition when rum became available to them which was not every day as for the navy, but in the trenches it did manage to get forward most days, often at the expense of other supplies which some might have deemed more essential.

To Jack the rum was essential. It had become more so since the arrival of the new RSM.

Ben his friend and accomplice in almost everything, also needed rum. But he had broken free from Jack to visit Cello the night before and he had watched fleetingly as he had stood at the side of the parade, standing out like a white feather on the back of a crow. His white underwear looking clean from a distance.

"Down it then mate, down the hatch," urged Jack. They

sat at the side of the hall that had been the school's dining room. Now it was the soldiers' canteen, the centre of their world. A grey smoke haze hung above the heads of the congregation of soldiers who hummed and droned steadily, sometimes intercepted by high-pitched shouts of mirth or vulgar laughter. There was a rumour spreading among the tables and benches where soldier's boots brought the knee into semi-rest for the elbow; that one of the French girls who had lately worked at the school was still there helping, somewhere in the kitchen.

"Those bastards in HQ Coy will have the drop on us there. Ain't that a fact, Ben?"

Ben had nearly finished his tot. "What d'you think's gonna happen to Cello?" he interrupted the flow of conversation.

"Due process it's called; COs orderly room, remanded for Court Martial…"

"Then?"

"Well this Regiment has got a bit of a reputation."

"For what?"

"Shooting soldiers…"

"Soldiers?"

"Our soldiers." He leered, as if this was the same subject as the French girl.

The leer hit Ben a bit, though he continued to go along with his friend. He hadn't told Jack about meeting up with Cello the night before.

"Yes I had heard about that." He hadn't really heard the detail.

"Five in one day, can you imagine that; from the same battalion. Five men shot for desertion or cowardice. Five men lined up and shot… Don't know if they used the same firing squad for all of them. What do you reckon? Like being on the range." He placed his mug of rum on the bench then held up two arms and feigned taking pot shots at five different targets lined up alongside each other.

Someone close by burst out laughing. Jack joined in. "Like at a fairground." It wasn't really like the range. When shooting at a target, although they might move down towards it, they shoot at the same target, anything else is unsafe.

"They wouldn't have done that would they?" Ben suddenly felt repulsion. He felt it had been building and suddenly had to admit it, at least to himself.

Jack continued with his play-act. He enjoyed the whole episode.

It was another Battalion in the Regiment and had happened two years before. It did echo through the ranks occasionally. No doubt the RSM knew of it well.

It gave Ben a strange feeling. Everything they did was about killing the enemy and preserving yourself. So why would you create more casualties among your own men. It seemed ridiculous.

Ben looked at himself for the first time; but not in a mirror of which there were none in the theatre of war.

There was more training in the afternoon which the men turned to with a bored shrug. How could training improve the chaotic moments of trench encounters? It was supposed to improve the overall tactics of set-piece battles. Except that those often did not go to plan, so any new tactics were quickly dispensed with as men were cut down by machinegun fire yet again or reached for entrenching tools in bludgeoning desperation if an attack was interdicted by the enemy before new tactics could be employed.

Cello did not take part in the lunch or the training. He was held in the 'guardroom', while due process gathered its materials. If they were behind the line, battalions always maintained a guardroom; a point of entry to their piece of territory when they were not in the trenches. Guards were needed to patrol the billets at night and stop vehicles which approached the area. A duty team led by an officer, with NCOs and junior ranks doing the patrols and other working parties used the guardroom as the point of control.

In this case the guardroom was a house at the end of broken terrace of unoccupied properties. In the front room the duty Corporal sat with books, including a diary recording the men on duty and any incidents that might take place. One important incident recorded was the taking into 'custody' of the 'prisoner' Cello. They used his real Name; Private Marcus Harris. The time of the incident was recorded as zero nine thirty.

The room he was held in was an upstairs bedroom. The stairs were creaky, the floorboards upstairs not sound. There was no furniture, no bed, unlike the school and the windows were boarded up with rough planks; nails, heads bent over, hammered swiftly and left. It was a bare, small room.

The guarding of Cello was in the hands of the Military Police, though the duty personnel were also used to add numbers and do tasks for him. There was only one way out of his bedroom and the stairs were guarded and the downstairs was occupied by the duty Corporal and other duty personnel.

Cello was not entitled to rum. But he did have to be provided with food and water. This was the task of those on duty. The options were for him to be taken to the canteen under escort or for one of the guard to collect his food and bring it to him. The RSM had given orders for complete isolation, so the latter option was chosen.

On bringing a mess tin full of stew and powdered mash potato, which was cold by the time it came to the still barefoot Cello, along with an enamel mug of water; the food bringer looked at Cello and his stare elicited speech. "Do you know Sergeant John Thomas Wall?" Cello asked.

"Sergeant Wall…" He said the name automatically so Cello knew the answer to his question. "He was one of our platoon sergeants."

"Yes? What happened to him?"

"They said he died in the bombardment."

"He didn't… I found him and rescued him but then he died. I buried him with some Germans… Didn't you want to find him after the bombardment?" He looked into the man's eyes, which were dull and after a moment they were diverted. "They said he had died," he repeated.

"But you didn't know that he had died."

"There were rumours," said the man, holding the food but this time looking up at Cello who was standing bare-foot on the bare boards.

"Rumours, about what?"

"Well… that he had deserted."

"How could that judgement be made?"

The man looked strangely at Cello. Then he shrugged, but it was not a submissive shrug because Cello was a pris-oner and a deserter himself. So he had no right to question. "Could you get me some clothes and boots?" asked Cello changing the subject.

"Corporal will need to agree that, I can't."

"Can you ask him?" Cello took the food. He needed strength. His anger was not enough.

CHAPTER TWENTY-TWO

The Colonel's orderly room

Men under punishment who were not employed in working party tasks, were put to their punishment without delay. If that involved detention they would be sent back to a suitable place for that to be done, at higher formation level, division or Corps level where facilities could be made available. After a term in detention they would be returned to the front.

Perhaps they would be sent home to England. But that was a reward. Everybody wanted to get home, to a peaceful existence. If that required a term in prison first so be it, they would be free eventually and they would be safe. So as far as possible few were held in detention. The alternative was to face the firing squad. But that was for exceptional offences. Crimes which could be deemed treacherous to the cause.

Cello's guards changed every day. He didn't see the same men twice. But the question that was to be faced was; what was to happen to Cello when the Battalion moved on, moved back; to the front? He could only go back to his section while due process took its course. If he deserted again of course it would go against him when he returned. All did eventually return.

So the decision would come to the RSM to make because he was the senior one to whom the duties of the guardroom fell. When a battalion returned to the front there was no need of it. All the men were effectively guards, all the company positions had their own sentries at the entrance to the Company Commander's, Platoon Commander's or Section Commander's trench. There was no rest and relaxation, no school dining room to congregate and smoke and laugh.

Every day the question; could he have boots and uniform, was left unanswered or just ignored. Eventually a decision had to be made. "What shall we do with him, you know… the prisoner… Sir?" asked the duty sergeant as the battalion was preparing to return to a reserve position at the front? "Do you want me to get him kitted out and returned to his section?"

The RSM had been unable to arrange for Cello to attend the Commanding Officer's orderly room as the Colonel had been away at Brigade conferences most of the three days they had spent at the school. So due process had been interrupted and he didn't know when it would continue. It would only be a matter of a couple of days. But in that time… *"No the man is not to be given a rifle. He will be kept with the QMs party. Hand him over the HQ Sar-Major. Let them give him uniform, no weapon though. Is that understood?"*

"Yes sir, very well."

Cello had his blanket, but nothing else for his bare cell. He had been accompanied to the outside lavatory and his food had been brought to him. He had not bathed. He was still barefooted and his underwear had some undignified stains about it. Holding his rolled blanket, he was marched to the wagon lines where the logistic elements of the battalion were forming. Every company and sub-unit had its horse drawn wagon and there were some old lorries for the ammunition and other supplies. They looked pitifully wanting maintenance even after the three-day period of rest. Men busied around them pulling tarpaulins down, feeding and watering horses, looking suspiciously into the engines of some of the tenders and cranking others into life; to start their whining and rattling. There was a tiredness about the engines as if they were on the point of breaking down permanently, as there was with the uniforms of men, the colour of mud, the black unkempt horses. Straps were frayed and tied where buckles had long given up. Webbing packs and boxes and crates were the commodities of the logistic area hefted by exhausted men, helmets tilted to the back of heads, rifles slung over backs; unheeded.

They were drawn up in a small farm square behind the street where the houses had ended with the guardroom. Cello stood as the rain started, on the periphery of the activity as the Orderly Sergeant, performing his final duty before returning to his platoon to prepare them to move, went in search of the HQ Company Sergeant-Major. They emerged together from a low hovel to conduct a consideration of the prisoner.

Cello stood there a bit like Jesus might have stood against his accusers. The simple blanket now wrapped around him like a Kaftan as a partial protection from the rain. On seeing him the Sergeant-Major paused in his stride, sort of tripped and coughed. Other soldiers had paused to stare. They all stood, semi-circular around him, but at a distance. Cello was discomfortingly alien. He knew that gave him strength, of a sort.

The Sergeant-Major didn't like the unsettling nature of it. It offended him greatly. "Get inside, get inside, *SMUGGER*," he shouted to an unseen man, "get some uniform for this man *now.*"

Suddenly a man rounded the corner of the farmyard. He was a Military Policeman. "Hey, hey, RSM says the prisoner is needed for the CO's orderly room now."

Everybody froze. "Well he still needs uniform. He's not going to appear like that is he?" The Sergeant-Major swivelled on the man, and talked into his face.

Cello had followed the man detailed to get him uniform into the hovel.

"Like what?" asked the MP.

"Dressed like that."

"The dress doesn't matter. The Colonel wants to see him, he's back now and he wants to see him."

He can't appear in front of the Colonel dressed *in a blanket. Its undignified*," retorted the Sergeant-Major.

"Undignified?" echoed the MP. "What do you mean?"

The Sergeant-Major paused and opened his mouth but nothing emerged. He couldn't put into words what he meant. "He must be in uniform," he merely replied.

They waited and soon Cello did emerge from the shed. When he had the blanket he was tall and straight and not short of pride for all that. Now he was uncertain again. It was just a loose uniform and boots. He wore no puttees. They could be used for some nefarious purpose. The RSM had specifically forbidden them.

"Right, now Private Harris RSM's orders. You are going for COs orderly room. It will be at the CO's office before the battalion sets off. So fall in. Sar-Major could you detail one more escort please?"

When being marched, a prisoner had two escorts and they would straddle the man front and rear very close so he was trapped between them. An escort was provided and the three having shuffled together, set off. The MP in the front giving the orders and leading. "Prisoner and escort by the left, *QUICK MARCH, LEFT... LEFT... LEFT RIGHT LEFT!"* They disappeared around the side of the farm buildings.

The Sergeant-Major shepherded his men back to work.

But it was not destined to be.

The Colonel on returning had been ambushed by the RSM into a rushed type of kangaroo court. He hadn't appreciated what was being set up for him. He turned around from putting his equipment down behind his temporary desk set up in the house next to the guardroom and was confronted with the RSM, Cello in the middle and the MP soldier. There was shouting outside as sub-units formed up combined with the noise of vehicles and under this cover they had sort of snuck into his office.

"What's this... RSM?"

"As I told you sir, the deserter, Private Harris. Thought you would need to get this done before we strike camp sir."

The Colonel slowed down. His actions seemed a little confused as if he had forgotten something at the location from which he had come. "Umm, well I... I can't do an orderly room here and now, I haven't the right... Do you have witnesses?"

The RSM coughed. "The case is clear cut. I know what happened and I will tell you sir."

The RSM was in command of the 'due process'. He stood at attention and looked out above the Colonel's head, way above his head as he was seated.

But the pauses in the room and the sweating expectation suddenly seemed to crack the atmosphere like the only window in the front of the building finally giving up. The Colonel was the only man to move and he shifted in his chair awkwardly. "Well RSM you know I must examine the evidence myself. And... where is the Adjutant?"

The Adjutant was the filter for all disciplinary matters. They went through his hands before reaching the Colonel and he prepared the orderly rooms, reviewed the cases and ensured the witnesses were available and present.

This adjutant was indisposed. He could not face the return to the trenches. His hands had shaken uncontrollably the night before after a bottle or more of whisky. He was curled under his blanket, curled like a foetus. No one dared to try to uncurl him. There would be tears and madness.

Better for the battalion to leave without its adjutant and let him catch up with excuses of illness.

"I... I believe he is sick sir," said the RSM

"Sick oh... well, then we have to wait. I can't see this man until the evidence is gathered and properly presented."

He did not look at Cello for one instant.

"Very well SIR." The RSM returned to his parade ground self, with everything corrected.

CHAPTER TWENTY-THREE

The evidence

The Battalion marched ten miles that day. They marched through Arras like ghosts. Although the town was the ghost. There were no people there, only soldiers passing and stopping in awe and moving on. There was nothing here for them, not the buildings or the supposed tunnels under them. Structures tilted and yawned emptily open, torn and hanging, as if apologising for still trying to stand, without their insides and legs blasted to nothing so that they were bowing over the devastation. Nothing survived the heavy bombardment intact. Apparently civilians darted in and out of the ruins trying to stagger on in a sort of life.

"What have we done?" asked Jack, surveying the carnage. But he had a sort of sneer on his face.

"Nothing," replied the Corporal who was a shadow of his former self having lost his pipe. He had lost hope as well and spent time sitting in any available shelter. The rest and time out of the trenches had diminished rather than recuperated him.

"You call this nothing?" said Ben suddenly in a flare of anger.

"Yea but we did nothing in this battle," pointed out the Corporal.

"The price of victory," said jack. He spat bitterly in the

dust, a desert of rubble dust at the side of the road leading into the town centre.

"There was an attack of sorts, but the victory is not complete," said a voice from the line of soldiers.

They sat in a line looking, not at each other, but towards the town, towards buildings, houses, streets. A huge slab of one stood up like a rock out of the desert. Piles of rubble and dust lay at its foot. Other buildings teetered on the edge of the square. What square had it been? What was its fame and worth now?

It shook men, seeing this.

"Why was this done?" asked Ben.

"Just like I said, it's the price of victory." Jack was angry.

"What's the victory when everything is gone though," questioned Ben?

"We fight for land, territory. Whatever is built on it – doesn't seem to matter," said the Corporal with a shrug in his voice though his shoulders had given up.

"It does matter though doesn't it," Ben wanted to know? "What are we fighting for, to preserve this land for its people? To defend the land?"

"It's gone mate hasn't it?"

"So what the fuck... is the point?"

The question fell swiftly to the ground. It had an exasperation about it. It voiced something that men couldn't face. They didn't look at it, didn't have to look at it.

Jack picked up a rock, which may or may not have been part of a building and threw it out from where they were sitting resting on the side of the road. Their boots had picked up the sand-like colour of the rubble, in contrast to the mud of the fields and trench land.

It seemed that only the army now inhabited this broken town. Trucks trundled by, horses and carts loaded with goods and supplies and ammunition presumably. Men who had been part of a so-called victory marched back. There seemed little jubilation in them. "How was it?" asked Ben as they passed.

"Bloody awful," was the sole reply.

This was only the beginning. They were set to go for miles, advancing. That was what they were told.

They marched on, skirting the heaps of rubble and the empty buildings and the centre of the city that seemed to echo a former bustling nature, but gave no justification in its ghostliness for the punishment it had received; or the impending 'victory' that was about to be visited upon it.

"Victory is ours is it," asked the Corporal?

"Not yet, not yet. Big push still to come," responded Jack who had taken over as the mouthpiece of reportage on the progress of this bogged down assault still in its early April stages.

There was no optimism in their trudging steps, kicking dust as they went. The dried boots would no doubt soon get wet again. They would soon be in the land of mud again.

It was getting towards evening as they stepped into the fields again away from the town. The land was no different; flatish, less damaged than the city. But it wouldn't stay like that for long, they considered. They moved further away from what had been a sort of civilisation across what had been a battlefield.

The Battalion was met by guides and taken off to their trenches which seemed strangely similar to the ones they had occupied a few days before when the whole Cello incident had been triggered. But they were in reserve. Other battalions had moved ahead and driven the Germans back but they had then withdrawn, leaving the reserve in a kind of front line. The gains that had put them there might soon be reversed though, as was customary.

There was a rumour of an attack to come which would

involve them, the next day. But being bored by the whole Arras affair now and with their minds questioning the legitimacy of the destruction of the city they had passed through; they fell into a relaxed trench routine with minimal sentries.

Behind them on the main road, trucks and supplies and horses moaned wearily up and down.

It grew colder in the night and they missed the real beds of the school. When you allowed humanity to creep back it was harder to take back the mantle of the animal. But sleeping could be done to hopefully forget everything; though that hardly ever happened.

They awoke to snow. Someone tried to gather a fist full and throw it at Jack. But it was mostly mud. Snow in its pristine form had a cleanliness which could never survive in the trenches. But clothing and equipment had a stiffness about it which somehow tricked the water out of it, or tricked the wearer into thinking it was dry. But when the temperature rose above freezing everything became wet again. It had frozen during the night and the snow had come lightly on the cold air. Now if you shook the snow off your equipment carefully, you could live with the illusion that your equipment was clean. Above the bunkers and sand-bags the light covering could be left like an extra coat; another illusion.

Soldiers, like children, seek a moment of lightness in which they can have fun, hence the snowballs.

But stand too brought an end to the hilarity. A message delivered by the platoon sergeant brought back the story of the Cello patrol. It had been forgotten, though few things are forgotten by the soldier, merely put somewhere in the mind that won't bring pain. "You gonna get a call to the CO's orderly room, Corporal, have you heard?"

"About that stupid Cello person…?" replied the Corporal with a little nervous push back of his helmet.

"Yes, about the same person, that patrol you did… bit of a cock-up wasn't it?" gloated the Sergeant.

But the Corporal objected somewhat. "No, Sarge it… wasn't really…"

"But you didn't bring all your men back did you?" The Sergeant leaned forward towards the Corporal's back. The men were still on Stand Too, at the trench wall, ready for anything, not all looking over the top but ready. They weren't proper trenches as this was a reserve position, but sand-bags were built up and the flatish ground was scraped into some defences where men could sit or crouch. But the inspection party, perhaps with some sort of bravado stood up and wandered around behind the men, as if they were immune to some stray shells being lobbed over.

The Corporal half turned. "But he chose to throw away 'is weapon, 'e chose to desert," he pointed out, lapsing into some slurred words, not the customary careful ones of his previous pipe-smoking reflective demeanour. "And I reported 'im didn't I?"

"Oh you reported him alright. And I reported him up the chain of command as well." He puffed out his chest at his part of the reporting. The RSM encouraged the reporting of things like that.

But the Corporal seemed suddenly to draw back from the blame. "Well it was my job to report him. I 'ad to… You would have found out… in the end."

"I would have found out very soon enough wouldn't I then?"

"Oh yes you would, you would, " agreed the subordinate.

Having come to a type of agreement that neither of them was to blame and that 'reporting' everything was their duty rather than snitching and that the Corporal had redeemed himself by making a full report, the Sergeant imposed the next part of his humiliation of the Corporal. "Well you gonna be needed for the CO's orderly room like I said, and don't think I will do it for you, cos you was in charge of that patrol, so you have to provide the evidence. You *are* the evidence."

"Just give us the nod Sarge, I'll be ready."

"The nod, what 'nod'? I'll give you a fucking kick if you want, to make sure you're up to the mark. I don't want the RSM looking at us like we not up to it."

There seemed no need for this outburst. It was as if the RSM's spirit was possessing the Sergeant and speaking through him. Any bond, any respect between fellows of lower rank was gone. It was a step between Corporal and Sergeant, one stripe, but the stripe was like a wall between territories of dislike where hatred could be expressed. Hatred had replaced respect.

Something broke in the Corporal then, some resistance that had made him and kept him as he was, had gone, with the pipe; broken, trodden into the mud. So he would do anything, go anywhere. His compass was not pointing anywhere, it just went round and round. It reacted to a shout and a shot. Behind a rifle it was steady. Anywhere else it was wildly whirring and knowing nothing.

CHAPTER TWENTY-FOUR

Logistic links

Cello had not lost his compass. Or he had found a deeper one. The depth was in the meaning of his music. The love had been there, but now he knew its purpose. He longed for it.

Those in the logistic detachment did not talk to him about his criminality or treachery. What was a deserter who had returned on his own? Was he still a deserter?

Soldiers in the rear area always thought themselves entitled to a bit of comfort. You had to take your luck when it was dished out, otherwise who was to know if it would come again. So they always found a barn or a cellar that was firstly dry and secondly could be made a bit comfortable. A fire brought comfort but usually was forbidden, too close to the front line. But there were the occasions when it was possible. Toilets were sometimes in the open, if they were far enough to the rear. Men sat together on a log over a trench full of disinfectant.

There were close to two hundred men of the headquarters and logistic elements of the battalion. Units of heavy machineguns, pioneers and mortars moved around the logistic area, although usually forward supporting the rifle companies, individually or in groups, known as strong points. Held back were the administration, transport, medical and logistic elements including stores people who brought forward the ammunition and food as well as those who dealt with records of the men and ensured that they were paid and their records of death, injury or illness kept.

Men coming forward to the front were the engines of information and communications, starting and spreading rumours of import to all the men about the future and the present. Often these were salted with details that enhanced the views already at the heart of the Battalion. Personalities such as the Colonel, the Adjutant or the RSM featured extensively in these communications.

There were many opportunities for these interfaces, bringing food and supplies up to the front were the main ones. Company Quartermasters came back to the logistic area. Transport went forward to deposit and collect. Some men did not wish to go forward. Others did. Risk taking, guilty shirking, blaming and accusations abounded.

Cello worked at separating ammunition into piles in response to requests from companies; individual uniform requirements and finding spare bits for weapons as armourer needs were many. He wanted to go forward. He wanted to find his section, for some reason he felt drawn to them.

But he was watched and guarded and he couldn't defend himself with a weapon. What if they were attacked behind the lines or when moving forward. It could happen. So he couldn't go.

"I met a Hun patrol. At that time I was without my rifle," he argued with one of the Quartermaster's SNCOs.

He looked at Cello, from under his cap. He didn't wear a helmet as he was mostly working among piles of stock, tunic off, vest sleeves rolled up. "You can't go up without a weapon."

"Where's your rifle Colour?" The man was a Colour Sergeant, the same rank as the Company Quartermaster

Sergeants. Cello felt empowered to be cheeky. He could see that the organisation around the NCO was breaking down. He was constantly overwhelmed by mountains of boxes of equipment. Yet if a Company asked for some needed thing which prevented them from carrying out their duties, often it could not be located. Paperwork, stock-sheets, receipts and demands were mixed and muddled together. Often forms and control sheets were not completed.

Logistics did not happen automatically. Requests from the companies had to be made for everything. Stock was carried at battalion level but only for a day or so. In turn it had to be resupplied by higher formation, Brigade and Division and above.

Certain activities happened at higher formations where staff officers were in abundance and they made sure their living was more comfortable and the stocks more plentiful. They did not move as the battalions did, in and out of the trenches. They occupied large houses and buildings and civilians often ventured back into these areas where food and even money might be made.

For women there was often regular employment in the brothels and further back, music and dance halls had even opened up where cities were not so destroyed.

"How can I carry my rifle when my hands are full of... all this?" The Colour Sergeant threw his arms around the chaos.

Outside the barn the sound of horses and men cursing their obstinance added to the situation.

Cello was not a horseman. But he had to work with them as they all did.

The Colour Sergeant looked up and his arms hung down, muddied from sacks of potatoes, not the dried mud of the trenches. "You set for Court Martial then?" He looked directly at Cello.

"I don't know," said cello.

"You gonna need a friend you know?"

"A friend?"

"Yes an accused's friend, or a defending officer."

"Defending officer?" Cello had not thought this far.

The Colour Sergeant peered at him intently, as the world teetered around him. "You do want to be defended, don't you?"

"Well I think a friend would be a good idea." He knew the friend he wanted.

"So you need to get one." He turned to the next pile. "Get those uniforms out into the Alpha stack."

"That's where I want to get too, Alpha."

"Well you had better take control of the stuff and make sure it all gets to them then hadn't you?"

Cello saw this as permission, but he knew a fight would be on with some regular storeman who usually looked after Alpha's needs. He had probably met him already. Most were suspicious and taciturn, while others tried to talk, but perhaps it was to mock.

He didn't care about mockery. He clung to tiny victories, like the sympathy shown by the Colour Sergeant, which he could then use. "The Colour Sergeant said I should stay with Alpha's stuff."

Transport was the key to every movement behind the lines. It seemed only that the poor bloody rifle companies marched. But in the marching was at least a coming together, a closeness where more than the man next to you could be your best friend as was the case when you attacked and inevitably got separated into pairs, if you did not become a corpse. Or those closest to you could be enemies. Cello had spoken to some men, but there was a suspicion in the bodies of those who grunted around the horses and boxes and piles of hessian and sand-bags and crates and the smell of hessian and cordite and horse manure and sweat. Looks were not given generously, eyes were down and whispers were kept for alliances between two men who shared the halter of a horse or box of ammo.

Not many shared a box of ammo with Cello so he laboured on in isolation. But non-enemies could be cultivated, of these the Colour Sergeant was the most important.

The Company Quartermaster Sergeants came back at different times. Their stuff had to be ready to go. Cello guarded Alpha Company equipment well, while he was guarded on and off by the Colour Sergeant. They were in a large barn, a beautiful vaulted one with a massive wood-beamed roof which was mercifully totally intact. The walls, great rough blocks, seemed at odds with the intricacy of the roof which defied any bomb to splinter it. The beams looked unbreakable and the grooving and slotting of the lighter supports too clever, the final cane-like wands on which the tiles were arranged, too lucky to be destroyed. Some men referred to it as a 'tithe barn', which dated back to medieval times. Instead of farm tithes to the church, the barn was now used for the individual company 'piles' of equipment.

Alpha Company Quartermaster Sergeant came in the evening. He was directed in through the dust and grit and stacks to where Cello sat on his charge. "Can I come with you Colour?" he asked.

"I don't think so," replied the man, fresh from the front with mud and a loaded rifle. But he was very tired and could do with the extra hands. He had heard about Cello but didn't realise that he was supposed to be under 'house arrest.' He was another pair of hands. "Well alright then, get this stuff loaded." He had to collect pre-cooked food and rum as well.

Cello used the horse to shield himself from others and soon they were ready. Feeling guilty Cello caught the eye of his Colour Sergeant, opened his hands and mouthed that he would be back tomorrow. The Colour Sergeant threw his head up and gave a brief nod. He knew that Cello would be under somebody's eye and he did not fear the RSM. He had a job to do, a never-ending job, without rest.

They trudged up to the front with Cello separating, walking alongside the horse, who seemed calm and without fear. This was part of the reserve area and other horses were around and the barrage was not heavy so there was nothing to make the horses really afraid.

Towards the battalion things thinned out. Logistic elements faded away somewhere. Occasional shells drummed and boomed in the distance; perhaps not so distant.

Cello knew he wouldn't need his rifle. Even if the artillery came close, a rifle round would not stop the shells falling. He had been in the middle of a bombardment at the German hospital and had no rifle then. Having his hands free helped treat the casualty. A rifle was a restriction which may have forced him to defend himself when at first confronted with the German patrol. That would have almost certainly led to his death. Now he was alive… and also free. Well, free to be stripped naked by the RSM on parade, then detained in just his underwear in a sort of prison.

But the freedom was a sort of mental thing. Standing with only a blanket around him before the Quartermaster's NCO, standing without shame against the looks of the logistic men, had given Cello a sort of pride. In a way he was commanding the NCO to find him a uniform and if he hadn't, then the blanket would had sufficed, impractical, but sufficient.

They got close to Alpha Company and stopped in a sort of crater. Night was due but somehow the evening's progress lingered. Platoon sergeants had been warned, they wanted food and ammunition and other things that had been ordered. The horse was quiet and the only sounds were the breaking open wooden boxes of ammo, to be dished out and the food containers.

Rendezvous were essential for communications and logistic delivery, but difficult to make in a land devastated and unrecognisable. A jerrycan placed on a junction of beaten foot tracks, a tiny plank bridge, sometimes floating, over a horrible pool of gunge, were the landmarks. In this reserve area, metal roads were closer and Cello had heard that some men considered crawling onto one of these and high-jacking at the point of the .303 a truck along the road into Cambrai, which apparently was not damaged like Arras and might even have young women still living there. But which way was it?

Guides had brought the men together. Some men knew their ground, by instinct. They might have been storemen, or officers' batmen; the soldier helpers to officers who cooked for them and helped pack and even carry their kit. Messengers, sometimes included both of these categories, or men in platoons who were willing not to stay cowering in bunkers.

The real communicators, sending electronic messages by wire were there, not always seen, but their wire was seen, though much of it was underground. At track junctions, wires popped up and were linked to junction boxes on stakes. Nobody touched these, but they used them for RVs.

CHAPTER TWENTY-FIVE

Nominating a friend

A meeting which is wanted and needed can also bring a levelling of conflict, a looking beyond the unstated and even unrecognised lump that separates and prevents men from sharing something that is in their hearts; from even revealing that they have a heart. This is because the meeting usually brings a benefit; food and drink being the favourite.

So Cello was allowed to go to his Platoon, the one he had previously been a member of.

He made his way as a kind of bringer of something to those in need, supper and rum.

They brought the metal containers and rum flagons that were like biblical jars, brown and corked. They were probably the ones whose contents Jesus had changed from water to wine, or rum in this case. They lugged them in carrying nets across craters while night fell. Cello's hands were needed, to carry things. Lights and sounds of heavy hard things knocking together did not seem to matter. They were the reserve battalion, one of them. In front of them was still No Man's Land, a nothingness which Cello knew about, though this No Man's Land was a different to the one he had inhabited; the one where he had buried John Thomas Wall. But that was not really No Man's Land as it was within the German trenches.

"So, the cello player is it, the bringer of food and drink now, is it?" The sergeant shone a flashlight into Cello's face.

"Yes Sarge," replied Cello. He had no fear. He felt nothing. He knew the worst sneers would come not only from this man. "Let me take the food to my section sarge?"

"Your section, *your section* is it?"

"It was yes."

The sergeant looked into Cello's face, at very close range. Cello's thoughts went back to the RSM's face on the parade ground when he had ordered him to strip to his underwear and stand on the edge. He hadn't recoiled. He hadn't backed away. He didn't do so now. He sort of absorbed everything. But how many knives of hate could he take?

Where did it come from, that hate? He was not a hateful person.

He knew one person wouldn't hate him. He thought he knew.

So he dragged the food, the corned beef stew now cold from its tin container being dragged across the mud and the flagon of rum, to the entrance to the trench in which his section whiled away the time, trying not to wait for the rum. But jack grabbed it. Behind him Cello saw Ben. "Can I ask you…?" he started. "Ben…?"

"Ask me…?"

"Yes."

Jack just glanced at them as he disappeared into the bunker.

They stood in half light, statues of the moment, statues that could carry the war away with them, like generals without rank, without weapons as Ben had momentarily put his rifle somewhere, perhaps the bunker. Cello without weapon did have a helmet which the Colour Sergeant had found for him.

The helmets tilted together. "I want you to be my friend… at my Court Martial…"

"Friend!" Ben glanced sideways from under his helmet. He complexion was dark. He had a Woodbine between his lips which opened allowing the fag to wag up and down around the word to show a hint of teeth which were surprisingly good. Many men's teeth were broken and black. Dental care of the army was not a high priority and many men joined with teeth already beyond repair.

"Yes." Cello glanced away to try to find words to explain better without passing his oppression onto Ben. "I won't be defended but I can have a friend and I want you to be my friend."

The words didn't stand up as earth-shattering. They fell down into the trench. No words could take them away from the trenches they were in.

"I will," said Ben without hesitation and without knowing what it meant. "What have I got to do?"

"I don't know yet. But they have to give me this, it's part of the 'due process'. I must have someone on my side."

"I won't be much good to you will I?"

Ben was just a common soldier. He had not met Sergeant John Thomas Wall. He did not realise the comradeship that the Sergeant had given Cello, even in his death.

"Yes you will," replied Cello.

CHAPTER TWENTY-SIX
A table

They were interrupted and Cello was taken away for duties elsewhere, another platoon needed feeding. But on returning to the logistic area some news was imparted to him by the Colour Sergeant. "You are to go before the Commanding Officer tomorrow. The CO gonna come down here to do it."

Cello knew that he didn't need Ben yet. The Corporal would need to come back to give his evidence, then he would be remanded and go back, under escort, for a Court Martial, somewhere further back than he had been. In a way he relished this. Perhaps there would be some sense amongst people who inhabited that area. Though none of the men in the front line would have given that thought credit. The disdain shown for those generals and their staff knew no bounds.

Empty sand-bags formed a better bed than ever you could get in the trenches. Life in the logistic areas always attracted envy. Buildings provided cover, although earth was a better protector in a bombardment. But no one would prefer a trench if they were offered a building, even though a bomb through the roof could do more damage.

So they settled down for the night, with sentry duty within the building. The smell of hessian filled their throats. It was like dry mown grass in the summer which had lain in the sun, Cello thought; a comforting and homely smell. He had been drawn into Sergeant John Thomas Wall's farm world. The barn they were in was part of a farm, many farms. But the tithes had long since been taken away and replaced by these war offerings. The animals which would have loved the comfort of the barn had been slaughtered in bombardments, been driven or run scared and screaming.

People came and went within the barn, searching some stores item which would need to be burrowed for. The Colour Sergeant got up, responded, went back to bed, got up again, returned to his sand-bag bed again. Horses whinnied outside, vehicles whined.

As so often, deep sleep came only in the dead hours just before dawn so that when the light came, men roused themselves exhausted from interrupted sleep rather than refreshed from a long one.

Dawn had only a few choices for its face; rain, dull cloud or occasionally sun. But the activity had many faces; Stand Too was no longer done as they were in a logistic area. Activity just gave up on sleep and exploded with a shout. On this morning the arrival of the RSM brought a shout. *"HAAARP."*

This was different from the greeting to the battalion on parade. But the RSM's eyes were focused on Cello, who was already standing up. The eyes were small, screwed smaller by fat cheeks, unadorned by whiskers, shaved and polished almost to a shiny surface, unlike any of the other men. Slowly he took his eyes away from Cello, who seemed to meet his gaze with a raised head.

He was looking for something which wasn't in the barn. His eyes darted about then fell on the Colour Sergeant, *"Table, table Colour…"*

"Sir?" queried the NCO, who didn't have his braces up. His uniform tunic, hat and equipment lay somewhere. His rifle was not in evidence. The absence of these seemed to take away his confidence.

This time the RSM used his hands, laying them in front of him and jutting his head forward. *"Table, we need one…"* Then he addressed Cello. "Get this… *Man*… out of here while preparations are made. *Get some MPs here… I want him detained until called, as per normal… Colour."*

A table! Had the Colour Sergeant had one he would have used it for his accounts and books which he had somehow to keep up, though whether anyone audited them and held him responsible was another matter. The Quartermaster nodded in on his account keeping now and again. But he also doubled as the Headquarters Company Commander and was constantly pulling together so many different groups, and the administration of the whole battalion. Letter-writing to the bereaved, the effects of the deceased and the burials of them, were often the things that occupied him. He was not due to attend this event. Had there been a table he would have probably laid hands on it for these managerial tasks.

So the table took over the war and had to be found while the RSM stood and twitched and turned around as if he was still on the parade ground. He wore a pistol, like an officer and a sort of Sam Browne belt. From somewhere, the Military Police who always seemed to hover around the RSM, ushered Cello away to the back of the building out of sight of the space which the table, when one was found, would occupy.

It would have been better had the Colour Sergeant been fully dressed. He could do his logistic job in his braces or even without them. But now he was the RSM's ball boy. He did not have the confidence for that.

The farm square was a place for animals and animal food, not office work. However eventually a kind of work-bench was carried in for approval. It was too low and the RSM sniffed as it was set out. However he opened his small back-pack and took out a big red book; *The Manual of Military Law*; to place on it.

Time jumped! There came a croaky hoot from outside. The Commanding Officer had found a staff car somewhere and commandeered it to bring him to the logistic area. He did not bring the adjutant with him.

Adjutants, always of captain rank, were a sort of lynch-pin of a battalion, or should be; more than a ball boy to the commanding officer. Care was taken over their selection. An officer was needed who maintained the heart of the battalion, whatever that should be. Some saw it as iron discipline.

This adjutant was not able to hold himself in any discipline, let alone an iron one. He shook a lot and had to make a supreme effort to control that, especially when he didn't have access to a whisky bottle. Prior selection of the adjutant appointment was not able to foresee the breakdown.

As to the iron discipline, the RSM was of course in control of that department, in the Adjutant's absence. So there was a coming together of dirty heels and a quivering puffing out of chests as the Commanding Officer entered the barn. The Colour Sergeant had even hurriedly thumbed his braces up. The RSM screeched out one of his expletives having had the hooted warning.

The Colonel sauntered in, touching his helmet with a leather cane acknowledging the attention of the men, though the Colour Sergeant quickly scrambled out of the way to stand near the door ensuring no disturbance. In a sudden moment of panic he wanted to check that the Corporal, who had been summoned from his trench, was actually there.

He was; standing alongside some of the men outside, near the staff car, which had become a bit of a thing of interest.

His mouth, without pipe was slightly downturned in nervous anticipation. He had his helmet on and rifle, chest slung. Equipment had been placed down beside him. Detail like whether to keep his rifle when standing before the colonel was not known or briefed down. But as Cello had been charged with throwing his rifle away the Corporal, almost without thinking, knew to have his round his body.

"Ah Corporal... you are here. What's your name?" enquired the Colour Sergeant.

"It's..." He stuttered a bit in getting it out.

"Right are you set for this? You've done a CO's before haven't you... Know what you have to do?"

"No I haven't but... Yes I believe I know what to do." His mouth was on the point of quivering.

"Very well chap, just be ready here and the RSM or me will call you in. Just give us some few minutes and we'll be set."

The Colour Sergeant disappeared inside and found things shaping up. The Colonel was standing behind his 'desk' and the RSM was leaning over from the front to have a few words. A sheet of paper, the charge sheet on the relevant Army form was in front of the Colonel. The RSM turned around, his face red; "Got the witness eh colour?"

"Yes sir all ready."

"Good... well I think we're ready to go sir, if you're..."

"Yes let's get this over with," moved the Colonel, bracing up for his task.

The RSM was back on his parade ground. "MARCH IN THE PRISONER!"

From the depth of the back of the barn came a command; "PRIVATE HARRIS QUICK MARCH LEFT RIGHT, LEFT RIGHT, RIGHT WHEEL; LEFT, RIGHT; *HALT.*"

The RSM cleared his throat. *"Sir, private Marcus Harris here is charged with throwing away his rifle in the face of enemy and desertion, SIR."*

The Colonel cleared his throat. "Are you…?" He confirmed the number and name of the accused reading from the charge sheet.

Cello nodded, then spoke. He was that man.

The Colonel read the charges, the very serious charges. Did Cello understand?

He did.

And how did he plead?

"I plead guilty to the charge of casting away my rifle and not guilty to desertion."

The RSM stiffened. He didn't know what the pleas would be. Perhaps he hadn't considered that Cello might have feelings and thoughts or had made plans for what he would say, including the possibility of a 'not-guilty' plea.

"Right-oh!" The Colonel stammered a little. "Shall we take the charges one at a time?"

The RSM leant forward. "The evidence is the same for each sir. So…"

The Colonel tripped over himself a little, perhaps realising the seriousness of the charges. "Yes well… as you have pleaded guilty to the first charge we do not need to hear the full evidence… But you might want to say something in your… On your own behalf. Or… we could hear the evidence as to the second matter…" He seemed unsure.

Cello seemed untroubled by the fact that he had been given a choice, although the RSM at his side snorted a disapproval. "I wish to hear the evidence on the second charge and I will reserve any statement until the end," Cello said calmly.

The only shuffling came from others, not him. He looked above the Colonel's head; being quite tall he was able to do that with ease.

"Let's hear the evidence then," blurted the Colonel somewhat hurriedly.

Shouts from the RSM summoned a stumping Corporal, a quick marching Corporal with an exaggerated parade-ground stamping halt and a rigid longest way up, shortest way down salute which slapped dust from his trousers. He gushed into a prepared speech about who he was and about to launch into his story…

But the Colonel held up his hand. "Corporal let me read the charges first."

The Corporal stopped, mouth open.

After the reading he continued, recounting the patrol quickly and the order given to Cello, his throwing away his rifle and his refusal to return to his own lines.

It was brief and the RSM gave a kind of approving grunt under his breath when it was complete.

The Colonel seemed at a loss for a moment then did, timidly it seemed; pose a question. "The purpose of the patrol Corporal?"

"Clearance patrol sir… No Man's Land."

"I see…" He looked around then seemed to focus on an idea. Before him stood the RSM, a Corporal witness, the accused a private and in the background a Colour Sergeant who now had his full uniform on. "Do we have the Platoon Commander at all RSM?" The Colonel was short of officer support. He was aware of the predicament of his adjutant, but he needed… something perhaps more.

"Gone on leave sir… yesterday."

The Colonel sensed some possible looming officer breakdown. He knew that the previous RSM, the Old Man, held the officers together as well, like some kind of fulcrum, balancing everything. In his absence there was a need for discipline to be maintained. "I see… well… Private Harris you have heard the evidence I believe you have something to say, bear in mind that you have already pleaded guilty to the charge of casting away your rifle…"

Cello needed no second bidding. "It was not a clearance patrol sir. We went to find a casualty who we had heard crying in No Man's Land... We found one... But he was already dead... But at that moment we heard the cries of the original casualty and I said we should continue to try to find him. The Corporal said no... So I cast away my rifle and refused to go on with the patrol... I mean go back with the patrol. "

"You cast away your rifle and refused to go back with the patrol? "

"Yes sir. "

"You know there is a possible third charge here of disobeying a lawful command."

Cello said nothing at first. But then he did look at the Colonel, straight at him. "But I have something to say about what happened after..."

But the Colonel held up his hand. "We know about how Private Harris returned don't we, a couple of days later?"

The RSM was back to his normal self. "Yes sir, all recorded, witness statement taken... As one has been taken from the Corporal... here."

"Good, good." He seemed more relaxed. "Well private Harris I think you will have to keep any further deputation for a superior authority." He raised his voice. *"REMANDED FOR COURT MARTIAL."*

CHAPTER TWENTY-SEVEN
The arrival of a box

The army form was written up and signed by the Colonel. The pleas recorded. The statements would be included. This was the smoking fall out of the orderly room event. On the army forms it all seemed clear and proper. Sighs of relief could be made, though they weren't recorded. No bombardment provided the church bells to announce the happy event. It was happy for the RSM.

"You're needed at HQ." The Platoon Sergeant summoned Ben in another part of the battalion area.

"HQ?" Ben was bemused.

"Yes Battalion, get your shit together. It's your *friend.*"

"Arhhh." Ben acknowledged the secrecy of the friendship, something despised by the Sergeant.

"Report to the orderly room so they can record you. Don't need a guide do you?"

"Well I…"

"You're not getting one. Take your stuff and get going."

Anyone going back for legitimate reasons, without injury, brought jealousy, translated into animosity. 'Cushy sod' was the politest of the possible send offs always accompanied by an invitation to 'fuck off'.

Ben was an experienced soldier. He did find the orderly room without guidance. It was in a part-broken hovel, part-tented complex at the road-side where a small motor tender was waiting. "Luxury for you and your prisoner friend today, you gonna get a ride. Only because he's a prisoner, wont get it when you come back." The Orderly Sergeant grinned. Then he ticked Ben off his list or recorded him as 'away on duty'.

Then his demeanour changed. "Oh and while you waiting for your… *friend,* to get escorted out, you might as well take charge of this." He extracted a large box from under his makeshift counter. His face was somewhat furtive. "It came for him but I didn't want to take it to 'im, you know with the RSM…" He made an attempt at a wink. "But actually, let me give you this first, the return label came adrift."

He passed over a slip of reinforced paper on which was written:

SENDER; MRS ROBERT HARRIS,
HARTWELL
COLEY AVENUE
READING, BERKS

"Best put it away, y'know a bit sharpish."

Ben stared and without asking further, stuffed the paper into his uniform pocket. "What is it?" He managed to ask. But the Orderly Sergeant put a finger against his lips. He bundled the box back under the counter. "Wait! let me see whether he is ready yet, sharnt be a mo'." He had the demeanour of a bustling shopkeeper anxious to make a delivery somehow without the prospective owner knowing about it, perhaps a surprise present. He bustled out of his hovel.

Ben waited. He heard the prisoner and escort parade, almost at the double; *"'EFT 'IGHT, 'EFT 'IGHT, 'EFT, 'IGHT; HAAAAALT. PRISONER EMBUS."* There was a scrambling sound as boots unfamiliar with the metal of the lorry bed, trampled up onto it.

The Orderly Sergeant literally flew back into his domain.

He grabbed the box and shoved it into Ben's hands. *"GO!"* he looked wild.

Ben had his kit on and his rifle slung. He went out onto the road. A canvas flap was held open at the back of the lorry which was already murmuring and thumping. The other red-cap escort was inside. Opposite him, hunched, long-limbed, without puttees and thinner than Ben remembered, head down; was Cello. His hair was clean and naked. He looked up and his face came alive. Ben pushed the large box in and scrambled after it. "What is it?"

Cello had his arms around the box. "Cello," he said.

After a grinding of gears they choked and whined away.

CHAPTER TWENTY-EIGHT

A prison

"Couldn't let the RSM get his peepers on that, wouldn't allow." Was all that was said by the one escort on the entire journey to the Court Martial centre at Corps HQ. Eyes acknowledged that even some Military Police were actually human.

They arrived at some logistic area. They could hear shouts and more vehicles than had ever been at the battalion locations. The driver had a word through his window and they droned on a little to where it became quieter. The three in the back were denied any view by the canvas loosely flapping but tied at corners. The driver spoke for moments again with some sentry then the engine was killed.

The flap was opened and a red-cap in full uniform with a white belt looked inside. Cello still held his box. Ben sat alongside him and the escort sat opposite. "What do we have 'ere then, prisoner, escort, friend… and a rather large parcel. We'll need to look at that. Got your kit as well I assume?"

"Yes…" replied Ben.

"Yes Sergeant, if you please." The man tilted his arm so that they could see the whole of his stripes.

"Yes sergeant," said Ben.

"Well we got a cosy little cell for you mister, er…" He

consulted a paper in his hand, "Harris... So you can follow me please. You as well Private..."

"Routledge, Sergeant."

"But you will be billeted back in the logistic area. This is just for Court Martial personnel. You can of course spend time with... Private Harris and you will be here for the... proceedings as well."

Ben nodded. They stood outside for a moment. Ben registered bars on the windows of the rooms that surrounded the little courtyard. It looked like some kind of prison yard.

The Sergeant led the way. "Worcesters again I see. You like sending your men up here don't you. I know it's been a while but I do recall the five," he said over his shoulder.

Ben and Cello didn't respond.

Then the Sergeant briefly addressed the escort and driver. "Thank you men, you can return now. Job done." They faded backwards to start up the tender and leave.

A door was unlocked and a dark corridor revealed. It had several cells leading off. They walked down and some soldiers looked out indifferently. "Just a few occupants at present," commented the Sergeant.

They rounded a corner and were met by another red-cap, a Corporal at an open door. "This is your one," he said. It had bars like the other doors and bars on the windows.

There seemed an efficiency about the place where everyone knew what was to happen.

Cello and Ben didn't know what was in store.

"Right; first the parcel. Let's open if you please."

There was a bed with folded blankets and a chair. The box was placed on the chair.

The brown paper came off eagerly. But there were several layers of it. Finally a dark brown box was revealed. The Sergeant jumped a little as perhaps he expected some kind of explosive device. But Cello turned to him then and spoke. "It's my cello, Sarge!" He found a catch in an instant and opened the lid of the box.

The Sergeant removed his cap which was probably something he didn't often do in that place. "Well I'll be damned," he said as he looked down at the jumble of things in the box, which were clearly not of a war-like nature. Then he put his head back and let out a belly laugh. "Ha ha ha, music is it. You gonna give us a concert then?"

"Yes, that's why we called him Cello," said Ben, released by the Sergeant's reaction.

Cello was gingerly taking out the pieces of his instrument from the box. "It's gonna take me a while to fit it all together and tune up," he said.

The Sergeant was a different man without his cap, not so tall and with almost a genial appearance. He had lost quite a bit of hair from the front of his head and wisps of the remaining locks were distributed unevenly over both sides. But then he remembered himself and covered the untidiness with the cap. "Well you got your play thing and I think we can allow that, but keep it hidden mind when the court officers are about. Now Corporal could you explain the routine to our new guest and I'll let you go down to the log area Private... to report to the orderly room there and get your billet. You can come back afterwards."

"Yes Sergeant," said Ben. He looked at Cello and nodded slightly. Cello had a mysterious look in his eyes and nodded also.

CHAPTER TWENTY-NINE

A concert in a cell

Ben came back to a strange sound. He knew what it was and he smiled to himself when he heard it, because the first sounds were incongruous. It wasn't music as he remembered it. But then he had never heard a cello being played. There were low rumblings and then it opened up to some sudden high-pitched shrills and a little warbling as if some gigantic bird had been set free in the prison complex.

The door was opened for him and the music became louder as he walked down the corridor. One might have thought that the other prisoners would react, maybe shout in joy. But they didn't. They had come to the door of their cells and one seemed happy. "Come for the sing-a-long pal," he said to Ben.

"No just for the playing," Ben heard himself say.

The Corporal stood grinning at the cell door. But Cello stopped playing when Ben appeared there. "Welcome," he said smiling.

He laid aside his bow. "Some people don't like the cello, but the staff here seems to approve." Cello had brightened. He sat on his bed. The cello was completely assembled and on the floor between his legs. Its box was part of the instrument, a sort of echo chamber as all such instruments had. An arm ran upwards along which the four strings extended and secured at the top. Cello was already tightening and tuning them with some pegs, pulling the bow that must also have been in the box, gently across with his ear turned down to listen to each low sound. "Got to keep it tuned up all the time, but that's not easy as I don't have the right tools. Just got to hope I don't break a string and the tighteners work," he said.

"They look pretty tight to me," said Ben looking at the white piece of wood that held the strings taught above the box.

Suddenly Cello launched into a tiny play. It started with a deep long mmmmm, a moan. Cello's right hand carved into a block of blue. Ben felt himself falling and being lost in the blue and dark. He shivered without cold. Cello's head was back and forward while he played. Then he changed. Little plucks higher on the strings caught Ben and petals of pink and yellow fell around him. Then a call, high from a far mountain, a child in white singing a high note.

Cello stopped. His concert lasted but a minute. It was a minute which took them away; perhaps each to a different place. The men were silent in stillness after the music. No one needed to say anything.

Cello commanded the room as he would a hall. "They've told me where the CM centre is," he said with a small glee in his voice.

"Have they given you food and drink," asked Ben? It was his job to look after his 'friend'. He did know that much.

"Yes the prisoner has had his evening meal," said the Corporal.

Ben looked at Cello. He took his cue. "Is it possible for us to be alone for a few minutes Corporal?"

"Umm right ho. I think so, but I will be in earshot, so no plotting if you don't mind."

"What would we plot. You got things pretty well organised here against all plots."

They laughed. Though it was a prison, there was a kind of feeling of release inside it, seemingly.

They were left on their own and Ben asked about the 'CM centre'.

"Yes it's in another building but quite close. All red table cloths and silent chairs. We had a look around."

"You seem…" Ben couldn't find the words.

"I want to get this thing over."

They both laughed. Was there an 'over' to this thing. Was there an afterwards?

"Yes but do you know… when?"

"Mine is scheduled for two days' time. There will be some senior officers gathering for the trial. I won't have a defending officer as such…"

"Do you know that…"

"Well I already pleaded guilty to one charge and that's pretty…"

"You pleaded guilty to…"

"At the COs… Colonel's orderly room. Pleaded guilty to throwing away my rifle… Also charged with desertion."

"But you came back."

"But I did desert. You can't say, oh I'm going now for a few days with the Germans – then I'll come back, therefore I never went. Doesn't make sense." He spoke to his cello. Head down, hair hanging, clean hair hanging.

"You still went at the time, you mean."

"I went… I threw away my rifle and went."

He gently began to strum the strings of his cello with his thumb. Dung, dung, dung, drummm, drum drum. Dung dong dung, dung, dung. He plucked individual strings.

He stopped and they listened and heard nothing. No sound of guns, no screaming of casualties, or whining of horses, or firing of rifles.

Had the war ended?

It was eerie, the silence.

Ears breathed; around the corner ears, down the corridor ears; down the windy corridors, through the locked doors, with their open bars; round the corner to the Court Martial centre. Ben hadn't been there. He did not know the process of the Court Martial. It was a different war there in a court.

They looked at each other and smiled. Words used as weapons in court might fall on ears that would not hear them. So they were powerless to change anything. They fell always, for or against 'due process'. The music however was more than words. It was about something that awakes within us, connecting with our very deepest being, Cello said.

CHAPTER THIRTY
Ready

Ben walked from his billet to Cello's prison the next morning, after a meagre cook-house breakfast. He did not hear the cello. He did hear and sense activity. There was a shout and the sounds of 'prisoner and escort', type of goings on; cell doors banging, quick marching boots. Perhaps the Military Police were taking the prisoners on exercise?

Ben was allowed in. There was activity in Cello's cell. An officer was there. Ben approached the door but stayed out of sight. "Your arraignment has been brought forward," he heard the officer say.

Cello did not reply.

"It will now take place this afternoon. Is that clear?"

Again Cello did not reply.

The man cleared his throat. Ben had assumed he was an officer. "You have not requested defence… Have you?"

"I have a friend," said Cello quietly, almost inaudibly to Ben.

"Right… Is that friend here?"

Ben was mechanical now. "Yes here." He raised his voice then entered.

Uniforms filled the cell. The officer was a captain, uniform straight, pressed and immaculate, Sam Browne polished and flashing slightly as he turned towards the door. Cap on.

"Ahh." The eyes narrowed. "Private… ?"

"Routledge… sir." He held his cap in his left hand and saluted. The rule was 'no cap, no salute'. But he did. If the cap had been in his right hand he might not have saluted. He felt foolish.

The officer did not return the salute. Being an illegitimate salute he probably saw no reason to. He narrowed his eyes as if trying to pierce Ben with them.

There was also the Corporal in the room. His red cap was firmly in place.

"Right, I'm the adjutant of the centre, but anything you need just ask the Corporal here… You may attend the arraignment. You won't need to say anything."

Ben felt himself relax. Cello looked down. He was standing, not to attention, just in a relaxed way.

"Right!" He seemed to like this word. "Two o'clock sharp. You Routledge make your way to the Centre by 1345, all seated by then… Clear?"

"Yes sir."

'Due process' was making its way. The wheels were grinding. That was the way things were, here, as well as in the trenches.

The officer paused, matter-of-factly. "Staff on hand to support you, medical and… there's a chaplain."

Cello looked up for the first time, but his eyes were unfocused. Ben tried to catch them, but there was no meeting of eyes, or exchange of glances.

"Carry on Corporal," said the officer.

"Very good sirrr." The Corporal did salute. This time the officer returned the salute, casually; then left.

After a glance, a slightly malicious one towards Ben, the Corporal also left.

Ben and Cello sat down slowly on bed and chair. "It's come quickly, I didn't…" Ben began.

Cello held up a hand. "I'm ready."

Ben didn't really know what he meant. So many questions hung there, unformed into words. So what was he ready for? One thing seemed unapproachable; the reason they were here; the real reason they were here.

But Cello seemed to be giving Ben reassurance, against his uncertainty. Then he leant back on his bed. "Did you like my playing yesterday?"

"I did, I… Are you going to play again?"

"Not now, not before… the *arraignment.*" He smiled like a youth who knew no boundaries, anticipating some excitement. His elbows supported him behind on the bed and he put his head back flicking his hair carelessly.

Ben had seen men with one too many rums act the same. They would usually be smoking deeply. He had his Woodbines in his uniform pocket but knew smoking was prohibited in the cells. "Don't want no one setting fire to their beds now do we?" the Corporal had said.

Cello didn't smoke anyway. They were allowed to smoke during the exercise period in the yard on the far side of the cells, on the way towards the 'Centre'.

Time weighed them into their places and they jumped at sounds in the corridor and from outside.

"Do you want to go back to the billet?" asked Cello.

"Not really, only sit there wondering."

"Yes… Thank you very much for smuggling the cello out for me. I know it wasn't easy."

"Some people are on your side, like the orderly sergeant."

"Of course, some people…" He paused. "What about the Court Martial people, what will they be like?"

"I've no idea," said Ben. He really did need a smoke. "Can I go for a smoke… Do you mind?"

"No Ben you go. Just ask the Corporal at the other end of the corridor. The door brings you out to a courtyard. The Court Martial centre is right opposite."

"I'll take a look then."

Ben went out. The Corporal, a different one, looked at him strangely, aggressively.

"Just going for a smoke," he said.

"Stay in the yard. I'll be watching you."

Ben thought; I am not the prisoner. His hand was shaking as he took out his woodbines and lit one. I am not! But perhaps they all were. He wanted rum. It was about the time for a tot. it usually came up in the evening but sometimes, if the weather was bad, they had a lunchtime nip. He drew heavily and held the fag tightly in his lips.

Prisoners!

They still got paid, a few shillings for smokes and to barter for extra rum. Some sent their money home. Some said money was all they were there for. Saving up – for a rainy day. Pretty fucking rainy here and now. It was not actually raining but the clouds looked threatening, as they always did.

You had time to think when you were out of the trenches; perhaps too much time.

Why had Cello asked him here, to be his 'friend'? Suddenly he felt a pang of loneliness. He couldn't play the cello or be anything; other than a soldier. That's all he could do. So why was he a 'friend'?

Yet he was drawn to Cello, like a prisoner might be to a free man on the other side of a wire cage. But with him as the prisoner.

He took out another Woodbine. His fingers were stained with tobacco. The hand had stopped shaking. 'I'm ready.' What did Cello mean by that? As if he had control.

The walls of the cell block stood like trench walls, but not as protection. What was there to protect them now. The 'yard' was small. On the far side was a wall, which looked less foreboding. Its door was not barred like the cell block door. It was wooden. Brown paint had long since peeled away and given up its coverage. Must be the Court Martial centre. The door through which they would pass.

Maybe it was nearly time. In the trenches they would have slept until someone told them it was time… Time to do something. Time for Stand Too.

They did not control time. They did not control their own time. Without planning for the future, even for the future of the next few moments, you could have a bit of a carefree attitude about the possibility of death arriving. 'That one's not got your name on it, you're all right until the next one comes over.' There might not be a next one.

But Cello somehow controlled his time. 'I'm ready.'

'Ben are you ready?' Ready for what? To try to play a cello, or a fucking violin.

Vehicles and activity happened on the other side of the Court Martial centre. The prison cell was at the side. It was a court house. Suddenly there was activity at the front. Very soon it would be time!

Ben retreated and asked the Corporal what was happening. Don't worry; soon they will be ready and I will call you, he was told. 'Soon they will be ready'.

Cello was 'ready'. But Ben, his friend didn't know what he should be ready for.

CHAPTER THIRTY-ONE
The arraignment

Suddenly there seemed to be more reinforcements to the prison and its Court Martial centre. Prisoners arrived and staff arrived. Shouting and marching came along also.

Ben was escorted out of Cello's cell. He had to be in place fifteen minutes before the prisoner was marched in. Everything had to be timed precisely. He didn't have time for more pondering. He wasn't frog-marched 'eft ight eft ight' style. He was delivered.

Through the paint peeled door they went, down another corridor and then halted outside a rather better maintained door from which the paint was not peeling. The Corporal's bustling stopped and he gingerly opened the door. From within Ben could hear some officers speaking in their customary manner. The Corporal held the door open and indicated to Ben some seats against a wall. Ben slid in.

The room opened up to him. It was a proper court room, with a high long desk decked with a blood-red cloth on Ben's left. Three officers sat behind it on high-backed chairs. A fourth officer, much younger, probably a second lieutenant though with his hands under the table top, this could not be verified, sat at a small table on the far side of the room. The three officers Ben noticed were a major, seated in the middle, flanked by two captains. The three had been in discussion but as Ben entered they looked quiz-zically towards him. They instinctively raised their heads as a sign of their superiority. They looked at one another to confirm Ben's identity, one of them whispered across and the major in the middle nodded. Then he opened a folder in front of him.

Ben saw that there were other desks and booths. But these did not have any occupants. There was a main door which seems to be guarded by two corporal MPs. Another MP hovered in the aisle between two sets of wooden benches. These were unoccupied.

There was some coughing and further hurried whispers among the officers before the President finally straightened himself and indicated that proceedings were ready. He had his blue paper in front of him and his cap was on straight, along with his Sam Browne, slightly shining in the weak afternoon sun. "Bring in the prisoner would you," he said.

It made Ben sit up, though he had been expecting some-thing like this. The main door was opened and Cello was marched in and straight up to the dock. The court officers watched him. He was shuffled into the position.

In a real court of law everything would be set before the judge entered. These were not judges; they were officers.

Cello stood in the dock.

"This is an arraignment only, you will be identified, the charges read and your plea taken. Your trial will be… set for…" He looked up to the two MPs standing in the gap between the benches, still empty. "You will be informed in next day or so… Is that clear?"

Cello nodded. He hadn't looked at Ben on the way in.

"Are you soldier number one three two one six private Marcus Harris of the Worcestershire Regiment?"

"No I am from the Artists' Rifles seconded to the Worcesters."

"Oh," said the officer drily. He made a mark or correction on the form in front of him and showed it to the other members of the court who nodded. "But you are private Marcus Harris of that number."

"Yes," said Cello.

"You are charged with; when on active service on the second of April nineteen hundred and seventeen you did shamefully cast away your arms in the face of the enemy. Do you understand that charge?"

Cello paused. Then he nodded.

"How do you plead to that charge?"

Cello was looking straight ahead and standing to attention. "Guilty," he said in a very clear voice.

The officer made a mark on his form. He looked up. "You are further charged that on the same day you did desert His Majesty's Service by leaving a patrol of which you were part of. Do you understand that charge?"

Again Cello nodded.

"How do you plead to the charge?"

"Not guilty," stated Cello.

The court stood still and the President seemed to look up towards the ceiling. Then he looked to his left but didn't confer with either of the other two members of the court. He looked back to Cello. "You don't have a defending officer."

Cello seemed to relax, back to the young man on the bed, which Ben had seen after his cello playing. "No I don't," he said in a conversational manner.

The officer stared at him for a very brief moment then looked down at his papers.

The court waited. The President spoke. "As I mentioned at the outset, this is merely an arraignment, which I now think is concluded. You will be informed of your trial date, which I'm sure will be in the next few days." He addressed the Orderly Corporal. "You may take the prisoner down."

And so it went. After Cello had departed the three offi-cers shuffled about, then rose and without a glance towards Ben they also left. The second lieutenant who was sitting almost opposite Ben did look at him, with large frightened eyes. Then he too departed, almost in a run.

Ben wondered whether the officer had ever been in the trenches.

So Ben left as well on his own, heavily.

CHAPTER THIRTY-TWO

Controlling the process

There was a word not noticed by Ben, not even thought about. A word exchanged between the members of the court, or rather passed on by the President, who was only a major and not really in full control of the process. 'Witnesses?'

When the army wants to move quickly it can. It can certainly move a word quickly down the chain of command and get a reaction. Words had even been sent down from Army HQ, the fifth Army and communicated to every man within a couple of days.

So the 'witnesses' message about a specific subject on an urgent 'disciplinary matter', could easily go from Corps to Division to Brigade and thence to Battalion in less than a single day. So it was. It happened to reach the ear of the RSM. It happened that the Brigade Commander was visiting the battalion on that day, at that time.

The message was conveyed via messenger. Radio communications were in place and telex machines similar to telegrams could be sent; which was done. On this occasion it was deemed that it should also be delivered by a messenger, who rode a horse and who didn't get blown up on the way but arrived safely and on doing so and seeing the RSM considered that his hands would be safest to receive it.

The RSM was momentarily diverted from the conversation

he was having with the Brigadier outside the HQ. The Brigadier was curious to know the contents of the message since it had obviously come from higher formation. He was the higher formation commander.

The RSM told him the whole story of Cello. When he heard about the German Red Cross apron he exploded. *"Good god. He actually arrived at your trenches wearing the damn thing!"*

The RSM enjoyed affirming the fact, mentally noting the sub-unit that had brought Cello in and from whom some-one might need to be sent post haste to corps as a witness for the Court Martial.

The Brigadier in his turn confirmed the fact. *"Get some-one; at least a Corporal, up to that court; TONIGHT. Where will the witness come from?"*

"The man's section sir; the Corporal who took the patrol."

"Get him up there! Now."

"Yes, SIRR!" The RSM, like a puppet, who had his instruction and was away on his mission.

The Brigadier, who had suspicions about the battalion, particularly as the absence of the adjutant was unexplained and there seemed a general air of uncertainty and lack of confidence about the decision making; was happy that the RSM was there. He would keep them steady, discipline wise at least. But a German apron! What were these men coming to?

An example needed to be set.

He journeyed back to his HQ by horse determined to see this one through.

CHAPTER THIRTY-THREE
Lullabies

"Berceuse," said Cello.

"What?"

"French for lullaby. That's what I was playing."

"Oh." Ben could still hear the echoes of the cello, soft but low, like a vibration of his heart, a deep heart. He looked up towards Cello. "That's deep."

"Yes of course and that was the purpose of a lullaby, to lull you to sleep. The cello is so good for that because it vibrates you and makes you full."

"Yes I feel it in my heart... I had better go and sleep then." He stood up, still with the heaviness from the court in his body.

"See you tomorrow."

Ben left.

He was free; to walk and move around, walk out of the prison. Yet he felt trapped.

The barred door clanged behind him. Prisoners had eyed him as he walked the corridor. They wanted to go out like him. The music had silenced them as it had him. It would send them to sleep.

He had mentioned his heart; the feeling in his heart. Instantly he had wanted to brush over that word. He had wanted to leave because of mentioning it. He felt for his

Woodbines. The hand was shaking. You are free. After this you will be free. After this…

Ben smoked as he walked, paying no heed to the sights and sounds of the area. A dark-haired soldier walking, smoking, thinking.

He coughed suddenly, from his stomach, not heart. The stomach, the arse and the shit coming from it, the mouth for food, cigarettes, rum and the insults and screams and shouts. These were the parts of a soldier. The eyes, one closed with .303 butt in the shoulder; squeezing and then the small jump as the round was delivered. Hold it tight to reduce the jump. More, more, more rounds. Fuck that; the entrenching tool, hand groping for it. Fuck that, ahhh fuck; chop it down on the neck, fuck fuck; desperate. Kill kill kill.

Or be killed.

The heart would stop. Stop its pumping, because the pumping hurts.

But this heart vibrating, moaning!

The music!

The dragging on the 'bine stopped the coughing. Ben spat. His mouth and lungs and teeth were dirty; like the pit of a trench. You didn't look into another man's mouth in the trenches. The smell and sight would be too horrible. Sometimes in death they would be cleaner. Corpses didn't need food, rum or 'bines. Still their mouths were often agape, as if wanting those things.

"Your mouth is like shit," was the oft repeated comment.

"Certainly got shit coming out of it."

It was always shit – the words.

After Cello played his music he didn't talk.

There was no need for it.

There was the lulling, but no talking.

CHAPTER THIRTY-FOUR
Convening

Signatures, from senior fingers, had more power than a rifle. One started the rot, in this case the Brigadier. That gave the document a power to complete its purpose. It enabled others to add their signature without wondering about the detail, like falling plates, tumbling justice. A signature setting responsibility meant agreement was easier than dissent. It didn't even require investigation. A nod went politely to chummy ones, perhaps cricketing respect, playing the honest game, with possible school alumni in mind.

That was the power of the pen in the hands of members of a club.

The Convening Order of the Court Martial had already been signed. The blue army form A3 authorising a 'Field General Court Martial' in this case was done by the Brigadier having been told about it by the Colonel. The FGCM could be conducted by a court consisting of three officers where the senior one could be a major. For the General Court Martial the President was required to be a Colonel. Pinning one such officer down, was never easy, but staff officers of major and captain were plentiful at the various headquarters.

The form had made its way back to the Corps level where some ink stamps made it even more official. The officers had been informed and the arraignment had been done and now the witness was making his way.

But there were words of encouragement needed to provide urgency.

The story of the apron would do that.

It found its way, as stories always did, especially from those who demanded respect; up the line.

That gave urgency and some rearranging of order of the various Courts Martial took place.

Prisoners were waiting in cells, waiting their fate. But they could wait longer.

Cello was the one to be dealt with.

There was a banging of doors and raised voices. "Private Harris!"

A head came round the door. "Tomorrow!" Followed by a smile; a sickly smile.

The staff of the Court Martial Centre didn't have a say, they smiled as men went to be shot. They had no free will, no independent thought or opinion.

Some of the staff Corporals, who changed every two days, seemed to have that sickly smile.

The cello was put aside and then slide under the bed. It was a real bed, off the floor, so something could be put under it.

Tomorrow! What is tomorrow? What shape will tomorrow take? How will the stomachs be; sick like the smile?

In the trenches, tomorrow could have a shape, even if it had no plan for activity in the mind. A soldier has no plan, how can he have? He can't have hope for the next day, in case that is cruelly snatched away. He can hope for a dry day or more rum, or a night's sleep at the end of it, or a letter or marching back to rest. He might know which of these may come according to the prophesy of his seniors or the rumour of brothers. This is the limit of his knowledge; though none of these that he has perhaps been told about, may actually happen.

"This is it then?"

"This is your time… Your time to shine!" Another sickly smile from the Corporal.

Ben couldn't speak. Cello could. But that was all he said. "This is it."

They were suddenly both on edge, ready to leap up, ready for now.

No, tomorrow. It will start tomorrow. It's not time yet.

Oh so we have one night until… Ben couldn't focus his thoughts. After tonight. Who knows? What tomorrow may bring.

A soldier couldn't change his future.

Perhaps they were paralysed in the knowledge of that; a soldier's future is always in the hands of someone else. You wait for orders. But then you were always shouted at to make you react. If you died you would be shouted at. So you reacted to stay alive. You could change that perhaps. But then there was the very strong feeling that if there was a bullet that had your name on it. It would get you anyway, whatever you did.

But there were other things that were out of all their hands. On the next day; the day on which orders had been given for the Court Martial to take place; the officer des- ignated on the Convening Order to be the President was violently ill. He was unable to rise from his bed, except to vomit. It was a comfortable bed in the accommodation des- ignated for the staff officers.

Servant soldiers scurried around seeing to the officer's needs; polishing Sam Browne belts and shoes. Shoes were the order of dress for staff officers, not boots and puttees. Some wore riding breeches, but not riding boots. They were left at the side of beds against the need for some visit further afield than the desks of the headquarters. Most did not get out. The commanders needed to do that, while the staff officers sweated over movement orders, logistic plans, reinforcement numbers and the preparation and passage of operational orders.

But this major would not be at his desk and he could not reach the Court Martial centre either.

Word went up to the office of the CAG, Corps Adjutant General. The department covered the administration of personnel, from pay to death. Casualty figures and the follow-up, which included the stopping of pay, sending of telegrams, burial and the recording of graves and the effects of the deceased, were part of their job. Courts Martial were also their responsibility.

There was always a daily issue to be sorted, as there was for the operational departments of the headquarters. "We need a Court Martial President to stand in pretty sharpish," said one of the junior captains hovering around the group of desks, pushed together with papers and files and signed forms, spilling over each desk. Clerk soldiers and another captain stood, rather than sat at the desks. They had taken over an office in the village. It might have been the mayor's office, not the mayor's council chamber which had been taken over by the artillery control centre, which had wires everywhere. The CAG department did not need instant communications. They did sometimes need instant decisions or instant answers.

"I'll do it." A voice came from behind.

"Colonel?" The captain turned. "You…"

"I've just arrived yes and well I haven't got a job yet."

"But you have…" The captain was taken off guard by the fact that this Lieutenant Colonel had no desk.

"Well I will be taking over one… soon."

The captain didn't want to make himself out to be

ignorant of some senior officer joining his department, otherwise why would he be there.

"Well the Convening Order will need amendment at the Court Martial Centre."

"That's quite close isn't it."

"Yes sir, it's about five minutes' walk down the high street, the old French court house."

"How very appropriate."

The Lieutenant Colonel was fully dressed for the occasion, with polished Sam Browne and some riding breeches and boots. He hadn't yet settled into the relaxed routine of shoes and negative Sam Browne. The abundance of leather was completed by a polished pistol holster on the right front of his Sam Browne belt. He checked the jutting black handle of the pistol occasionally with his left hand as the pistol butt peeped out towards that hand.

"Convening orders gone down there, MPs'll look after you... sir."

Somehow it seemed too easy. The Convening Order was the main piece of the jigsaw to be completed. That was out of the captain's hands, although normally he would have sweated over its preparation and the procuring of the signature of the relevant senior officer, usually the brigade commander of the accused soldier.

The Lieutenant Colonel was untroubled. Not for him the mundane amendment needed to the relevant form. He marched the high street with his head held high, or tipped up a little more if some questioning eyes, perhaps of fellow staff officer, caught his; aware but perhaps ignoring that he was in an alien environment. The captain hadn't noticed but the senior officer was all too aware, of the lack of a single medal ribbon on his tunic. The war was over half way through its third year. But he walked as though he had served in every theatre in those years, with a jaunty confidence, waving his cane to passing individuals, NCOs and groups who chucked him up a salute. "Cheerio, chaps."

All would be well in the world.

After this job he would have some medals on his chest.

On reaching the Court Martial Centre like a sort of messiah, he breezed up to the Red Cap on the main door. "The er... Private Harris Court Martial, I'm the... President."

"Yes sir, the new President, this way sir, right now, just in time sir."

He waltzed past the other sentries and red caps standing their ground. This was their ground, but the convening order was not for their eyes or their responsibility, unless some discrepancy invited their attention. But any alleged falsehood could invariably be filtered by something such as the glaring eyes of an RSM or the authority of some senior officer, even if he had only a cricketing excuse.

No one knew the Lieutenant Colonel's excuse but the certainty that he had one for being there was accepted.

The moment came when he sat at the table with its red cloth after a nod to the other members of the court and the Convening Order was in front of him, neatly handwritten and signed by the brigadier, probably with his own fountain pen.

The Lieutenant Colonel had no fountain pen, no pen at all. In front of him, laid out assiduously by one of the MPs was a pile of finely sharpened pencils and sheets of average quality foolscap. There was an India rubber there also and a pencil sharpener next to the red *Manual of Military Law*, should he need to consult it.

He looked at the Convening Order and was suddenly a tad nervous. A Lieutenant Colonel should have his own fountain pen. He had a revolver and a scabbard for his sword on the Sam Browne belt which accoutrements made movement in his chair a little difficult. It was not all meant to be worn sitting down. He needed a pen however. For as he had heard or read somewhere; 'the pen is mightier than the sword'. It certainly was more useful when sitting at a desk or table on which this convening order needed amending and where the details of the court proceedings would need to be written down.

Written down and recorded.

Gingerly he turned the blue page of the convening order. The amendment could wait until tomorrow or whenever the completion of the court would be. By that time he could have acquired a pen. Meanwhile… He picked up a pencil and laid a couple of sheets of paper onto the back cover of the convening order, neatening it together. "Uhhhum." He cleared his throat. The court waited. "Prosecution?" He looked at the court from his central seat. He had already acknowledged the members of the court sitting to his left and right. They were officers who would do as he directed. They would interpret the movement of his body and the intonation of his voice to ensure they complied with every rule of procedure and every due process.

But the other speaking parts of this theatre were more important.

"Yes sir." A captain stood from the desk to the left of the long table.

"The witnesses are ready?"

"Yes sir."

"The accused is arraigned?"

"Yes sir."

The escorts and court orderly were standing at expectant distances, at the door and a small table respectively; all Military Police NCOs; all smartly dressed. This was the parade ground, not the trenches. There was certainly no smell of the trenches, the only smell was old wood and leather.

He began to take control; to settle into his surroundings, which were not unfamiliar, being a lawyer himself.

"Right march in the accused, when you are ready Corporal."

CHAPTER THIRTY-FIVE

What did you want to hold?

Cello was marched in with a whirlwind. The 'left right, left righting' was overemphasised. Then the court of law took over.

He was escorted to the dock but allowed to take his place with dignity, unruffled by a parade ground semblance of discipline.

There was no oath to be taken by the accused. It was the job of the President and his board of officers to ensure that the truth will out. That was the purpose of the trial.

The charges were read again and the pleas were read again. Guilty to the charge of 'shamefully casting away his arms;' not guilty to the charge of desertion.

The President looked at Cello during the reading process, noting that he did not move or flinch or look at anyone else. The President let his eyes stray to the one occupier of the 'public' benches; a private of dark hair and striking pale features who yet seemed more uneasy than the accused. Ben's eyes did not catch any other person in the room.

After the recapture of the arraignment, the President tapped his pencil on the foolscap in front of him, as yet still virgin white. He gave a brief nod to the prosecution, who stood and took two strides into the centre of the room. Then as a sort of afterthought, the President stopped him in mid-stride. "The charge of 'casting away his arms' does not concern us at the moment. You will bring evidence for the desertion charge will you not?"

The prosecuting officer nodded. "Sir, the evidence in this case… err the case of desertion, is clear. Private Harris… on the evening of the second of April, this very month, was tasked as part of a patrol into No Man's Land. This was a routine activity to dominate the area in preparation for what might have been further operations by the Battalion." He named the Battalion. "The patrol was led by Harris's section Corporal…" Again he gave the name.

The President cut across his bows, making his judge-like presence felt again. "Do we have Corporal…?"

"Yes sir, he will be called."

"Let's call him." He seemed anxious to get on with the proceedings.

The previously pipe-smoking Corporal was marched in. He did have to take the oath, which was duly administered by the court orderly. Then nervously he looked out at the court, without his eyes appearing to fall on either Cello or Ben.

The prosecuting officer took the floor again. He began by verifying the identity of the Corporal; Frederick Ives; yes. Then he mentioned the charges facing Cello. Then he started his direct questions. The President had his pencil poised. "Did you lead a patrol out into No Man's Land on the night of the second of April?"

Yes.

Was Private Harris a member of that patrol?

Yes.

Tell the members of the court what happened on the patrol.

The Corporal turned slowly towards the row of seated officers. He raised his head on which his hair, unlike that of Cello or Ben, appeared to be thinning somewhat. His face was also thin and clean shaven and the upper lip seemed to lift, momentarily revealing a very discoloured tooth. Then he sniffed loudly. "Well sir… sirs. I took the patrol out from our own trenches into No Man's Land…"

The President interrupted him. "May we know the purpose of the patrol, the mission if you will?"

Corporal Ives quickly looked at the prosecutor, who took the cue away from him. "It was a routine clearance patrol of the sort carried out on a nightly basis with the aim of dominating No Man's Land and gathering intelligence for future operations… sir."

The President nodded and then turned to Corporal Ives. "Was that your understanding Corporal?"

The question hung as Corporal Ives adjusted his feet. Then he swallowed visibly. "Yes… but…"

"But?" asked the President.

"Well we 'ad another job, which was… we were supposed to find a casualty."

It was not clear whether the Corporal would dance to whatever tune he thought the court wanted or whether he would find some words of his own and how far he would take those words.

The prosecuting officer took over again. "And did you find the casualty?"

The court waited as the witness shifted on his feet and sniffed again and put his hands on the witness stand frame. They were very white. "No sir."

There was an intake of breath, just audible, from Cello. Though he did not move.

That seemed to spur the Corporal into a new memory. "We did find one… dead man, sir, already dead."

The court seemed to settle its attention back to mild interest. After all there were many dead men out in No Man's Land; lying waiting to be discovered; or not waiting.

"Did you think this was likely to be the casualty you

sought," asked the prosecuting officer, feeding words to the Corporal which did not require a discomforting recall of memory to respond.

"Yes."

Ben's interest was more than mild. Something had been missed. But he thought 'due process' might fill in any gaps of detail in the account. He did not know whether he would be called to speak. In this court where the officers seemed to be talking things out in a reasonable way, his confidence was restored. This was not like the trenches. There was no RSM here.

Calmly the prosecuting officer took over again. "And what happened then Corporal?"

"Well we 'ad already been gassed see and I was worried that we might be discovered by a German patrol or we might give ourselves away some'ow." He reverted to the dialect of his upbringing although the men under him previously had all thought he was refined with a degree of worldly wisdom. Perhaps that had come from the pipe; whose wisdom was now wanting. "So I ordered that the patrol should be ended and we should return to our own lines."

"And what did Private Harris do?"

"'E threw down his rifle and said he wasn't going back."

"He cast away his rifle?"

"Yes sir... sirs."

"And what did you then do?"

"I orrrdered 'im to pick ut up and come with us, several times I did."

"And what was his response?"

"'E said he weren't comin' back, and 'e didn't pick up his rifle."

"And what happened then?"

"We all returned without 'im. And one of the other members of the patrol carried his rifle back."

The President had been listening and shifting occasionally in his chair whose worn leather upholstery allowed him
manoeuvre. It was a chair, with arms to get comfortable
in. But now he felt the need to intervene. "Corporal did
you know that the definition of desertion is that a soldier
is said to have deserted only if he has the intention of not
returning."

"Urmm." The Corporal was a bit lost now.

The prosecuting officer helped him out. "It is understood
that Private Harris did subsequently return."

The Corporal was ready for this. "Yes sir 'e did and what's
more 'e came back wearing a German medics apron."

Had there been a public gallery full of spectators this
might have been the cue for some sort of reaction, a gasp
perhaps, or even a laugh.

Nobody in the court reacted. There was no intake of
breath. Cello looked straight ahead.

A defending officer might have objected to the fact that
the Corporal was giving evidence on aspects which he did
not witness personally as Cello had not returned into his
piece of the trench system. But this was not perhaps appreciated by the court and the Corporal was not about to correct them on the technical aspects of hearsay and actual evidence. Besides he had seen Cello during the journey back,
after they had been relieved that time.

The prosecuting officer wasted no time to further
besmirch Cello. "if I may, we have heard that Private Harris
mentioned that he had been with the German forces, even
wearing uniform given by them when he returned."

"I hardly think that a medic's apron could be classed
as uniform, but I take your point; the act of joining the
armed forces of another country, particularly the enemy, is
an indicator of the intention of not returning at the time of
absenting himself."

"Thank you, sir." The prosecuting officer smiled at the President.

The President leant back in his chair. It appeared that the case had been made and of course there had already been a guilty plea to 'casting away the rifle'.

The witness waited. The prosecutor waited. The President leant forward perhaps in a moment of decision, over the desk. "Do you have any further questions for the witness?"

"Just the one I think sir… Corporal, did Private Harris mention to you or any that you heard from, about his time with the Germans?"

The Corporal looked around and swallowed. He did not look at Cello. "He said he was doing a much more worthwhile job there… 'E said that he had come back for the Court Martial only, otherwise he would have stayed with the Germans."

The members of the court did react to these words. Their bodies assumed postures of suitable reprove, a look, a frown, a cough, a movement which was as good as a full stop.

"Job, he was doing a job, what precisely?"

The prosecutor did not bother to refer this to the witness. "I understand it was as a medic sir, hence the medic's apron."

The Corporal nodded. He was dismissed and there being no one else to meaningfully address, the president turned towards Cello. The Court Martial changed gear.

Ben's mind burnt with the things that had not been mentioned.

"So Private Harris; of course you have pleaded guilty to the charge of casting away your rifle and I would firstly like to hear from you, why exactly you did that?"

This might have been the time for those things to come out. Ben waited

"I didn't want to hold it any more."

"But you are a soldier... So what did you want to... hold?"

"My cello."

CHAPTER THIRTY-SIX
Bach is announced

Had the President worn glasses he would have removed them. Without them he screwed his fists into his eyes, to try to change the view in front of him perhaps. But it was the word that had struck him like a… like some sort of warlike projectile. "So you play, but what are you…?" He faltered.

"I'm in the Artists' Rifles. I was apprenticed to the ENO… English National Opera orchestra and they… well a lot joined up."

"ENO, yes I am familiar, loved classical music all my… So what are you, were you… What's your favourite… ?"

"I was working towards a recording of J S Bach's solo Cello Suites when we were… I was… I joined up."

Suddenly as if released like a boy from boarding school, the Lieutenant colonel shouted. "JOHANN SEBASTIAN BACH… German… Yes, wonderful, English player doing a recording, German composer. Wonderful." He stared forward moving his eyes away from Cello, he seemed… changed. "You seem too young. How old…?"

"Twenty-three."

"Ahh yes, your date of birth is here, silly of me. But there is no mention of your… vocation… Cellist. No mention of it." He searched around for some excuse for his foolishness at not knowing he was in the presence of someone who perhaps could be a great musician.

"Here, I am a private in the Artists' Rifles."

"You are!" His eyes stayed on Cello, in lingering agreement, as if he were looking at his son, or a potential son; not a soldier who had pleaded guilty to a heinous crime, a crime created by the war.

As a cellist he would never have cast away his cello. And as to a rifle he would never have held one. How could a cellist hold a rifle? His cello was far more important than a rifle. Had he picked up such an item in the orchestra pit instead of his cello, yes he would have cast it aside, of course he would.

The Lieutenant Colonel trembled a little, unsure at first what he should do. The papers in front of him could not tell him. The orders of the Brigade Commander could not tell him. He had no way of consulting that officer for clarification. He had to decide for himself. "I am going to adjourn for today," he said, quietly at first. "Orderly please clear the court." Nobody moved. As if the order was to be complied with automatically, he continued. "I want the board to remain for a moment please." He looked at his fellow board members. There was a stillness in the room.

The normal procedure would be for the board to leave first. But nobody knew what to do with this unexpected order. So the Lieutenant Colonel exploded and shouted it. *"I SAID CLEAR THE COURT, ORDERLY, NOW!"*

The escort to the accused standing at the door would not normally have responded to an order, other than being told to march the accused out. So he blurted out. "I'm not an orderly... sir."

The Lieutenant Colonel lost something in his reply, as if he had suddenly gone under the table to find a deeper self. *"YOU, YOU ARE AN ORDERLY."* He trembled somewhat.

"FOR THE PURPOSE OF THE CLEARING OF THE COURT YOU ARE AN ORDERLY." He was screaming now, in an uncontrolled manner not befitting of the haloed place that those present stutteringly knew they were in. *"NOW DO YOU THINK YOU CAN DO IT, CAN YOU CLEAR THE COURT?"*

He didn't need to because he was an escort so he marched up to the dock and met Cello who stepped down from it and with the other escort stumbling forward from the door, they all joined together. They didn't put their hands on the prisoner. He was not handcuffed. He was not a reluctant criminal. He was marched from the Court

The President was unsure whether he was a criminal. How could he be a cellist and a criminal?

As to clearing the court Ben quickly made the door, the prosecutor almost ran after the accused but turned the other way once outside. The Court Martial board remained. They stood but didn't walk. They looked ahead woodenly, as if turning to the President would be an anathema.

CHAPTER THIRTY-SEVEN
Bach comes in

They banged back through echoing doors, Ben catching up with Cello. They had to be together. Ben did not hesitate or allow any separation. He wanted to swear; fucking hell, he wanted to say. He wanted a smile to be on his face because he sensed a victory.

At his cell, Cello was not smiling, not celebrating. He went straight, head down, hair dropping over his eyes, to his bed and drew out from under it, slowly and with intensity, his instrument. He flicked his hair back from his face. Once he held it, he did smile, very slightly, for he was a serious young man. A man for whom being a soldier was a temporary existence and one which he never fully embraced.

However with the cello, it could be instantly seen, that this embrace was a familiar and expert one. Ben did see it. He watched in awe.

The player tweaked and strummed and listened and turned the strings tight, holding his ear down. Then applied the bow to make a few little moans with it.

"Bach," smiled Cello a little more broadly.

"Who is this Bach and why did the President...?" He couldn't finish, for the bow hit the strings and his friend came alive. A great deep-throated draw filled the world. It didn't seep out of the cell, it blasted. At first the sequence started rumblingly low but notes rainbowed out climbing stairs, climbing and climbing in a sort of uncontrolled reaching for a sky of colour and joy; yes joy.

But then it started again on another higher stairway, pulling at hearts, unable to be imprisoned. Music could never stay in a cell. It vibrated out. It burst out. Cello and Ben laughed as they knew it would be heard outside, but didn't know how far it would reach.

In fact it reached the courtroom. The President had slumped into his seat. In a very correct procedural manner, a jug of water and an actual glass had been placed on the table. This was a life preserver for he reached for it, poured and drank heavily as if he was already at the officers' mess bar refreshing himself after a hard day. He had had a day of sorts, a strange day, which was far from over yet.

The other members of the court, sat down gingerly. The President looked at the youngest member, the second lieutenant who was probably no more than twenty-one. The President seemed to retrieve some composure. He looked across at the young man and nodded. "You can go," he said.

The young man got up and clicked his heels together. He saluted, turned and left without a word.

As if the opening door had let in the sound of the cello it could be heard as the officer departed. But the closing of the door behind him did not close the sound off. In fact it came from small open windows high in the wall behind the table where the three Court Martial officers sat. But it didn't come in thinly, it came in strongly even though from a distance. It filled the court room immediately. There was no other sound on this seemingly quiet day of staff and logistic work. Only an occasional distant boom gave a reminder of where they were.

The music gave a different reminder perhaps to the President and he seemed transported to that place. Slowly he got up. At the low notes he did a little bobbing bow and at the high ones as the music climbed an invisible stair he reached his head up, as if looking towards some distant horizon, a distant green pasture. A small smile of recognition played at the corners of his mouth.

He walked around the table listening. "Number one in G," he said now facing the other two officers. "It happens to be my favourite."

They stood up, stood still, not moved in a bodily way by the music as the President seemed to be.

"What do you think?" The President wanted some fellowship in his transportation.

"... Colonel!" One was trying to bring perspective. This was bizarre, not at all the time or the place.

The president was getting deeper into it. "Oh I know, not appropriate, but its beautiful don't you think? Imagine, a cellist, playing Bach right here, right here and now, in this... in this..." He seemed unable to continue.

The music did continue. It seemed to take control where he could not. It rose again on its vibrating stairway and he looked higher, weaving his head a little this way and that at the backward and forward quickening movement of the bow, which he could not see but with eyes part closed could imagine and follow.

Suddenly the President did something strange. He unbuckled his pistol holster. His face was red and he continued to have some motion about him but he was smiling and he seemed jolly. Perhaps it was all a joke. There was no buckle on the holster, just a leather flap with a hole to fit over a metal stud. He had got that flap open.

In the officers' mess holsters were opened on many occasions, pistols were drawn and brandished. Shots were also fired, perhaps in some game or prank, or in frustration. So the unbuckling of the holster was only strange given the formal environment of the court.

But still the other officers of the Court Martial board remained in their spots. He was after all two full ranks senior to them and a Lieutenant Colonel, who could be the Commanding Officer of their battalion, was a revered figure, an all-powerful one.

By now the President had got the revolver out and some brandishing was being done, but he still seemed to be transported by the music and so the weapon became a sort of conductor's baton.

His mood changed and he stopped his little prance. He levelled the revolver in the direction of the other members of the Court Martial. "Why are we killing men like this. Why are killing soldiers… cellists?" He pointed his weapon at first one and then the other of the officers standing in front of him. His voice became more unreasonable and higher pitched. "Think of that… Listen to the music."

One of the officers did now begin to move. "Colonel he is a soldier!"

"Yes but… its wrong, don't you think." Now his voice had gone. It had become a sort of whine.

The other officer raised his voice. "Colonel it doesn't matter. That is not our concern."

"But it is dear boy, don't you see?"

Suddenly the music reached a crescendo as if at the top of the stairs it opened to a wide vista of joy and freedom in the music of a shrill dancing bow, backwards, forwards, up and down the scale. "Oh god!" And the President did actually himself begin a sort of dance; a hop and step to the rhythm, then a hop step on the other foot. Then he went too far. "Chaps it's time for us to take control, it's time for a… mutiny I think." Her waved his revolver wildly.

The captain acted. "Colonel *NO!*" He jumped over the table and trying some sort of restraining move caught the President with an outstretched arm.

It was too late, the revolver went off with a crash, muffled a little, caught as it was somewhere between the officer's Sam Browne belt and his tunic.

The captain stepped back. The President slumped down and blood began seeping onto the courtroom floor.

CHAPTER THIRTY-EIGHT
Another outburst

A page turned but the story stuttered and missed a beat. The original Court Martial President arose from his bed and the ailment that had laid him low the previous day had left him. He nodded to the other two Court Martial officers at breakfast but discussing the case was not permitted. However another staff officer quietly mentioned to him that the CAG would like a word.

He arrived at the senior staff officer's desk before zero nine hundred hours.

"… Unfortunate incident." The full colonel, the Corps Adjutant General, looked up into the cigar smoke halo that was collecting over his head. He got the cigars from a friend in the industry. Rather proud of it he was. He ended the brief account of the previous day's events. He hadn't mentioned the music playing. "Need to get this wrapped up though, today if possible, clear?" The other officer was after all only a major.

"Do me best Colonel," responded the new President instantly.

"Good, good. General seems to be rather keen to get this one out of the way, not sure why. Here's the convening order, no changes made, so you're still the Pres…" He handed over the blue document.

The major left the office, or the church hall it seemed to be and began his walk to the Court Martial centre. He was passed by Ben going towards Cello's cell. Ben saluted, his arm quivering; to which the major merely waved his gloved hand towards his cap in acknowledgement. Ben frowned to himself. He recognised the man and his stomach somehow told him what was afoot. In the back of his mind had lain the possibility of some sort of reprieve. But the purposefulness of this officer quelled that.

On reaching Cello's cell his stomach churned further. Cello was already on the point of being escorted out. He smiled at Ben secretly. Don't worry, said the smile.

Ben followed.

For the resumption of the trial no chances were being taken and the court was assembled before the board entered.

On arrival the major had been shepherded to a back room which would have been used by the French law makers and judges. That law seemed to have fallen under layers of dust in the room which had not been included in a sprucing up by some working party from the logistic area. The board members stood in the middle without disturbing the dust. Their Sam Browne belts shone. The President also wore his medals and a sword. To complete that regalia required sword gloves.

Mention was made of the music but the captain who spoke, also the one who had tried to restrain yesterday's President, made Cello and his music playing out to be some sort of renegade act, one of defiance; and the President's 'heart attack', as just a natural and highly unfortunate occurrence.

They went through the statement made by the witness and the pencil written notes made of it and the major decided that this would suffice to take proceedings forward.

It was time. A knock on the door told them that the court was assembled.

They emerged from their lair. All clear. Their shoes heralded the approach and arrival in court. Chairs grated on the wooden floor. They sat down with the President making sure he did not sit on his sword, the sword frog held it, but only so that it could hang down the flank of a horse.

The others had revolvers like the previous President, as was normal for staff officers.

This President looked directly ahead. "Good morning, please relax and stand at ease… Uhhum." He placed the convening order on the table in front of him. "With regard to this hearing… It will continue. There has been, a slight hiatus… but the evidence presented yesterday in front of the members of the board here," he indicted the two captains sitting to his side, "still stands, as part of the prosecution case."

He turned to the prosecutor. "So um… do you have anything to add to your case?"

The prosecuting officer who had sat, on the instructions to rest at ease, stood briefly. "No sir, not at this stage." He knew he would get a chance to fire some more bullets into Cello.

The President, like the turning of a weathercock without wind assistance, focused on Cello. "At this stage you have the chance to make a statement, explain yourself if you like… Whenever you are ready."

"Is there justice in war?" Cello spoke suddenly, in a low voice. His head was slightly bowed, his hair hanging down.

The court stood still.

"Sorry could you say that again?"

Cello lifted his head this time and looked straight at the President. "I said, *is there justice in war?*"

The President sat back in his chair. "No this is your opportunity to speak about the case, about yourself if you like and anything that has a bearing on it."

240

"I know, this is part of my statement. Let me put it another way. Maybe in a way you might find in a dictionary. Is there the quality of being morally just or righteous, or the observance of any divine law, which says; thou shalt not kill? In war killing is a righteous act, justice is therefore overturned. Or justice is void and shamed under a new law, giving the hand of freedom to those who might become murderers, judge, jury and executioners in the vacuum; holding up a sneering excuse of a noble cause… *IT IS NOBLE IS IT NOT?"*

There were statues in the courtroom, everybody was still for just an instant

Cello did not wait though for an answer to his amazing speech. "Your silence gives the lie. Or I know you won't reply, it is not in the… procedure. Noble or not matters little, for to kill is righteous and that requires the production of killing machines. The rifle is a killing machine, to discard it is an act of cowardice even though doing so might show the quality to be morally just and righteous… I am a just and righteous person!"

The members of the court moved. There was a visible sigh, though the audible side of it was not detectable.

"No one is doubting this," blurted out the President.

"But acts of wilful cowardice in the face of the enemy are punishable by death. To kill in war is righteous."

There was no answer to this.

"SO DO IT. YOU HAVE WEAPONS, SOMEONE SHOOT ME." He pointed first vaguely towards the sidearms of the board. Then he held up his hands, very steadily searching the major's face.

The President's face grew red, starting with small spots on his cheeks. He looked affronted. Suddenly he was not a soldier you may have encountered in the trenches. He was a logistic man. A major from the base, grown a little

241

fat. In some way he despised those who were constantly in action. He didn't call for that. Yet he had not avoided it either. Because of his age he fell easily into the staff-officer mould. Younger and leaner he could have been a battalion second in command, perhaps ready to assume command if his commanding officer should become a casualty.

But no, he did what he could in his staff job. Touching soldiers where he had too, usually on paper. But now, something aroused his anger. A tent-peg carefully malleted deep into the ground to achieve a military encampment of purpose; had been ripped from its moorings.

Cello's outburst was extraordinary also to Ben who couldn't take his eyes off his cellist.

But Cello seemed to sag. The energy had left him.

"I've never heard such disgraceful nonsense," the President eventually managed to ejaculate.

But it wasn't, thought Ben. If Cello was to be sentenced, why not carry it out here and now.

"You don't have the courage." This was delivered quietly but firmly by Cello. As if he, who was a coward to cast away his rifle, knew exactly what courage was all about.

This must have done it for Cello. He was clearly some sort of subversive. The major quickly leant over to fellow board members, one after the other. The second lieutenant, sitting apart was not involved in these exchanges.

The President turned to the prosecuting officer and asked mildly; "Do you have anything to add on the prosecution side."

That officer, probably thinking that Cello had sealed his own prosecution, said. "I don't believe there is any need sir."

The President looked down at his papers, then up again abruptly. "This court finds you guilty on all charges and sentences you to death. The sentence is subject to confirmation by the convening authority of this Court Martial and the General Officer Commanding the expeditionary force of His Majesty's Armed Forces in France. This court is adjourned."

CHAPTER THIRTY-NINE
The bare cell

The shock of everything left Ben speechless. He smoked with a Woodbine hanging from his lips in the corridor outside Cello's cell adding some yellow wispy stains to those already making the walls a dirty brown. With his outburst Cello had made himself a hero of the prison. Everybody heard about it very soon and prisoners set about calling out from their cells. Some even clapped.

Ben and Cello hadn't heard what had happened the afternoon before. They knew nothing of the 'suicide'. The clearing of the court by the then President and this new departure with the 'old' President had a stink about it. That much was clear.

But Cello's challenge to the court might have sealed his fate. At least that is how it looked from the faces of the MPs who escorted them back to the cells with an air of finality. The rapid completion of trials was not so normal. But some expected more anger in answer to Cello perhaps a banging of the table and an order to 'handcuff the prisoner', to prevent him pointing and gesturing. Even though those gestures had ended in a sort of surrender. The words did not concur with that body language.

Cello sat on his bed, intent on his instrument. He forced out a comment. "You are not surprised Ben, are you?"

"Are you though?"

"I suppose not… In view of…"

"What you said."

Cello looked up as Ben stood at the door. He was almost smiling. "Yes in view of what I said."

"But you don't regret saying it."

Cello did do a sort of laugh then. "No, no I don't regret it." Then his face turned serious. "Why do you think I shouldn't have said it?"

"Well… Not in your character. Never seen you like that before. No… I mean; yes, you should have said it." Ben was learning. He had not been out in No Man's Land with Cello and Sergeant John Thomas Wall where they had learned a sort of independence.

Though Cello was now realising that even with this independence he could not fight the system, the 'due process', at least not with any hope of victory.

So the victory would need to be a personal one. He knew he would have to prepare for that.

Ben was still confused and needed clarification. "What happened yesterday, to the old, well yesterday's President, you know the Lieutenant Colonel?"

"Ask them," Cello tipped his head up. Behind Ben unheard above the noise of other prisoners, an MP Corporal had appeared.

The MP Corporal cleared his throat. "Yesterday… was a day like we're never again gonna see 'ere I wouldn't think." He was all official and tall, though there was a softness to his voice.

"So what did happen… I mean after the President…"

"Didn't you lot 'ear the shot?"

Cello looked up. *"SHOT!"*

Yes 'e shot 'imself, poor sod."

"The cello… so loud," said Ben, as if in apology.

"Yes… it was during… the noise. We rushed in when we heard the shot. 'Course we was closer, just outside the door… There 'e was… shot 'isself."

Cello looked at Ben, a look which held no guilt, only curiosity.

Then Ben's thoughts went back to his salute to today's President as they passed on the way to the Court Martial centre and Cello's cell respectively. The purposefulness in the officer's stride brought forth his dread, a feeling that everything had been decided.

What did they expect? Cello hadn't expected anything. Once his treatment by the RSM had started he knew how things might turn out. But he had the satisfaction of delivering his partially prepared speech; perhaps a little earlier than previously he had thought. But the satisfaction was still there.

Ben still held a confused view of things. No one had told him what his job was to be. No one had given him orders. He understood that perhaps there should have been something for him to do beyond any orders. He had waited for an opportunity to do something, which had never come. Now it was too late.

And his dread now was that Cello didn't need him as a 'friend' any longer.

But he needed information, where Cello seemed to have accepted something…inevitable. "What is going to happen now then, Corp?"

The Corporal looked from him to Cello, then at the floor, the cold flagstone floor. "Well confirmation usually takes a few days but it can be done sooner if… Though usually the CinC commutes the sentence to…"

"To what?" asked Ben.

"Imprisonment."

Ben saw hope spring up, though not from the Corporal's

eyes which were still cast down. "See, Cello, see… pal." He didn't know how to refer to Cello so he used the word 'pal' awkwardly and began to smile.

Cello didn't smile. "Usually…?" he questioned.

"Yes, but I don know, not bin 'ere that long meself and so I… s not familiar."

"Well we will know soon wont we?" Ben was a little excited now.

The Corporal maintained his reserved disposition. "You will know, just as soon as it's made known."

'Made known', seemed a little formal and unforgiving. The 'due process' was as cold as the floor.

"While we're waiting I want a bare cell," announced Cello suddenly.

"A bare cell!" Ben and the Corporal spoke together, almost as one.

"Yes I want the bed cleared. I don't want a bed."

"But…" Ben felt hopeless just then; powerless. "How you gonna sleep?"

"The same way I slept in No Man's Land, on the ground… floor. I just need a blanket. That will be luxury compared with what I had there. This is all I want."

He held his cello.

CHAPTER FORTY

A visitor

Solo musicians cannot be interrupted. Watchers will never break a link with the high secrets of classical performance art. Musicians are the soldiers of the composer. Soloists and lead instrumentalists are the Corporals and officers, individual players are the troops, conductors are the Generals and Field Marshals. They are not fighting a battle. They are making a movement or moving an emotion, combining sounds to bring to layered hearts, a kaleidoscope of images and a lifted world.

Some lone musicians do not need an orchestra. They are complete on their own, regardless of where they are playing.

When Cello had been in No Man's Land he needed his instrument. Now that he had it, he did not need a bed. He even turned away food.

Ben arriving at his door and seeing a bowl of breakfast porridge left on the floor there, saw a shaking man, seated on a stool in the corner of his bare cell. A man with closed eyes controlling the music and letting it take him at the same time. Cello's hand was quivering as he pressed his fingers high on the strings to make notes.

It was not the shaking man of those times he had spent with Sergeant John Wall. This was a man seeming vulnerable by music which controlled him, jerked him, took his strength. At the same time made him strong. So strong he needed no external assistance.

He needed no 'friend'.

So Ben stood and felt jobless, yet moved in the heart. The music was giving him strength as well as to the man who played.

Cello stopped playing eventually. Ben did not applaud as a concert audience might have done. He dropped his head in a sort of nodding motion. There was some desultory clapping from other cells however, who formed an unseen audience. "Do you like it?" asked Cello.

"Of course I do. It is your... You are a musician."

"I try. A musician is never complete. He has to bring in the composer to interpret that person's mind."

A pause fell between them.

"What is that thing you do with your hand?" He imitated Cello's hand, vibrating as he pressed fingers on strings It seemed to him strange to ask about it. But he couldn't think of anything else.

Cello demonstrated it with his left hand. "It's called vibrato. It gives the note a resonance, an echo if you like. I don't use it for every note but I do use it a lot."

"Yes." But Ben had no idea what he was talking about. "That's good isn't it."

"Well it is a technique used by all players in the more advanced..."

"You are good, I know; a very good... I think that's why the President shot himself. He knew how good you were."

"Why would that make him shoot himself?"

Ben shuffled his boots which he had cleaned since arriving at the logistic area. The music sort of demanded clean boots.

He had no real abilities, no music or art or... real opinion. "I don't know."

Being a soldier was not really a skill. You followed orders. Some followed them like lumps. At least that is what the Platoon Sergeant called them, whose limbs were for work and using the rifle. You were a rifle and a bayonet; nothing more. Except when working, which in some cases was done in the manner of a mad man. Leading men to be sent again and again to the same piece of wire to redo and redo it. Until someone got sacrificed just to make the wire firmer.

Perhaps the President; who shot himself, also believed the soldiers were 'lumps'. Then came a cello player, not a 'lump'. Somehow that caused the shooting.

That was something worth drinking to. Jack would have loved it. Ben smiled to himself at the thought. Suddenly he missed rum to drink to something. He wished Cello did actually drink rum.

He didn't drink, or eat; only play music.

Ben sat on the floor, the only place to sit.

They waited; which was a skill that all soldiers did have, though Cello seemed restless, not nervous, unable to shut his mind down in the waiting.

They listened to the other prisoners moving and getting fed and then going out to take exercise. Finally Ben and Cello did also go out.

Meals came from the cookhouse and Cello refused his. Ben did eat; the ubiquitous mess tin of stew, which he didn't have to go to the cookhouse for. In an act of passing generosity an MP private brought it to him.

The day wore. Very little light came into the cell block.

When Cello was not playing he glanced at his instrument often, perhaps to check it was still there.

Prison routine was only punctured by visitors.

One came late in the day. The Corporal brought him, unlocking and stepping slowly down the corridor, stopping at cello's door; an officer. But eyes were attracted to the 'dog collar' instead of a tie. He was a chaplain as well as a captain. He had a naked head which was balding badly, which most captain's heads wouldn't be.

He addressed the cello which was not being played, with some surprise at its presence. "Private Marcus Harris?"

"Yes."

The chaplain looked from the cello to Ben. "Do you want to talk in private?"

"I'm Private Routledge," said Ben.

"He is my friend," said Cello.

"Yes," said Ben.

The chaplain smiled in a sympathetic way.

"Well... You both... then, should know... Should know, that the Commander-in-Chief, Field marshal Douglas Haig; has confirmed the sentence."

CHAPTER FORTY-ONE

A lieutenant

Cello and Ben's eyes flashed naked at each other. The heart is the source of hope, still present while it beats. But the shock as a band of hope breaks from the heart, takes the veil off the eyes.

But even made flimsy, hope can start rebuilding straight away if there is strength to do it. "It's not over yet Ben." There seemed an edge of panic in Cello's voice though.

The chaplain looked from one to the other. "Well... it's signed now, so there is no way back from that. No appeal is possible I'm afraid."

"So what happens now then, what happens, because cello is... He didn't desert. He came back. He didn't do it." Ben had caught the tone of panic in Cello's voice and his heart began to race.

The chaplain held up a hand. "What's your first name Private Routledge?"

"It's Ben, Benjamin."

"Benjamin or may I call you Ben... I'm sorry. This is hard for you both. I am not permitted to speak about the details of the case. I have no jurisdiction in the matter. It is my job to support you at this difficult time." His voice had a funny sort of purr to it.

"Support, what support," asked a defiant Cello?

"Well pastoral support." The chaplain, looked around

and his eyes fell inevitably on the cello, propped against the wall. "Ah… do you play?" He even touched it which prompted a sort of defensive movement from Cello.

"Of course I play." Why would the cello be there if it were not to be played? But he declined to say that. "So when…?" he asked.

The chaplain responded quickly. "I don't know. I am not entitled to know the details. But I am in residence here and when you want me just ask one of the staff and they will make contact. And I will pay a visit on the night…"

"The night before they shoot me… No thank you… that won't be necessary."

"Do you want to pray now, with me."

"No, I don't."

There was a silence of finality, during which the chaplain seemed to take a place with the Court Martial board. "Well I will remember you in my prayers Private Harris, you may rest assured of that."

"Rest, rest-assured. What do you mean by that? I'm not resting, assured or otherwise. As you can see perhaps. I have no bed on which to rest."

The chaplain responded with some embarrassment. "Yes I was wondering about that."

Cello let his embarrassment grow, while he reached for his instrument. He took it across his chest as he sat on his playing stool toying with the strings gently.

"Have you been in No Man's Land father?" asked Cello suddenly using the Roman Catholic style of address for a man of the cloth.

"I have been in the front line, on many occasions."

"Yes but have you been in… No Man's Land… Alone?"

"Well no, no I haven't."

"At least you admit it. It changes you, being out there… Alone."

"I can only imagine." The chaplain was breaking now.

The atmosphere dropped a little. The three looked at the floor.

Ben needed a smoke. He needed rum. Cello's strength gave him back a little bulwark of hope. Time surely was on their side. It would take time for the army to do… anything. Afterall there weren't men marching around who could form a firing squad.

The chaplain, made a swift sign of the cross over Cello then, his duty done; he slunk away.

They had not an idea of how quickly things outside the prison complex could move. Their army, of the trenches and the waiting, was not this one.

But the day wore away. A parcel arrived for Cello to break the evening's monotony. It was a small book which he did not allow Ben to see.

Ben smoked and went for food to the cook house.

Cello poured over the book with hasty anxiety. Ben asked him casually about it on return.

"Some music and songs and some very new music from a composer who will be England's greatest…probably."

"England's greatest."

"Yes although he did want to study in Germany. Strange isn't it. This war is everything. It is the monster of monsters. Yet it is nothing if you were to be on an island in the middle of the ocean. Music, composing goes on; in England, Germany, where ever. Music creates another world."

Ben felt his mind being stretched. "Another world! Island in the middle of the ocean!" He laughed grimly and ended up coughing. "I wish we were. Then we would be away from all this."

Looking intently at the book, Cello picked up his instrument, or rather positioned it in the playing mode. He looked at his bow and seemed to dust it with one hand gently.

Suddenly he struck the strings with the bow and drew it four times, across and back, across and back. Four low notes erupted, rumbling the walls almost. Cello stopped. "Ha, how was that."

Ben stood shocked. "Incredible, like a tank perhaps in the war."

Cello dropped his bow and looked with a little despondency at Ben's inability to lift himself above the war.

"It's the beginning of a new concerto. Dramatic isn't it?"

"Certainly is."

"My mother sent it. She knows the composer and thought I would like it."

Ben couldn't speak. Music was a mystery. He had caught a glimpse of the music written in hand in the book Cello had received. It was a kind of mystery that it had arrived. But the arrival of the actual cello had been as well. Ben was happy about his part in that. So he didn't question or look further into the mystery.

That it made Cello happy was something also of tiny satisfaction for him and gave birth to some new little bandage of hope.

He journeyed back to his billet without the need to salute any officers.

His night was interrupted. "They need you at the prison." He recognised the MP Corporal who had found him.

He ran breathless and was admitted to Cello's cell.

It wasn't even dawn yet.

A lieutenant was inside with Cello. They had some pieces of paper. Cello looked over his shoulder as Ben stopped at the door. "It's today... well soon," he said casually. Then went back to studying the paper.

CHAPTER FORTY-TWO
No birds

"There's a song I want them to sing first." Cello again spoke over his shoulder. "You can sing as well. And the Lieutenant has agreed to it."

"A song. Cello what's happening?"

"They are despatching me today, don't really want me around I guess, not after what I said. So I'm being shot at dawn, which I guess is in about, what." He consulted the lieutenant's face. "One hour sir?"

The Lieutenant straightened but didn't respond except for a slight nod.

Then cello, with a false brightness turned away from him paper in hand. "But first we will have a song!"

"A song." Ben went back to the word.

"Yes the officer has agreed to instruct the firing squad in it… and lead it himself. That's decent isn't it?"

"Cello!"

"BEN, DON'T BE AFRAID. I'm ready."

Ben had seen death too often perhaps for this. It took his stomach away; this calculated and prepared and deliberate death was not like the others.

"Here's a copy of the song." Cello held out a page, handwritten. The lieutenant had taken a copy for each of the firing squad, in a matter-of-fact way. "It'll be like church parade. But instead of an organ I will play my cello." Cello was actually smiling.

Ben couldn't speak any more. Whereas before he had wondered about his dirty boots against the purity of the music, now he had no inside, no stomach or heart. Though a dull feeling emerged in his gut, below his stomach. With Cello being so calm he couldn't scream out in some mad way as the Lieutenant Colonel had done when he was President. Ben couldn't have a breakdown, not now.

He wasn't the one about to be shot.

An escort of MPs appeared in pre-dawn quietness.

The other prisoners had not succumbed out of the silence. They slumbered on oblivious during this time of the night that demanded sleep more than any other. Or if they were awake they ignored the world, perhaps in fear.

Cello's little procession did not show fear. It was not a time for that. The fear came before in the preparation, the anticipation.

Or should have done.

Ben's stomach was still twisted. As he walked, it was twisting even more.

It was a strange procession. The MPs were leading, with Cello in between two of them. Instead of carrying arms at the shoulder, he carried his cello, which was larger than an arm, a weapon-like arm. But somehow it held some threat. Perhaps because of its unusual size.

The Lieutenant came next, followed by Ben. They moved as though their shoes were somehow muffled. They crept, wordlessly, secretly. There were no prisoners watching, as they usually did when Ben came to see Cello. The patrol passed all the cells and went out through the bottom door.

The chaplain did not keep to his word and met them at the door, adding one more who took up a place at the back of the line.

They turned away from the logistic area, away from the village complex, or town that had been reduced to a village along a rubble road, then down a track with high walls on each side.

Cello looked up to search out any approaching sun, or grey smudgy dawn. He noted that no birds sung, unlike when he had buried Sergeant John Wall. John Wall had died. He would die. There was no hope of that not happening. But his hope lay in the music, in one more thing that he had to do in that regard.

The small road became a track and the walls widened.

A scene awaited them, a small farmyard, a rubbishy type of backyard where the lives of previously useful implements met their end and waited to rust. War had intervened and now a sand-bag wall was placed towards one side where a high stone wall bordered the yard. At the other side a section of soldiers who carried shouldered arms, stood in a group smoking.

"Still no birds then," commented Cello.

CHAPTER FORTY-THREE
Harmony

The squad ground out their Woodbines to prepare for their secret mission. They unslung their rifles.

The Lieutenant walked across to them apologetically and stopped them in the unslinging.

The MPs stopped Cello's little team at a short distance from the men with rifles.

A low grey light of the coming dawn enabled them to see each other better.

Cello had been carrying his instrument balanced in the crook of one arm lengthways, not up and down like a rifle. Yet he unslung it from his arm and rested the small stake that protruded from its base on the ground. He looked towards the sand-bag wall then unbidden he picked up the cello again and walked over to it. The MPs, Ben and the chaplain watched. They had no control.

He needed something to sit on or he could play standing up.

The Lieutenant had finished passing the sheets around to the squad and talking to them. They looked uncertain but they still kept their rifles slung.

Cello tuned his strings until he was happy with the sound, which was at first weak in the open air, intermingling with the uncertainty of the men and their shuffling and the fragility of the dawn, struggling to make itself seen.

Cello was bare-headed and as he bent his head and shoulders forward his hair fell in its customary way over his face like a student over a desk about to write his exam; a boy even.

Then he threw the hair back and became a warrior. Elgar's unpublished cello concerto erupted forth, at least the first six bars. The sound did not reverberate as in the cell. But Cello used vibrato on each note which added strength. It caught every man's attention just as the RSM had on the day he had arrived and announced himself to the battalion. This was a different announcement. He stopped. "Right, now I have your attention. We are going to sing a song and I will play. You have your words… You can come a little closer… can't they Lieutenant."

The men shuffled forward. But not too close.

"Okay I will play the tune first and then we will add the song… Ben could you lead the singing."

Ben looked down at his sheet for the first time.

Cello played; this time without power or vibrato. He just concentrated on the tune, playing it through once. Then he looked up, as a teacher might look over his pupils. "Are you ready, don't worry we'll do it a couple of times, until…" His face was wet. But no one saw that. They didn't know what was in his mind. They knew they had to sing. They held up the sheets

"Out of the night that covers me,
Black as the pit from pole to pole,
I thank whatever gods may be
For my unconquerable soul."

Ben heard himself. He was standing apart from the squad, whose voices came a little thinly and unevenly.

Cello stopped playing. "Come on we can do better than

that I'm sure. We'll take it from the top and this time carry on for the four verses."

"*SING, ALL OF YOU, SING!*" Suddenly the Lieutenant caught the atmosphere of the moment and his call came like a battle cry.

Out of the night that covers me,
Black as the pit from pole to pole,
I thank whatever gods may be
For my unconquerable soul.

This time It came louder and stronger and rose and went on effortlessly to the next verse, as the playing grew in harmony with the singing. The chaplain, who stood aghast, should have been proud.

In the fell clutch of circumstance
I have not winced nor cried aloud.
Under the bludgeoning of chance
My head is bloody but unbowed.

Beyond this place of wrath and tears
Looms but the horror of the shade,
And yet the menace of the years
Finds and shall find me unafraid.

It matters not how strait the gate
How charged with punishment the scroll,
I am the master of my fate,
I AM THE CAPTAIN OF MY SOUL.

The song echoed and stood strong, then died as the dawn took its strength on. And Cello was exhausted and laid his instrument aside as if to rest. He nodded to the officer.

The sheets were collected, the rifles unslung. A little parade ground was formed and the men were spaced out into a line facing Cello.

"READY." The bolts were ratcheted back and rounds fed into chambers. *"AIM…FIRE!"*

One volley rang out as if rehearsed by the singing. Cello turned slowly, his head tilting slightly towards Ben. He dropped.

Birds did then sing, as if in applause, not alarm.

End

Other books in the trilogy

The Cellist's Friend

After the execution of his friend, Ben is gripped by a terrible guilt at not having done more to save him. He is obsessed with the song sung at the execution. He returns to the trenches and is badly injured on an operation. Rescued by a Jamaican soldier who is a reinforcement to the Battalion, he is sent back to England to recover. He writes to the wife of the soldier who rescued him, Pearl, only to discover she has become a widow. They fall in love through the exchange of letters.

Despite massive racial prejudice Pearl journeys to England. But how will her presence and that of a writer friend help Ben redeem his guilt and face the parents of his friend the cello player.

Rest Not These Dead

As the war ends Ben and Pearl struggle to find a life in England. She suffers a tragedy which makes her want to return home for a visit. Ben convinces her to marry him before she goes but he needs to find work if he is released from the Army as expected, to support them both and convince her to return.

Still desperate to right the injustice of the execution of his friend, Ben finally returns to France to help clear dead bodies from the battlefield. He believes that this might help him find out the full story of the cellist and recover the cello that he played before his execution which is desperately desired by the parents.

With the help of a journalist Ben and a soldier friend hatch a plan that might right the injustice, but it has huge risks. If it succeeds though it will challenge the whole culture which led to the war in the first place.

Also by the author

All About the Boys The last days of Wilfred Owen

A play about the last battle of the WW1 poet, one of the greatest of the war, Wilfred Owen.

The play shows the effect of Owen's poetry on his men as they prepare for and fight the last battle. A battle which claimed the life of Owen and resulted in one posthumous VC in his sector. The play shows how poetry could have played a part in this fierce battle to cross the Sambre-Oise Canal.

About the Author

Robert's dream of writing a novel about this war dates back almost fifty years to his reading of *All Quiet on the Western Front*. At the time he was serving in the British Royal Marines. The book led him to question his chosen career. Hearing about relatives who had served, including his uncle, killed in 1917; spurred him on. Much learning and practice brought him to the opportunity of the centenary of the war.

A Cellist Soldier began as a play, his second about the war. A week after starting writing, an actual cello played in WW1 was found in an attic in England. On finishing the play Robert was struck by the story of the cellist's friend and what might happen to him. So he wrote *The Cellist's Friend*. This novel is the prequel. The whole trilogy challenges the injustice and the loss of values in war and its affect on many lives and the culture of nations.

As well as novels, Robert writes plays, poetry and other stage events for an award-winning Arts organisation in South East London. He lives in London with his family.

www.ingramcontent.com/pod-product-compliance
Lightning Source LLC
Chambersburg PA
CBHW030325200626
46816CB00006BA/1939